OASIS SERIES

Book Two: Evolution

Jeannie van Rompaey

London | New York

Published by Clink Street Publishing 2016

First edition.

ISBNS: 9781910782934 (paperback)
9781910782941 (ebook)

Man is by nature a political animal.
Aristotle *Poetics1,2*

The child that's born must be kept.
1605: R.F. School of Slovenrie, The Epistle.

Also by Jeannie van Rompaey

Novels

Life Drawing
After
Devil Face
Oasis Series, Book One: Ascension

Short Stories

Betrayed
Afternoons on the De Keyserlei
The Idealists
And her mother came too
Anna-Belinda
Swap
Recognition

Contents

The Chronicles of Planet Earth edited by Odysseus

Introductory Contribution by Michael Court

After the unbelievable had happened, the catastrophe that pitched us all into shock towards the end of The Big Event, Odysseus asked me to record my impressions of that day for the Chronicles of Planet Earth. I could hardly refuse. In spite of the fact that I would have to relive the horror in order to write about it, I felt honoured to have been asked to record such a milestone in our history.

Later he suggested that I should include further journal entries, based on my life. Odysseus has asked others for contributions as well of course. As he never tires of pointing out, history is not a definitive account of the past but a compilation of distinct contemporaneous versions.

Up to now, my journal has only ever been intended for my own eyes. It's a place where I can write freely and express my personal opinions. By allowing sections of it to appear in *The Chronicles of Planet Earth* my private thoughts will be accessible to others. I have to admit I'm not completely at ease with that idea. But Odysseus has convinced me that my entries will provide a valuable piece of primary material about the history of these times, both on Earth and on Oasis.

I imagine my work being pored over by academics, maybe long after I am dead, studied in detail for clues as to how the changes in our worlds took place. What a grandiose opinion

I have of myself to think that my little journal could prove so important. Still, I do like the idea that I am to play a role in the telling and unravelling of history, so have agreed to become a contributor.

For those of you who don't know me and wonder why I should have been chosen to contribute to this chronicle, I would like to introduce myself.

I was born a mutant humanoid and brought up on Earth by Kali in Compound 55. Some of you may remember me. I was known as Mercury, often as Little Mercury, because of my diminutive stature.

Four years ago, at the age of sixteen, I underwent various operations and therapy in Hos-sat to remove my mutations and after two years emerged as a complete human being, "a complete." I became Michael Court and went to live on Planet Oasis, not really a planet, but a man-made satellite. My father, Alexander Court, is the person responsible for this change. It was this good man who searched for me, eventually with success, made arrangements for the necessary changes in my physique and brought me to live with him on Oasis. For this I shall always be grateful.

I would like all of you reading these journal entries to know that I am not only proud of being a complete but also of having been a mutant humanoid. Even after my transformation I still feel part mutant.

I haven't always felt positive about this duality, but it has made me appreciate how you, my fellow humanoids, must feel as you gradually leave your compounds to start new lives outside. It can't be easy. It wasn't easy for me to get used to a different way of life on Oasis. There was a lot to learn. I was often confused and unsure of myself. But every day that passes I have come to regard this dual personality as a special gift to help me understand our disparate worlds.

I hope that in the not too distant future I can use this gift to good effect to build good relations between Earth and Oasis.

Chapter One
Oasis, Land of the Free
(according to Michael)

Journal Entry

1.0 p.m. I leave my computer cubicle at the University of Oasis in search of some fresh air and a sandwich. I poke my head round the adjacent cubicle to see if Jonathan would like to join me, but he's not there. Probably chasing skirt in the junior common room.

As I walk through the campus on the neatly tiled paths that criss-cross the greener than green lawns, I find myself whistling. I don't immediately recognise the song I've chosen or that has chosen me, but it's a happy little tune. It fits my mood as I think about this satellite that's become my home. I've never quite got over its beauty. It's a pristine place, fresh and bright. The buildings, lakes and plazas gleam in the sunlight; the lawn and flowers on campus and in the park glow, luminous as jewels. Open to the ever-changing sky, you have to be prepared for those biting showers, ready to run for shelter when the rain assaults you with sheets of liquid metal. But the clouds soon roll back and the sky is blue again and the grass and leaves look and smell newly-washed. Refreshing. Invigorating.

Suddenly it comes to me. The tune in my head is "Always look on the Bright Side of Life" the satirical song that the crucified men sing at the end of *Life of Brian*. I stop whistling. The song is oddly appropriate, not because of its cheerful optimism but because of its irony. I've come to realise that all is not perfect in this paradise we call Oasis. This clean beauty is a veneer that conceals a dark side. Every day I become a little more disillusioned. Why is it, the historian in me asks, that the utopian ideals expressed in the original charter of Oasis are being forgotten? Ignored? I pull up short. Is it possible that Oasis is falling so short of its fundamental principles that it is destined to deteriorate further until it can truly be labelled a failed state?

I shake my head to get rid of these pessimistic thoughts and make my way under the giant arches that mark the division of university and town.

As I emerge, I catch sight of a familiar figure loitering on the corner of the street. The figure is familiar. The loitering isn't. Stella Jameson isn't the type to hang around on a street corner. It can't be her. But it is. There are the chiselled cheekbones, the immaculate blond cap of hair, the Dallas blue business suit with gold epaulettes and cuffs. And the matching shoes with metallic spiked heels.

I dodge behind one of the twin pillars that hold up the rather pretentious arch, hoping to see the person she's waiting for. Too late. She has seen me. She waves and click-clacks towards me on her stilettos, her mouth forced into a bright smile.

'Michael! I was just passing, not dreaming I'd see you. What a lovely surprise.'

I am somewhat disconcerted to discover that the person she's been waiting for is myself.

'I'm just on my way to buy a sandwich,' I explain.

'I'll buy you lunch. Wouldn't you rather have a proper lunch?'

'Thanks,' I say, trying to sound appreciative. 'That would be great.'

Father and I often lunch together, whenever he can get away from his duties as Minister of Culture. But I've never before had lunch with his wife, the woman I refuse to call Mother.

As we walk side by side, I think about my ambivalent relationship with Stella. To be fair, she has done her best to make me welcome as her stepson. Not an easy task. I am eight years older than Stuart and ten years older than Bella, her children from a previous relationship. I've tried to fit in with this readymade family. I really have. But neither my efforts nor Stella's have been entirely successful. We hold opposing views on a variety of subjects and both of us are reluctant or downright unwilling to compromise.

Our polite acceptance of each other for Father's sake is the only concession we are prepared to make.

We pass the Symposium where Father works, a circular building with a crystal dome in the centre of the main plaza, surrounded by statues of famous men. On the other side of the square stands the marble-fronted museum, its grand entrance supported by a series of Corinthian columns. Ornate. Imposing. Inside are the treasures rescued (or pillaged) depending on your viewpoint, from a contaminated Earth.

I remember how sick I felt the day I saw Durga's golden warriors displayed there, marching up and down in a glass cage. They've been returned to Earth now and, hopefully, never again will there be live exhibits, mutant humanoids or completes, in Museum Oasis.

As we enter the park, the sky darkens. Granite-coloured clouds blot out the sun.

'Quick,' says Stella and begins to trot briskly on her excessively high spikes towards the nearest shelter. I jog along beside her and we make it just in time. Down comes the metallic rain, silver spears slashing through the air like a bodiless army.

A few moments later the shower is over, the clouds roll back and the sun comes out again. A steaming mist rises from the ground leaving the dahlias aflame with an unearthly radiance that never ceases to amaze me. As we emerge from the shelter, we grin at each other, momentarily united by this piece of magic.

We lunch, Stella and I, in the park restaurant with its dazzling view of fiery flowers and shimmering lawn that stretches down to the lake.

Stella's raised eyebrow shows me she's surprised that I know exactly what to order. It occurs to me that Father hasn't told her about our lunches here. I'm pleased about that. I like to think of them as trysts at which Father and I exchange confidences not shared with her.

I know that Stella has contrived this meeting. That means she has something specific she wants to talk about. It isn't until we've finished our meal and are having coffee that she broaches the subject.

'Michael, I am aware that you are now a young man – an adult.' She hesitates and runs a long, blood red fingernail around the lip of her coffee cup. 'It's natural that a moment will come when you decide to leave Home-Court-Jameson and set up on your own.' She takes a deep breath. 'When that time comes I want you to know that your father and I will help you find the right home and support you financially if necessary. We brought you here from Earth and you are our responsibility, whether living at home or not.'

I'm flabbergasted. OK, Stella and I have never been close, but I've had no previous indication that she wants me out of the house.

She hasn't finished. 'Sooner or later you will meet someone you want to live with.'

I feel my neck muscles tense. She must have found out that I've been seeing a girl from the Project, and this is her way of preventing our relationship from developing further. She's about to tell me that unless I give Lizzy up, the offer she's just mentioned will be withdrawn. My cheeks are burning. What shall I do? Deny all knowledge of the girl? Or admit I know her and try to engage Stella's sympathy?

'You may not think it will happen, Michael, but one day, sooner or later, you will fall in love. And when you do and you feel ready, you will want a home of your own.'

Does she know about Lizzy or doesn't she? She's still speaking hypothetically about the partner I might have one day.

She leans across the table and places her hand tightly over mine. 'This is a difficult thing for me to say, Michael, but I must say it.' She pauses and looks me straight in the eye. 'You do realise that you must never father a child.'

I stare at her. Of all the subjects she might have talked to me about I had no clue it would be this.

Mutant humanoids rarely become pregnant. The Great Plague that spread over the Earth made most of us sterile. I was the youngest child in C55, probably the youngest in all the compounds. Isis, two years older than me, was the only other child I ever met or heard about.

But things are changing. A miracle has occurred. Isis, now twenty-two, is pregnant and has been taken to Hos-sat to have the baby. Is it because of Isis's pregnancy that Stella has turned her attention to this subject? Does she think that because recent research suggests that Planet Earth is no longer polluted, the likelihood is that mutant humanoids will be able to reproduce again?

Stella releases my hand and picks up her table napkin. The red of her nails catches the light as she pats her matching red lips to remove an imagined crumb. The lipstick is not smudged. Come to think of it I've never seen Stella without immaculately painted lips. 'Of course, I don't expect a young man like you to abstain from sex. That wouldn't be natural.'

To my annoyance I find myself blushing. 'I'm not having sex with anyone,' I tell her.

She looks relieved. 'I'm not suggesting that you are,' she says, putting down the napkin. 'Yet.'

I feel my temper coming to the boil.

'Anyway if one day I do have a mutant baby would that be so terrible?' I blurt out.

Because this is what this conversation is about, but as usual, Stella doesn't want to use the m-word.

'How can you say that when you know what happened when you were born?'

'That was twenty years ago. They wouldn't take babies away from their parents these days.'

'I don't know what they would do.' She reaches for my hand again and grips it, her nails biting into my skin. 'It mustn't happen. Do you understand? If you do find someone to love, you must tell her before you move in together, that you don't want children. That would be the only fair thing to do. Naturally you mustn't tell her why.'

'I don't need a lecture on being fair to an imaginary girlfriend.' I withdraw my hand and look down at it. Her nails have left little dents in the skin.

'As long as you realise how important this is.' She narrows her eyes. 'What I suggest you do is to go to Hos-sat and have a vasectomy. To be on the safe side.'

I feel the colour rising up my cheeks again. "That's ridiculous. The chance that I will have a baby is minimal as you well know.'

'We did believe that the humanoids on Earth were permanently barren, but now it seems they're not. That female in Hos-sat for example.'

'Isis, my childhood friend.'

'You can't afford to take the risk, Michael. You must see that.'

I'm becoming hotter and hotter. "Mercury rising!" Kali used to say that when I was in danger of losing my temper. Kali, who brought me up, the only mother I've ever known.

I take a deep breath. 'It might be a good thing for public relations between Earth and Oasis if a mutant humanoid was born here. Show people that mutants are not so different from completes.'

Stella purses her lips. For a moment she looks quite ugly. 'Now you're being ridiculous.'

'In a few years time mutants and completes may be living side by side and mixed blood babies may become the norm.'

It's Stella's turn to go red in the face. 'That won't happen. It mustn't. In any case it will be years before there is genuine integration. Maybe never.'

It's true that attitudes on Earth and Oasis will have to change drastically before it can even be contemplated. '

'At the moment, as you know, the few humanoids who are here live in the Project,' Stella continues.

'Yes, they're kept well away from us and only come out under cover of darkness to sweep the roads or clean the public buildings, doing low paid jobs considered too demeaning for completes. It's exploitation. Slave labour. I can't believe Athene agreed to such a scheme.' This is a jibe at Stella. As Head of Worldwideculture, it was Stella who appointed Athene as CEO of the compounds on Earth.

'She thought it was a start, I suppose,' Stella says.

'A bad start', I snap.

'It's working reasonably well. We hardly catch a glimpse of them or they us – which, to be honest, suits us all.'

'Segregation,' I say. 'Apartheid. Have we learnt nothing from history? Mutant humanoids are not another species. They are just as good as completes. You know that. You should anyway. You live with two of us.'

Stella looks as if she's about to explode. 'You and Alexander are not… '

'Not mutants? Oh yes, we are. Just because we've had surgery to remove our "unconventional bits" doesn't mean we've changed inside.'

'That may apply to you but not to Alexander.'

'Are you sure about that?'

Our raised voices attract a few looks, but most diners have left and our table is tucked away in an alcove.

The flush on Stella's cheeks subsides. She looks pale now, her lips drawn in a straight line. 'Please don't be flippant, Michael. I'm alerting you to the consequences of fathering a child for your own good. And for Alexander's. I don't know what he would do if the truth came out about his past. It would kill him.'

It won't kill him, but he would be distraught, that's true. He goes to great lengths to keep my past, and his, a secret.

If the effects of radiation and plague that caused mutant humanoids to be infertile are wearing off, and if I do father a mutant baby, Father will be afraid of the repercussions, both personally and as far as his political career is concerned.

Journal Entry

Back at the university, in my computer-cubicle I think about what Stella has said. It's strange. Until today, I've never thought about the possibility of being a father. What young man does? Now I find myself feeling quite passionate about the rights of this unborn child. I consider several possibilities.

One: to have a vasectomy to make sure I will never be a father. Game, set and match to Stella.

Two: to persuade my imaginary girlfriend to take the morning-after-pill as my friend Jonathan makes sure his many sexual partners do. Stella hasn't recommended this option because she is aware it is not a hundred percent effective. Oasis encourages its citizens to propagate and does not want a foolproof method of contraception.

Three: if I do become a father, to take the moral high ground and keep the child, mutations included. It would cause Father distress, but maybe I could persuade him to take my side. He's already shown himself courageous by seeking me out and claiming me as his son.

I think about what could happen to the potential child. He or she would be unlikely to be taken away at birth and put in an institution on Earth as I was, but Father and Stella would surely try to whisk the baby to Hos-sat to have any mutations removed.

But I wouldn't want my child to turn into some kind of split self, half mutant, half complete, like me. I mustn't let that happen. It's taken me a long time to come to terms with my mixed status. I wouldn't wish that on anyone else.

A shocking thought occurs to me. It would suit completes if this generation of mutant humanoids were to be the last. I wonder, not for the first time, if mutants are being fed something in their food packoids to make them infertile. That the results are not infallible doesn't mean it isn't happening. On Earth, when I was a mutant, I may have been given such substances in my nutri-rations but that amount of control would be impossible here on Oasis. That could explain Stella's concern that the effects are wearing off and that I might be capable of fathering a child.

My suspicions grow about the unscrupulousness of the Oasis Symposium. Why did the contamination of Earth last so long? It's nearly two hundred years since The Great Plague. Were the wilderness years deliberately prolonged by using some sort of spray such as Agent Orange? The fact that it would be callous, not to mention immoral, to deliberately pollute the Earth in order to keep the mutant humanoids imprisoned in compounds is unconscionable, but not impossible. Add to that a plan to sterilise mutants by putting medication in the food and my disillusion with Oasis would be total.

I start to tap into my computer, determined to find out more. As I continue my research a key question keeps returning: why can't completes accept mutant humanoids as equals?

The answer comes to me quickly. Because they are afraid of us.

Journal Entry

A message on my mob-fone, from the implanted chip behind my ear: 'Please help me, Michael. We're in terrible trouble. Meet me at the Obelisk at five o'clock?'

I sigh. Much as I like Lizzy there are times when I wish I'd never become involved with her. She relies on me too much, expects me to find the solution to all her problems.

I'm sure that The Oasis Social Project started off as a good idea, a way to help those members of our society who had fallen on hard times. They are provided with basic accommodation in a separate urbanization and supported until they find new jobs and are ready to be released back into society.

Like many philanthropic schemes, it doesn't always work. Some people abuse the system, preferring to continue to live off the state rather than find work. I don't know if that is the case with Lizzy's family or not. She says her father can't find a job that pays enough for them to live in the city itself. Meanwhile they continue living as second-class citizens, dependent on charity.

I do my best to help Lizzy. Sometimes talking to her is sufficient. Sometimes I give her money. Not much else I can do.

Jonathan says I'm too soft, that I must understand that she's not my responsibility. Jonathan is the only one who knows about my relationship with Lizzy. It would have been almost impossible to keep such a secret from him. He knows my movements throughout the day. We attend quite a few of the same seminars, have adjacent computer cubicles and take our coffee breaks together. We're really good mates and I know I can trust him not to tell anyone else. It's good to have him to confide in, just as he finds it good to tell me about the girls he goes out with. Lanky Susie has long gone. Now he has a series of girls of all shapes and sizes. He takes pleasure in telling me when he "scores", as he calls it. He boasts a bit about his conquests, considers himself an Alpha male. His floppy fair hair and laid-back attitude to life do seem to attract females, mainly students at the university.

As for me, I don't go out with other girls. I don't really go out with Lizzy. We meet in the Project from time to time. Safer for her than venturing outside again, she says. Her brothers have agreed to our friendship, an ally in Oasis town proving useful. And profitable.

When we want privacy, Lizzy and I go into the garden shed in her uncle's back yard. Once there, we hold each other close and exchange a few kisses. I spoke the truth when I told Stella I don't have sex with anyone. I'd like to make love properly to Lizzy and I know she'd be willing, but not in that dirty shed and there's nowhere else to go.

Besides, something holds me back. Deep down I know that if we did make love it would be an act of irretrievable commitment.

Jonathan says that's stupid. He's slept with lots of girls and feels under no obligation to any of them. He's a free spirit, he says. Maybe I'm made differently from him or maybe it's because Lizzy is so vulnerable that I couldn't bear to hurt her. Part of me wishes to be relieved of this burden that my relationship with Lizzy is turning out to be.

I allow myself another sigh but I do reply to Lizzy's message, telling her I'll be there at five.

Chapter Two
Nasty Neighbours
(according to Michael)

Journal Entry
She's leaning against the obelisk in her blue dress, tracing a circle in the loose sand with a pointed toe. A dancer: that was my first impression of her. I feel my heart race at the sight of her, but not, perhaps, with the same urgency it used to.

She kisses me lightly on the cheek and launches into an explanation of her current problem. She and her family have new neighbours.

'Mutants,' she says. 'Ever so many of them, all packed into one house. They're really ugly. One man has two heads. Can you believe that? And another one three legs. They sit outside on the doorstep all day long and munch food. It's disgusting. Thing is they're always there. Every time we leave the house there they are, staring at us. You'd think we were the mutants the way they gawp. Why can't they stay inside like everyone else? No one else sits on their doorsteps.'

I take her hand in mine. 'You've got to realise, Lizzy, that on Earth they were shut up in compounds for years because the air outside was polluted. Being outdoors is a treat for them.'

'I don't know anything about that. I just know that half the time I'm afraid to go out.'

'Have they done anything to make you afraid of them – threatened you or anything?'

She sniffs. 'Not exactly. One of them smiled at me – well, not a smile – a leer. Definitely a leer. I ran back indoors and slammed the door. I was totally wrecked. Couldn't go out again for days.'

'Perhaps he was just trying to be friendly.'

'Well, I don't want to be friends with him. We had good neighbours before. People like us. But the government got rid of them.'

'Do you know why?'

'The usual excuse. Said they were making no effort to find work and couldn't expect to live off the state for ever.'

I ask where they've gone but Lizzy doesn't know the answer to that and doesn't seem interested. It strikes me as odd, her lack of interest in the plight of her previous neighbours. It doesn't seem to occur to her that the same thing could happen to her family. She is so obsessed with the "horrible mutants" next door, she can't think of anything else.

'Have you any real complaints about your new neighbours?'

'What do you mean real complaints? Isn't it bad enough them being there? But yes, there are other problems. They're so noisy. We can hear them clomping about, up and down the stairs, bumping into furniture and walls and they shout at each other all the time. Even at night. Their voices are so shrill. They do my head in.' She pushes out her bottom lip in a pout and looks at me to judge my reaction. Her way of flirting.

It's true that mutant humanoids aren't co-ordinated. They have little control over their arms and legs and their voices tend to be high-pitched. I remember what I was like before surgery, physiotherapy and voice therapy. Lizzy wouldn't have thought much of me then. I try to make her understand that her neighbours are probably finding life very different here. 'It will take time for them to adjust.

'But they're not even trying to adjust. They just do what they want, regardless of anyone else.'

'Lizzy, you have to be patient. I'm sure things will improve. It's a culture shock for them living here.'

'A shock for us you mean, living next to these – these monsters.'

'Just because they look different from you – from us – doesn't make them monsters, Lizzy.'

She bursts into tears. 'You don't understand. You don't have to live next door to them. You live in your beautiful home in Oasis city. You can't imagine what it's like here.' She pounds her fists on my chest. I put my arms round her and try to calm her. She stops sobbing and raises her blue eyes to mine. 'Michael, I want you to do something for me.'

'You know I'll help you if I can,' I tell her, stroking her silky fair hair. I'm sure she washes it to make it shine like that just before she meets me.

She takes a step back and gets an envelope out of her bag. 'Take this letter to the Symposium for me. It's from my father. He's been round all the houses in the Project collecting a list of people's names. We want the government to do something about it.'

'A petition?'

'Is that what it's called?'

'How many signatures are there?'

'I don't know. Nearly everyone signed it – apart from one or two families too scared to do anything. Afraid of losing their benefits I suppose.'

'What do you expect the Symposium to do?'

'Send the mutants back to where they came from. We don't want them here.'

'That's not going to happen, Lizzy. You see, the Symposium invited them here.'

She stares at me, wide-eyed. 'Why did they do that?'

'Because they needed people to do the menial jobs – keeping the roads and buildings clean for example.'

'They're taking our jobs.'

'They're doing the jobs you – we – don't want to do. The kind of jobs that don't pay much.'

'And they don't mind?'

'On Earth, in the compounds, there's no monetary system.'

Lizzy looks at me blankly.

'They don't use money. Their food and clothes are provided for them.'

'Who gives them these things?'

'We do.'

'So they get everything free, while we have to pay for everything. That's not fair.'

I don't know how to start to explain. It's like talking to a child. I sit Lizzy down at the foot of the Obelisk and start to give her a potted history of Earth. If I could make her understand what it's like to live there maybe she'll be more sympathetic to her neighbours.

'The completes who escaped to the satellites were the lucky ones. They escaped after The Great Plague. The unlucky ones suffered from mutations and were left on Earth.'

Lizzy snuggles up to me, 'I know all that.'

'Some of the completes felt sorry for them,' I continue, 'and decided to help them. They built the compounds to keep them safe from further contamination.'

'Yes, I get all that,' Lizzy says, her head nestling on my shoulder. 'We were taught all that at school, but what I don't understand is why they are here.'

I start to explain how the completes ransacked the

Earth and took its resources to create a rich new world for themselves on the satellites creating a standard of living much higher than in the compounds. 'Now that the atmosphere on Earth is no longer dangerous the humanoids feel they are entitled to share our luck....'

I stop talking, jump to my feet and turn away from Lizzy, a lump in my throat. I can't do it. I can't justify this venture. Not to Lizzy, nor to anyone else, including myself. What was Athene thinking of to agree to this stupid scheme? It's misconceived from start to finish. For one thing people like Lizzy and her family do not enjoy a high standard of living. They are as confined in the Project as the mutant humanoids in the compounds.

Another thing, these particular mutant humanoids, the less educated ones from C1, were brought here to work for completes, not to share the culture and higher standard of living. The entire enterprise is an anathema.

I face Lizzy, pull her up and grip her shoulders. 'You're right, Lizzy. I agree with you. You shouldn't have mutant humanoids as neighbours in the Project. And yes, I will take your letter to the Symposium – if that is what you want.'

Her face lights up and I think again how pretty she is. 'Thank you, Mr Darcy.'

Her reference to *Pride and Prejudice*, an old joke of ours, embarrasses me. I realise, perhaps for the first time, that our love story, unlike that of Darcy and Elizabeth, will not have a happy ending. I will always be Lizzy's friend, but not her husband. We are too different.

In spite of Stella's warning that I must never tell anyone that I was once a mutant humanoid, I know that I will never ask anyone to share my life without being completely honest about my past. There is no way that person will be Lizzy.

Her reaction to her new neighbours makes it clear that I can never be able to share my secret with her.

Journal Entry

When Stella goes upstairs to say goodnight to the children, I give Father the envelope containing the petition. I tell him that a fellow student gave it to me and asked me to make sure the Symposium received it.

Father asks me if I know what it's about. I tell him that I do.

He opens the envelope and frowns. 'The migrants from Earth weren't supposed to live mixed up with the Project people, but in a separate section,' he says. 'We can't expect them to integrate straight away.'

'Father, you are on the sub-committee that came up with this suggestion. If you don't mind me saying, wasn't the scheme doomed from the first?'

'Doomed is a bit strong, Michael, but I have to admit that there are some people in the Symposium and even on the sub-committee who think of this venture as an experiment and will be only too pleased if it fails. They will use this petition as further proof that integration of mutant humanoids and completes won't work.'

He fingers the envelope thoughtfully. Is he wondering whether he should pass it on to the Symposium or withhold it? The petition from the Project will only add fuel to the views of those who object to any sort of integration with those on Earth.

'If only Athene had refused to send them,' I say. 'She should have sent students from Headculturedome to study at the university instead.'

'That's what she wanted to do but the Symposium rejected that suggestion. Bringing in the blue-collar workers from C1 was a compromise. Some of us thought it was better than nothing and would keep the peace between Earth and Oasis for a while. Seems that was a mistake.'

'Seems it was.'

Father sits brooding in his armchair for a while.

I have something else I want to ask him before Stella comes back. 'What happens to the Project families who lose their houses?'

'You mean the ones who break the rules, take advantage of our generosity and don't try to find work '

'My uni friend told me that a lot of families have been turned out of their homes in order to make room for the mutant humanoids. Where do they go?'

Father is still playing with the envelope containing the petition, moving it round and round between his fingers. 'I think there has been a bit of a blitz, yes. But it was one that was well over due. Some of these people are very lazy, Michael.'

'But isn't it difficult for them to find employment? Isn't there a kind of stigma about living in the Project that makes companies hesitate to employ them?'

'You seem to know a lot about it.'

'I only know what I've read on line and what my uni friend told me. He has cousins who live there. They didn't want to accept charity, but the father lost his job and couldn't get another and, as they have three children, they didn't have much choice.'

'What are their names? Perhaps I can help them.'

'I don't know. We were only talking in general terms. My friend's cousin told him that they were caught in a trap, that he couldn't find work and had no choice but to stay in the Project. They've been threatened with eviction if he doesn't get a job soon. That's why I asked you what happens to the people who are evicted.'

'Depends on the situation.' Father sits back and makes a church of his fingers, the envelope as the steeple. 'If they are criminals, deliberately abusing the system, they are sent to Pris-sat. If not and their problems are deemed genuine they go to another place to be – ' he hesitates for a moment, 'to be re-educated.'

'To learn new skills to help them get work?'

The church collapses and the envelope drops to the floor. Father leans over to pick it up. 'That's more or less it. Yes.'

I get the feeling he's not telling me the whole story. 'What's the satellite called where they receive this re-education?' I ask.

Father pauses again. He doesn't want to tell me but he's promised to answer any questions I may have.

'It's not a satellite. It's a building here, on Oasis,' he says. 'It's known as The Rehabilitation Centre.'

I don't ask him any more about it. I can look it up on the Internet later and find out exactly what the rehabilitation involves.

I note that Father puts the envelope back in his pocket when he hears Stella returning. She drapes herself on the peach-coloured sofa next to him, ready to engage us both in conversation, but I don't want to hang around any longer in this lush drawing-room with its stylish colour combinations chosen by Stella. I jump to my feet and excuse myself saying I have some work I must do for uni tomorrow. Is it my imagination or does she look relieved? I think of our lunchtime chat. It occurs to me that she will be not be happy until I have left Home-Court-Jameson and she can have Father to herself.

Back in my room, I type in rehabilitationcentre.inc and up it comes. It's not a very informative site, but it tells me enough to make me realise that although job skills are taught there and linked to work experience, the emphasis is on psychoanalysis.

What exactly does that entail? It seems that the centre is designed to re-educate "miscreants" defined as those who have abused their civil rights and need to be "re-processed."

After treatment and tests, they may be eligible for work experience, unpaid jobs, that may lead to them being taken on as paid employees, acceptable as citizens of Oasis again.

From the few details described on screen the process sounds a viable method of making sure that the participants are ready to go back to live and work in the community. Why then do I feel uneasy? I think it's the terminology, all those words beginning with "re". Reprogrammed, repatriation, reprocessed, re-educated, reconstituted. They all suggest the stifling of the individual. Could Oasis be degenerating into the kind of regime that imposes its will on those who do not conform, a regime that turns those it considers dissidents into model citizens through force? I intend to find out.

Enough of that for the moment. I must plan my paper for tomorrow's seminar on Russian politics.

No. I can't concentrate. Too many new thoughts whizzing round in my brain. I'll make "a things to do list" instead. I often use this method to prioritise my work schedule, but this time my list is shorter than usual.

1) Write essay 2) Visit Rehabilitation Centre 3) Visit Isis in Hos-sat.

I had no idea I was going to write the third item, but as soon as it's written down, I know it's something I must do. It won't be just a social call. If Oasis is as corrupt as I'm beginning to believe, the future of the latest mutant humanoid to be born could be in jeopardy. I need to make sure my friend and her baby are safe. I cut and paste and put the visit to Isis at the top of my short list. I stare at the three items and once they're imprinted on my mind delete them.

The next evening I tell Father and Stella that I've decided to go to Hos-sat. Stella's face glows. 'Well done, Michael. You're doing the right thing. You won't regret it.'

Father offers to come with me.

'No, that's not necessary. I'm a man now. I don't need you

to hold my hand. Besides, I've got friends there. I won't be alone.'

The team who did my surgery to transform me from mutant to complete will pleased to see me again: the surgeon, nurses and the therapists, Janey and Moira.

Father agrees to let me go on my own. 'This is a simple operation compared with the ones you had before and, as you say, you'll be in good hands. When would you like to go?'

'As soon as possible,' I tell him. 'Tomorrow if possible. Better to get it over with.'

'Tomorrow might be rather short notice, but I promise to do my best to get you there as soon as possible.'

'Better make it quick before I change my mind.'

Stella and Father exchange concerned looks.

'Just joking,' I assure them but Stella whispers in Father's ear and he gets up to use the phone in his study. I plump up a peach-coloured silk cushion, plonk it behind my head and close my eyes.

When Father returns he says everything is arranged. I can go to Hos-sat tomorrow. Stella grins like the Cheshire cat in *Alice in Wonderland.*

If she knew what I was really planning, she wouldn't be so smug. I have no intention of having a vasectomy. Isis is due to give birth any day now and I intend to be there to prevent anything that may affect the safety of the new baby.

Chapter Three
Diversions and Duplicities
(according to Heracles)

My darling boss, that bitch Athene, has invited me to supper in her superior pad in Compound 99, Earth's flagship. No sign of anything to eat. Straightway she leads me by the hand to her double bunku.

She doesn't tie me up like she did last time, but allows me to sprawl on my back, my three legs spread wide, my huge square head propped up on the pile of pillows.

'No need to bind you,' she says. 'You know the rules. I trust you, Heracles.'

She trusts me? There's a thing. Does she really believe I'm the sort of person likely to stick to rules? I quite liked the idea of being in bondage to her but it's more comfortable un-tethered and I can decide whether or not to take advantage of my freedom later. She leaves me lying on the bed for a few minutes to prepare myself for the treat she has planned. I close my eyes.

It was a shock the first time she danced for me, when she revealed the jungle print on her body: the exotic multi-coloured trees and flowers, birds and creatures in colours the Fauves would have died for. I shall never forget the anticipation I felt as the lights flickered and the music rose in pitch and swelled in volume, the build up to a storm. Her movements grew faster, her body twisting and turning, keeping pace with the bellow of thunder, the streaks of lightning, the lacerating rain, the panic of squawking parrots flying sky high and the howl of tigers crashing through the undergrowth. Magic. Amazing. And afterwards as the storm subsided and the music and lights faded, I swear I could smell the dampness of the earth and hear the drip, drip, drip from the branches of the trees. Climax achieved, followed by calm, peace and togetherness. Yet it was just a dance. We hadn't touched. It was all spectacle all illusion, a thrilling, oddly satisfying trick.

Having experienced it once, what will be the effect of a second showing?

Repetition of sex with the same partner is often disappointing. Will this pseudo sexual ritual be similarly lacking in excitement when revisited? I don't have long to wait to find out.

Slow music with a persistent beat invites me to open my eyes. In she comes dressed in a long white robe. She stands in a spotlight, her back to me, and begins a striptease. Slowly. Small sections of her body are revealed one at a time: a shoulder, an elbow, a buttock and a sole of a foot. I see enough to know that her body is not painted, printed or tattooed as a jungle as before, but as a collage of libidinous, female body parts. A jolt as nipples, pudenda, neck, mouth and eyes appear in unexpected places. One breast on a shoulder blade, another on a thigh; vaginas and labia stamped on her back like lipstick kisses, red, raw. The displaced erogenous zones make a pornographic pattern. She swings round to face me. The lights change colour from green, to pink, to purple. A saxophone moans. Her hips swing, her body twists, the images merge.

An apparition materialises of a dark beauty, lips pouting, eyes sultry, dark breasts with darker nipples. I draw in my breath. A change of light and another female appears, a cool blond with alabaster hips and thighs. A redhead follows.... How can this be? Athene has made herself into a series of sensual females. Each has her own particular shape, her own manner of moving and her own, very personal scent.

'Take me,' each body pleads 'and you will possess all the women in the world.'

I ease myself up on to my elbows but make no further shift towards her, honouring the trust she has in me. Or so she thinks.

She slinks round the bed, encircling it, tempting me. I can't help but be aroused by the ever-changing female representations.

The disparate images become a whole, disintegrate and combine again to form a different face, a different body and a different apparition of beauty. Stimulating. Suggestive. Titillating. All the images are versions of Athene, bent on seducing me. That's what this is about. Seduction. Shapes unite and divide, fuse and dissolve with smooth subtlety, transforming into yet another female. Elegant, graceful and sexy. Wow!

One of them slides on to the bed and lies beside me, up close and personal. I lie still. I don't want to break the spell, because I can't help thinking that this is some sort of witchery. If this is foreplay bring it on; but I refuse to touch her unless she touches me first. There is something about the colourful amalgam of voluptuous images combined with the sad, beguiling music that I find unsettling.

Witch, bitch, what's the difference? Athene, all women all woman, is offering herself to me unconditionally. Or is she? I have the feeling that if I so much as reach out to touch her the music will stop, the lights black out and she and her alter egos will disintegrate. She's a tease. Nothing more. It's a power game. She's testing me and I'm determined to pass the test. Or shall I teach the bitch a lesson and take her, show her what a dangerous game she is playing, what a brute I can be?

She's very close to me now, our bodies almost touching. Her sweet breath brushes my cheek. There's a glint of power in her eye. I can smell her sex. I roll away from her and stand up straight on my three muscular legs. I have an erection, but I will not allow her to seduce me. I don't want to give her the satisfaction.

She too rolls over and slips off the bed. I turn away from her and leave the dormo-cube. The music fades. The lights cut out. I wait in the living-cube. I have won this round of the contest. Of that I'm sure.

In she floats, her white robe a complete cover-up of her decorated body. Her smile is cool, confident.

'Well done,' she says. 'You haven't betrayed my trust.'

I smile back, certain that in spite of her praise she is disappointed.

'That was an enjoyable – supper,' I tell her. 'What next?'

'Champagne,' she answers, determined to keep me here.

'No thanks. I need a clear head. I have work to do.'

Like hell I have. I'm going to find a real female on whom to slake my lust. I'll visit Sati, my prisoner. She's just the medicine I need.

Thor, my friend and number one groupie, is lounging in a comfortable shaper in the dino-cube. His ugly mug lights up as he spots me. 'Hi, Boss. I've saved you a place,' he says, tapping the seat of the shaper beside him. I'm not really his boss, but as Athene's deputy I have considerably more power than him.

'Very kind of you,' I say, with a hint of sarcasm that's completely wasted on him.

I make myself comfortable in the shaper, stretching my three legs out in front of me, which attracts the attention of the females nearby. I haven't lost my touch.

Thor leans forward, anxious to hear my news. 'Well? Tell all. I understand you were with the delectable Athene last night? How was she?'

'Totally delectable.'

'Did you kiss and make-up?'

I yawn. 'How little you know me, Thor.'

'I know you well enough to realise that whatever happened between you and Athene won't change your plans.'

'Too right.' I punch the top of his arm. '*Our* plans.'

Thor grins with both his mouths, chuffed with my response. I know he's totally loyal to me.

When I first came to C99 I managed to rescue him from a nasty piece of business. He was accused of rape. Ridiculous. All the females here are up for grabs and this particular one, Artemis, was always gagging for it. What did I do? Fucked her myself. Consensual sex, of course. I've never found it difficult to bed females. My irresistible charm, I guess.

Afterwards I asked her about the incident with Thor. Turns out he did force himself on her, pinned her down and just went for it. I told her many females liked a bit of rough. To call it rape was an over reaction. It wasn't too difficult to get her to retract her allegation and stop her taking her complaint to a higher authority. If Artemis had officially accused Thor of rape he could have been deported to a compound of lower status. Or even spent time in a prison cell.

Thor has always been grateful for my intervention. That's how I know I can trust him to keep my secrets. He is aware I intend to be CEO of all the English-speaking compounds one day and I assure him he will be my deputy when the time comes.

Since that time he has shown time and time again that he is willing to do anything for me. No job is too dirty to give to Thor. Any little bit of "persuasion" needed to coerce someone to do something and he's my man. When Athene asked me to find the source of the rumour that was spreading round the sectoid that she had killed Ra, our previous leader, Thor managed to find someone willing to confess. Whether the selected female was actually the source or a scapegoat I didn't know. I didn't care. And I didn't question his methods.

Thor is also my main source of gossip. 'A new two-headed has arrived,' is his latest news.

I've just come from Sati, the ultimate two-headed beauty, one head topped by long, straight dark hair, the other crowned with a curly mop of blond curls. Sati's still officially my prisoner, but, to keep her amenable, I've set her up in a sumptuous boudoir, a whore's chamber, with a huge circular bunku topped by pink satin coverlets. She adores it and we've started from scratch with our exploration of what she calls love-sex, investigating different ways to satisfy each other. For two people as experienced in sexual matters as we are it's quite a challenge, but you could say we are rising to it. We enjoy trying to outdo each other in inventiveness.

When Thor mentions the arrival of another two-headed I'm immediately interested. Maybe I could try out some of the sexual experimentation explored with Sati on the new female.

'Where is she?' I ask, looking round the dino-cube.

Thor grins. 'It's not a female, but a male giant. And guess what, his skin is as black and shiny as polished ebony.'

I resist the temptation to ask him how he knows what polished ebony looks like. 'Why is he here?'

'They say Athene has brought him here for her own pleasure. That's why I was a bit taken aback when she chose to spend the night with you.'

He shoves his nutri-ration into both of his two mouths, one above the other. Not for the first time I think how revolting he looks when eating. Females seem turned on by his two pairs of bulging lips. I can't think – or perhaps don't want to think – why.

I didn't spend the night with Athene. Only the evening. Was the time I spent with Athene a rehearsal for the night she was to spend with the new humanoid? I'm not exactly jealous but the idea doesn't exactly please me either.

'Where is he now?'

'In Athene's office. He's been in there the entire morning. Apparently he's got a good brain as well as a muscular physique. You'll have to watch out, Heracles. She may be thinking of him replacing you in more ways than one. How would you like that?'

'She's in for a shock if she tries a trick like that with me. I intend to replace her, remember.'

Thor gives me a sly look. 'And when that happens I'll be your Number Two?'

'Of course. Won't be long now, Thor, my friend.'

In fact, I doubt I will make him my deputy. Better not give him too much power. I'll have to persuade him he's more useful to me undercover.

I think a female deputy would be a good choice. More malleable. More agreeable. Maybe one of my prisoners, Durga, the demon slayer, or Sati. No, not Durga. She's too power hungry. Sati then. She is not unintelligent and certainly more compliant than before.

Thor nudges me, and places his coarse face next to my ear. 'Here he comes,' his two mouths say in tandem.

A massive black humanoid strides into the dino-cube. Thor is right. The giant's skin is as smooth and glossy as polished ebony. (I've never seen ebony either, but I've seen pictures and read about it online). The giant carries himself with dignity, his two heads held high, but he does not intimidate me.

One of his faces is elongated and impassive and has an

uncompromising slit for a mouth; the other has a broad forehead, a stubby nose and puffy lips. I'd rather do business with the latter. His huge neck is encircled by a copper collar. His bare arms are half-covered with bracelets of red, blue and black beads. The top half of his arms are stamped with small circles, seemingly embedded in his skin. The rest of his body is clothed in a long, loose robe with wide coffee and cream coloured stripes.

He takes his nutri-ration from the bar and sits down at a table on his own. I note that he eats with the more generous of the two mouths. The other face remains blank. Mean and hungry!

Everyone is sneaking glances at the newcomer, not sure what to make of him. He's certainly unlike anyone we've seen here before.

I wait until he's taken his last mouthful and amble over to him, careful not to bump into the tables and chairs on my way. I've been practising my walk lately, determined to move less awkwardly. As a potential leader I need to cultivate poise. I'm quite pleased with my progress. My three legs move in a more co-ordinated manner now and I've developed an athlete's roll, which suggests I'm a sporty type. Not a bad image to project. I'm conscious of everyone's eyes on me.

'Welcome to C99,' I hold out my hand. 'I'm Heracles. No doubt you've heard of me.'

He stands up, towers over me and shakes my hand. He's a good foot taller than me. Shit.

'Kata-Mbula,' he says. '109th King of the Kuba, from Zaire, deep in the basin of the River Congo.' His voice is amazingly low-pitched for a mutant, yet loud. It resounds throughout the dino-cube without any conscious effort to project it. 'But please call me Kat. Everyone does. Oh yes, I've heard all about you all right, Heracles.'

He motions for me to sit at his table but I need to assert

my authority. Show him I'm in charge. I remain standing and suggest that we go my office for a private chat.

He agrees affably enough. All eyes are on us as we leave the dino-cube. I wink at Thor as I pass.

My office is large with a huge workstation and a state-of-the-art compu. I show off a bit, explaining how I am able to view other compounds on the multi-screens and even Oasis. I think he's quite impressed.

'So – you're a spy,' he laughs, a booming laugh that resounds round the walls.

'I suppose I could be, if necessary,' I'm trying to size him up and I suspect he's doing the same with me.

I gesture for him to take a seat on the opposite side of the desk and he eases his long frame into the comfort of the shaper, his legs set wide under his robe. He exudes genial self-confidence.

'Which compound have you come from?' I ask.

'C97 or Compound Creative as we prefer to call it,' he tells me with a wide grin. 'We concentrate on the creative arts, you see.'

We all do that to reach our targets. There's no need for him to boast about that. 'I think you must be a warrior, a big guy like you,' I can't resist saying.

He leans forward, hands on his wide apart knees and opens his four eyes wide. The thin mask-like face says, 'Kata-Mbula is a peaceful king. He doesn't fight, but he has many troubles. Many problems. Sometimes he feels like he wants to kill himself.'

Before I realise what he intends to do, he stands up, pulls out a knife from inside his robe, holds it high in the air and plunges it into his heart. Uttering a mighty cry he collapses and lands in a rolling heap on the floor. He twists and turns, shrieks and groans. A few more tortuous rotations of his body, one final jerk and he lands flat on his back, eyes wide open, unblinking, silent.

I stumble round the desk. Good Zeus, he's killed himself and I'm left with a dead humanoid giant in my office.

I stand staring down at the lifeless body. What the hell am I supposed to do now?

One of the four eyes blinks. He sits up, pulls himself to his feet and starts to laugh, that deep booming laugh. It seems he will never stop.

He goes on and on laughing and puts his hands on my shoulders to pull himself up. Whether out of relief at him being miraculously restored to life or shame at being duped, I start laughing too.

I can't believe it. The devil really had me fooled. 'For a moment I thought you'd topped yourself.'

Another huge guffaw and, his arm slung round my shoulder, he says, 'Forgive me, brother. I couldn't resist it. Once an actor always an actor you know.'

He hands me the knife.

'The famous Kuba King, my ancestor, Shamba Bolongongo, substituted this wooden knife for war weapons and always carried it with him as a sign of peace. We at Compound Creative follow in his footsteps. We are all men of peace. Performers. Actors. Dancers. The only deaths we know are on stage. So far.'

I finger the wooden knife. It's carved with images of birds and animals. I hand it back to him. 'It's beautiful.'

In Compound Creative we have many beautiful things. We're passionate about creativity.'

I'm not sure why he's telling me this. Again I think that all mutant humanoids are encouraged to be creative.

I decide to ask outright what he's doing here. 'Did you ask for a transfer?'

'Oh no. Athene invited me. Didn't she tell you?' The thin lips of the elongated head attempt a tight smile.

The other head adds, 'I think it's wonderful what she's doing. She's only been CEO for a few months and already she's visited all the compounds and talked to many of us personally. She wants to know what we would like to do now that the Earth is no longer polluted. She's a true believer in democracy.'

He's a fool. Athene's frequent visits to the other compounds may be in the name of democracy but their intention is to consolidate her position as CEO.

'She has made very few decisions as yet,' I point out.

Poker face nods ambiguously. Big face grins but says nothing. I screw up my eyes. What does he know that makes him so smug?

I stroll round my workstation, back to my swivel-shaper and sit down. 'Tell me, why did you agree to come here?'

'Athene made me an offer I couldn't refuse,' says poker face.

'She asked me to dance at her inaugural ceremony,' says the other.

Shit. She asked me to organise that ceremony but I haven't got round to it. To be honest, I hoped I would have managed to replace her as leader before it took place. Seems she's going ahead without my help.

'To dance?'

'Yes. The Kings of Kuba have always been dancers as well as rulers,' explains wide face. 'Just wait until you see our costumes.'

'And masks,' adds poker face.

I can't help thinking that a face that inscrutable doesn't need a mask.

The two heads look very different, but, like Sati's, each head seems to think as one, often finishing each other's sentences.

I stand up. 'I have a treat to look forward to then,' I say, holding out my hand. 'I look forward to seeing you perform.'

'I shall be honoured to dance here.' Kat takes my hand across the desk and gives a bow.

'Especially as Athene has agreed to dance with me,' adds the other head with a smug smile.

A sick ache in the pit of my stomach tells me how I feel about that.

Athene has an office even more spacious and luxurious than mine. She has personalised it since it belonged to previous CEO, three-headed Ra. Feminised it. The pictures on the walls are swirls of colour and the shapers are covered in pink and silver silk.

'Heracles, take a seat. We need to talk.'

Sounds ominous.

I choose a double-shaper and lounge on it, one of my legs splayed over the back, another over an arm and the other stretched out on the seat.

Athene frowns at my casual pose. 'I hear you've met Kata-Mbula. A fascinating humanoid don't you think?'

I raise my eyebrows. 'Fascinating indeed.'

'What do you know about him?'

'That he's to dance at your inauguration.'

She smiles, 'And....'

'That he's a man of peace.'

'What else?'

'Nothing else.'

'He didn't tell you why I've brought him here?'

I shake my head.

'As I thought, he's discreet. He's left it to me to tell you. I've brought him here, Heracles, because he's a brilliant designer.'

'He told me about the costumes and masks for his dance. Says they're really something.'

'When I visited his compound, I was knocked out by

the performance he put on for me. You do realise that Kata-Mbula is the Head of C97, Compound Creative. What he has achieved there is astonishing. He uses everyone's creative talents to the full, puts on pieces of theatre and dance and involves the entire sectoid. Those who want to dance or act or perform in any way do so. Others design the sets, costumes and lighting or compose music. Those with a more practical bent construct the scenery and make the costumes, wigs and masks. The show I saw was a veritable spectacle. It told the story of some famous Kuban king from the seventeenth century in dance and mime. I was gripped from beginning to end.'

'That would be Shamba Bolongongo. He was one of Kata-Mbula's ancestors, the most famous of the Kuban kings. He brought peace to his people.'

Athene's eyebrow shoots up. 'How do you know all that?'

'I make it my business to know.'

'You continue to surprise me, Heracles. Well done.'

'You were so impressed with his performance you invited him here to dance?'

'Not just him, his entire sectoid. Kat is to be the artistic director of the biggest spectacle that mutant humanoids have ever performed or witnessed.'

I sit up. 'You want his entire sectoid to come here and perform here for us?'

'You're thinking too small, Heracles. They are going to perform not only for us, but for everyone.'

'Ah, you will transmit it on the big screen.'

'For those who can't come yes, but every single humanoid from every compound will be invited here to see it. The first to apply will be awarded seats. This will be the first big event to be held on Earth, since before The Great Plague. The first of many I hope.'

'In the open air?'

'Kat is to design a huge amphitheatre. It will have a roof, but an adjustable one that can be rolled open if the weather is fine and closed if it's wet or cold.'

I sit up. 'What can I do to help?'

'I'm glad you're so enthusiastic, Heracles. There have been times lately when I've wondered if you are really with me.'

'I'm with you all the way, Athene. You should know that. I'm sure I can incorporate some of my own ideas into this project.'

'I'm sure you can. I want this to be an experience that everyone can share, something to remember forever. An inspiration.'

'It sounds great, really great.'

She needs Kat more than me. I am merely a bit player in this event she's dreaming up. I feel power slipping away from me.

I pull myself to my feet. 'I'll give it some thought, Athene, see what contribution I can make to this – this spectacle.'

I'll make sure it's a spectacle all right, a spectacle that will result in the end of her reign as CEO. I start to amble off, hoping she notices my athlete's roll.

'Don't go yet, Heracles, there are several other things I need to discuss with you.'

I look over my shoulder at her, amble back and sink back on the shaper.

'The first concerns your prisoners, Durga and Sati. I've allowed you a free hand with them. After all, you saved C99 from invasion and you deserved your show of power. But it's time for an amnesty. I want you to pardon them both and give them their freedom.'

That makes me sit up again. 'But….'

'If you don't release them, I will.'

I stand, stride up to her workstation and face her across it. 'This is not just, Athene.'

'It is just. You've had your revenge and made your point. Now let them go.'

I can't believe what she's saying. 'What the hell are they going to do once they're free?'

Athene shrugs. 'That's rather up to them. That's what freedom means.'

She hesitates, moves smoothly round her workstation, perches on the edge of it next to me, her one eye looking deeply into the central one of my three.

'I need Kata-Mbula to stay here to design the amphitheatre. But that will create a power vacuum in C97. My suggestion is that you go there as head administrator and oversee The Big Event there. By the way, that's what I've decided to call the inauguration ceremony: The Big Event.'

I don't say a word.

'What do you think about this opportunity I'm offering you – to be Head of Compound Creative? It will give you a real chance to try out your leadership skills. Good experience, as you've never been in charge of a sectoid before. You'd still be my deputy, of course. That goes without saying.'

In spite of that last comment, I can't help thinking that this is her way of getting rid of me. She wants to replace me with that two-headed giant. That's what all this is about. I try to keep calm.

'What about Durga and Sati?' I ask.

'Leave Durga to me. She can stay here in C99 for the time being, until I find a position appropriate to her skills. As for Sati....'

'I'd like to take Sati with me,' I interrupt.

'As your concubine?'

'As my assistant,' I tell her. 'Remember how useful she was helping Kali to reorganise the recreational facilities in C55 before she....'

'Decided to take over?' Athene smiles.

'That won't happen this time. There's no way she'll get the better of me.'

'I'm sure she won't.' Athene slides off the workstation. 'But just remember, Heracles, she isn't your prisoner any more. The amnesty is for Sati as well as Durga.'

Athene is fobbing me off by presenting me with my own compound and my own workforce. At first I'm furious with her, but the more I think about it, the more convinced I am that this solution is not so bad. It's Kata-Mbula who is being deposed, not me. I am to be in charge of the sectoid that was previously his. He may take over my office and multi-screen compu for the project in hand, but I am still Athene's deputy. She has left me in no doubt about that. This is a chance for me to prove myself a valuable leader.

There are advantages of moving to another compound, away from Athene's eagle eye. I can spend time plotting a takeover without her looking over my shoulder.

I am just about to leave her office again when Athene adds, 'By the way, you do realise that when I say everyone will be welcome to attend The Big Event that I mean completes too. I intend to send invitations to every single member of the Symposium on Planet Oasis.'

I go to see Durga first, tell her I forgive her and that she is free to go.

She tosses back her red hair. 'Free to go where? Back to C98, my compound, to turf out that traitorous sister-wife of mine, Jagadgauri?'

'That's not my decision,' I tell her. 'You must discuss that with Athene.'

Durga scowls at me and starts to gather up her possessions.

Sati doesn't seem grateful to be set free either. 'Gee, thanks for nothing,' she says. 'Actually I'm quite comfortable here in this luxury aparto.'

She spends most of her time lounging on the huge circular bunku watching filmograms, with breaks for her beauty treatments. It's only at night when I return to the boudoir that she has to work for her living.

'Comfortable, eh? That's a pity because I thought we'd go on a road trip.'

She becomes curious when I speak the lingo of the filmograms and badgers me until I tell her what sort of road trip I'm talking about. 'I'm to be Chief Administrator of Compound 97 and you'll be my Number Two,' I announce.

'I don't intend to be anybody's Number Two.' She shakes her curly blond hair. 'I'll be Number One or nothing,' adds the black-haired head, dark eyes flashing.

'OK. You win. You can be my Number One.'

Christ, females are so stupid. Unbelievable.

Sati spends a lot of time deciding what to take with her. She'd like to take the circular bed.

'I'll buy you a new one when we get there,' I promise.

The only thing I want to take is my drive-saver. I copy all my files on to it and wipe the compu clean. I don't intend to make it an easy changeover for Kata-Mbula.

He wanders in while I'm doing this, but doesn't seem to notice.

His main concern is that I look after the members of his sectoid.

'They need nurturing,' he tells me. 'Make sure you give them lots of praise, even the less talented ones.'

'Yeah, yeah,' I say. 'I get it. Lots of encouragement to reach their targets.'

The thin face looks at me a little oddly. The broad face says, 'Make sure they rehearse everyday. I'll be back from time to time to teach them new choreography, but I've got to spend most of my time here, designing the amphitheatre and overseeing the building of it.'

I go to say 'Goodbye' to Athene. She glides round her work-station and looks up at me, her deep blue eye piercing my middle one. 'We'll see each other soon, Heracles. I'm going to miss you.'

'I'll miss you too,' I say dutifully. I give her a sly grin. 'Kata-Mbula told me you are going to dance with him at The Big Event. Is that true?'

She lowers her eye-lid and gives a little laugh. 'You'll have to wait and see – just like everyone else. But it would make a fantastic climax to the event, don't you think?'

Chapter Four
Welcome to Compound Creative
(according to Heracles)

As Sati and I step out of the teleport, our first impression is of a blaze of colour accompanied by a mighty noise. The colour emanates from the swaying floor length robes of red, blue, silver and gold displayed by what seems to be the entire workforce of C97. The noise comes from the banging of drums competing with humanoid cries of 'Hi,' 'Welcome,' and 'Great to meet you!'

A tall, dark-skinned female in a black and gold caftan heads the group. She raises her hands above her head. The drumming and voices cease. The robed figures stop swaying.

'I am Bathsheba,' proclaims the imposing figure, her deep voice resounding around the entrance hall. 'Delighted to make your acquaintance, Heracles. We have heard so much about you from our beloved Kata-Mbula.' She turns to Sati. 'How beautiful you are, my dear! Welcome to Compound Creative.'

Sati and I exchange a look. This Bathsheba is keen to show us she's in charge.

At a gesture from Bathsheba the music starts up: drums, cymbals, violins and some sort of wind instrument. Hips sway, mouths open wide and everyone bursts into song, the most amazing sound I've ever heard. The acoustics of this hall or theatre, whatever it is, make the voices soar.

At the end of the song Sati and I applaud and everyone joins in, clapping, cheering and laughing.

Bathsheba raises her arms again and opens them wide. The crowd splits into two sections leaving a central passageway for us to walk through. Moses crossing the Red Sea has nothing on us. As we pass through, I take the opportunity to demonstrate my athlete's roll.

The singing and clapping continue. Sati holds her two heads high and takes dainty steps on the tips of her toes. Hands reach out to touch us as we pass.

Bathsheba leads Sati and me to our adjacent aparto-cubes. Detailed tapestries hang on the walls, each depicting mythical stories, based on the culture of the countries of the members of this sectoid.

'Their ancestors knew these stories and we try to keep them alive in embroidered wall hangings, carpets and paintings, as well as in our theatrical performances,' Bathsheba informs us. 'Make yourselves comfortable. I'll be back to show you around later.' And off she stalks. Good riddance.

Sati tiptoes around her aparto. I lean on the doorframe and watch her. She takes off her shoes and sinks her toes into the fake fur rugs in the shape of tigers, leopards and lions. There have been no animals on Earth for several hundred years, but someone has taken the trouble to research what they were like.

Sati lies on her stomach on a double shaper and runs her hands through the soft white fleece cover, closes her eyes and breathes in deeply. She springs up and flings herself on top of the red and blue striped velvet bunku-spread, kneels up and draws the matching curtains around the four-poster. She parts a curtain to make a small gap. A provocative blond head peeps out. She pulls the curtain closed again, but a moment later the other head, dark hair pulled seductively over one shoulder, takes a peek at me.

She stands tall on the bunku and drapes a curtain round her lovely body: Cleopatra in a carpet. I grin. She can be fun when she chooses. When she's tired of playing peek-a-boo, she pulls the curtains wide open, jumps off the bunku and runs her fingers over the decorated surfaces of the carved statuettes in the corners of the cube.

'These must be their gods,' she says. 'Or kings and queens. The humanoids who live here must be very talented to carve these.'

'They must indeed,' I say, almost as impressed with the quality of the arts and crafts as she is.

Sati goes into the lavat-cube. I hear her quick intake of breath. She peers round the door with both heads.

'Come and take a look, Heracles. It's like a garden.'

The walls are painted with trees, leaves and flowers and there's a huge shower comparto with a double spray.

My aparto next door is very similar but more masculine. Every single tapestry, painting, rug and carving is distinct. Originals. When I worked in the histo-lab with Odysseus we had many original artefacts, all from the past; but this is contemporary work. There's a double four poster in here too, but my bunku-spread and curtains are in earthy colours, brown, terracotta and green, the colour of the jungle, and the jungle theme continues in the lavat-cube, with huge trees and giant tropical plants. How imaginative of these humanoids to bring the outside world inside in a windowless space.

Bathsheba returns and asks imperiously. 'What's the verdict?'

'Stupendous,' says Sati. 'I could live here.'

'I certainly hope so,' says Bathsheba. 'And you, Heracles. What do you think?'

I don't want to sound too enthusiastic. 'I think you've gone to a lot of trouble to prepare these apartos for us. Very gracious of you to decorate them with examples of your best work.'

Bathsheba chuckles deep in her throat. It is only at that moment that I notice her mutation: three extra fingers nestled round her neck. She may have more mutations than these of course, but the long black djellabah covers the rest of her body. I am reminded of Athene's long white robe and what it conceals, the ever-changing bodily patterns that come alive when she dances.

What secrets does Bathsheba's gown hide, I wonder?

I have little desire to find out. If I ever do rip off her clothes and take her it will be to teach her a lesson, to make her realise who is boss. I don't fancy her at all. I find myself shivering.

'Cold?' asks Bathsheba with a toothy smile. 'Come, I'll show you the rest of Compound Creative and you can judge for yourself the general standard of our artistry.'

All the art and craft on show is of a similar standard to the items in our apartos. No wonder Bathsheba chuckled when I suggested the apartos were decorated especially for us. I'm knocked out by everything I see, but try not to show it, determined not to encourage Bathsheba's superior attitude by giving her cause to gloat.

She points to a particular painting and proudly informs us it is her creation. It's a powerful piece, dark and forceful. Again I feel sceptical about this female. How much power does she have? Is she friend or foe? She shows us a large dormo-cube that contains a series of double bunkus. 'Some of our members prefer to sleep in communes.' She allows the door to slide shut quickly as she moves us on.

I take Sati's arm and steer her away, remembering the disruption she caused with her love-sex orgies in Kali's compound, C55. Better not to give her any ideas.

Bathsheba slides open another door. 'This is Kata-Mbula's office. Yours now, Heracles.'

The office is laid out with specific care. It has less carvings and paintings than the other rooms and only one tapestry. I fail to understand why Kat's office should be so basically equipped. He is, or was, their leader. You'd think he'd want to demonstrate his power by exhibiting a generous amount of artefacts and paintings.

Bathsheba explains Kat's viewpoint. 'Kat displays ten new pieces of creative work each week. It's a competition that everyone wants to win.'

'Good motivation for the workforce,' I remark. 'Plus he is able to assert his power by selecting the ones he likes.'

Bathsheba frowns. 'It's not like at all. The members vote for the ones they like best and he accepts their choices.'

My turn to frown. 'But suppose he doesn't like the pieces they choose?'

'He only has to look at them for a week before the next ten arrive.' She strolls to the door. 'In any case, Kat is not one to spend much time in his office. He likes to be out there working alongside his colleagues.' She gives me a sidelong look. 'Athene says you're a bit of a whiz on the compu. Not a skill many possess here, so I guess you will have your uses.'

A snide remark, belittling compu skills as an art form and suggesting I won't be much use at anything else. I have no wish to join in with this acting lark, but I am determined to show her I'm in charge. On the surface she seems to be helping us settle in but I sense her resentment. She thinks the sun shines out of Kat's arse and is determined to make me feel incompetent.

I see that I shall have to make myself felt as a different kind of leader.

'From now on I shall choose which pieces I want to decorate my office.'

Bathsheba opens her mouth to protest, changes her mind and closes it firmly. 'As you wish,' she says, her voice cold.

Before the tour finishes, Bathsheba takes us outside. The creativity of these humanoids apparently extends to the making of a garden on ground that has been barren for years. The flowers are grouped artistically in groups of colour. I don't know the names of the plants, but I do know the effect is striking. One of the borders features yellow and lavender coloured flowers, another orange and magenta and there is a square of green lawn, surrounded by bushes and what I believe is called a hedge.

On the lawn sit several humanoids holding pieces of paper. 'Learning their lines,' explains Bathsheba. 'I've told them they must be word perfect by tomorrow.' That's her way of telling me that she's in charge of rehearsals.

'As with the other sectoids, we can decide to leave the compound if we wish, build our own houses and live separately. But we choose not to do that. Why? Because we are a close-knit community, used to living together and working together on our creative projects.'

''It will take time for most of us to get used to living outside,' I agree, 'but in the future I assure you we shall all live in houses and flats, just as human beings did in the past.'

'Not the humanoids from Compound Creative,' insists Bathsheba.

I smile. Not worth arguing about. I'm going to make it happen. Against the skyline, I note a dome-shaped building. That must be C98. Between these two compounds, I will build my city.

I screw up my three eyes and look across the wide space that once was the wilderness and visualise it. First The Heracles Tower, then houses, shops, cinemas and sports grounds. My original plan B.

Plan A was to build the tower and the city on a satellite in the sky, but I will build a city here first.

'Thanks for showing us round, Bathsheba,' I say,

dismissing her. 'I am going to spend some time in my office now.'

She smiles. 'That's fine. I'll look after Sati. I have something very special for her to do.'

'What's that?'

'Suffice it to say that we are going to prepare for the party this evening. See you later.'

First we've heard about a party. Sati prances off with Bathsheba and I sit down at Kat's compu and look at his files.

Designs for stage sets, costumes and masks, notes on choreography and ideas for theatre productions: nothing of any importance.

I plug in my drive-saver and upload my files.

When I return to my aparto I hear excited voices and laughter next door. I knock and enter and there is Sati surrounded by a group of females, some kneeling at her feet, others standing, others sitting watching. Is Sati up to her old tricks, initiating some kind of love fest? No. They are making her some new clothes, dressing and undressing her as if she is one of those Barbie dolls seen in old adverts. Two of them are winding a long sheath of scarlet silk round her body, drawing it neatly over her breasts and pinning it on one shoulder. The kneelers are tacking up the hem.

'What do you think?' asks Sati, pushing the women away and giving a twirl. 'Does it suit me, Heracles?'

I stand in front of her nodding and grinning and the females start to clap in rhythm as Sati spins. I join in – the clapping that is, not the spinning.

'You next,' they say and although I protest it makes no difference. Two or three of them approach me holding a long sky blue piece of cloth and begin fitting it over the jump suit I'm wearing.

'Just a minute,' I say, pushing them away and handing back the swathe of material for them to hold. I strip off, letting the discarded jog suit slip to the floor. I kick it away and stand there naked, my wide shoulders, strong chest, three muscular legs, penis and testicles exposed. Nothing to be ashamed of: I'm well hung and happy in my skin. I lap up the stares.

I grin. 'Come on, then.'

The two females with the fabric come towards me, a little tentatively at first, but soon their professionalism takes over. They drape the length of material over one shoulder and begin to adjust, pin and tack it together. Others have been putting the finishing touches to Sati's costume. That's what these are – stage costumes. Nothing is real here. We've entered a fantasy world.

In the other compounds we take little notice of what we wear. Joggers and T-shirts arrive regularly and we put them on and take them off with little thought of fashion or aesthetics. In Compound Creative it's quite different. Everyone wears long robes, which, apart from looking elegant and colourful, also serve to hide most of their mutations. I'm not saying they look like completes. Some have extra heads or eyes and such mutations cannot be hidden under a robe. But let's say one is less aware of the mutations here than usual, because of the caftans, sarongs, djellabahs or gowns. When we next meet these creative humanoids we shall be dressed like them.

A special supper has been arranged for us. No food packoids or nutri-rations tonight. Apparently one of the skills my new workforce possesses is the ability to prepare tasty food. I have no idea what the ingredients of this meal consist of, but everything tastes and smells delicious. Not only that, it is presented artistically too. Attention has been paid to colour and the arrangement of the food on decorative serving plates in the centre of a giant table. A great deal of effort and imagination has gone into the preparation. I glance at Sati. She arches her four eyebrows and licks her two pairs of lips.

I'm not sure how we are supposed to eat this meal so keep an eye on the others. They eat with their fingers as we do but they don't thrust the food into their mouths. They eat in what I can only describe as a delicate manner, holding their fingers with elegant precision. They don't snatch at the food but take a little at a time and bite small pieces off before chewing and swallowing.

I note Sati observing the way they eat and copying it. She manages very well, much better than I do.

I'm so worried about looking like an oaf that I don't eat as much I'd like to and get up from the table still feeling hungry.

Bathsheba whispers, 'don't expect to eat like this every night. This is a special feast to welcome you.'

I feel quite relieved to hear that. I'm not used to eating in public with so many people watching me. The dino-cube in C99 has a series of small tables. They are not well lit and I usually sit alone or share a table with Thor whose table manners are infinitely worse than mine. He can't resist stuffing his nutri-rations into both mouths at the same time. Gross.

That reminds me. The change in my life took place so quickly I didn't have a chance to tell Thor I was leaving. I must send him an auto-mail tomorrow. Or perhaps not. Let him wait. Do him good to worry.

After supper we are led into the theatre. The members of the sectoid appear fascinated by us. They touch us as we pass or come and sit beside us and let their fingers play on our hands and forearms. I find it a little disconcerting but strangely soothing.

We are treated to another dance performance. I can't say

I enjoy it. All that smiling and leaping and gyrating. When will it end? I can't wait to curl up in my bunku with Sati, make love-sex and go to sleep.

Much later that's exactly what we do. But when I wake up the next morning, Sati has disappeared. No doubt she's sampling the commun-dormo-cube. Up to her old tricks again.

Chapter Five
New Broom
(according to Heracles)

The next day I am determined to show Bathsheba and the entire sectoid that I am in charge and they'd better understand that fact.

I find Bathsheba in the dino-cube at breakfast time and tell her to gather everyone together. She asks me to sit down beside her for a moment, takes my hand in hers and advises me that such a confrontation would not be wise. 'At least not before you've talked to the council.'

I get the strange idea that she intends to seduce me. True she's a handsome woman, but she's far from young and not my type at all. Her deep voice and touchy-feely behaviour give me the creeps.

I have no idea who or what the council is but she soon enlightens me.

'Kat knows that the best way to get humanoids to co-operate is to give them a share in the decision-making. He's all for democracy. The council consists of colleagues who wish to share their ideas with him. The members tend to change from week to week. A nucleus remains, but there are always some who have to relinquish their duties on the council because they are busy working on a particular project and can't devote enough time to attend meetings; but there are always others bursting with enthusiasm ready to take their places.'

All this democratic stuff is not my bag. I'm a tad bored with it already and am aware that Bathsheba senses this. Still I mustn't rush in "where angels fear to tread" – an old cliché that one – or "like a bull in a china shop" which is probably a more apt expression in my case. I did rush my doomed visit to Oasis that time and look where that got me. Locked up in a cage and put on show like an animal in a zoo.

I agree to meet the council. Bathsheba looks relieved.

'Very wise, Heracles,' she says and encloses my hand in hers. I feel my skin crawl and am pleased when she leaves. Patronising bitch.

The members of the council assemble in my office later that morning, nodding and smiling. I really can't tell one individual from another. If the council changes from week to week it hardly seems worth the effort to get to know them anyway.

I tell them about the proposed general meeting. They look surprised. One of them says, 'It's quite a good idea in principal. You could give a short speech to introduce yourself. It would give everyone a chance to see and hear you, but it must be handled carefully.' The speaker is a humanoid with two ears one above the other on one side of his face. He only has one mouth but seems more interested in talking than listening. 'You could express your ideas in a very general way, saying such things as we are all working toward the same goals and that you are as keen as we are for The Big Event to be a resounding success.'

Wow! That's original, I think, but I'm sure my sarcasm wouldn't be appreciated, so I bite my tongue. A lot of nodding is going on and I find myself nodding too, to keep them happy. They are looking at me, expecting me to say something.

'Who doesn't want The Big Event to be a success?' I make a gesture, the palms of my hands uppermost. 'The meeting would be an opportunity to get everyone on my side.'

'We don't do sides here,' a red-faced female with frizzy hair informs me. 'We are all so devoted to our Kat, you know. You'll have to give us time to get used to you.'

'With a few changes, such as new schedules, I'm sure we can all get on well together and achieve a good result.'

A rather stern looking female with three piercing eyes says sharply. 'New schedules! No need for that. An excellent timetable is already in place. I drew it up myself and it's working well. Let's keep to that. '

More nods from the council. I let her comments wash over me. I have agreed to listen but I don't have to take their advice. After all, I'm in charge.

I try again. 'I will be able to judge if changes are necessary when I make my daily inspection of rehearsals.'

The male with two ears placed vertically above each other proffers another piece of advice. 'It wouldn't really be prudent to talk about inspecting our work. Why not just say that you wish to attend rehearsals or workshops from time to time to take an interest in what we are doing. It might put a few backs up if it's felt you are checking up on us.'

It doesn't occur to these cretins that "putting a few backs up" might be my intention. To let them know who is boss.

Red face adds, 'You must remember that negative criticism impedes creativity and none of us want that, do we?'

Yawn, yawn. I stand up and summon up a smile. 'Thank you all for your time and advice. I'll think about what you've said and get back to you.'

They seem surprised that I'm cutting the meeting short.

The female with piercing eyes and a voice to match turns at the door in a last attempt to get some sense into what she no doubt perceives as my thick skull. 'You really must understand that creative humanoids – especially actors and dancers – must be handled with great sensitivity.'

'Oh, I do understand that,' I assure her. 'Being creative myself, I understand all about sensitivity.'

She frowns as if she doesn't believe me but can't call me a liar to my face.

They are all reactionaries, resistant to change. They want to keep the status quo at all costs. What's the use of being a leader if you have no power to initiate change?

Feeling a bit disgruntled, I shut myself in Kat's office, now mine. I'm in the mood for a vigorous bit of hacking.

Half an hour later I break into the Symposium's website on Planet Oasis. Great!

Another half hour and I manage to access the personal account of The Minister for Foreign Affairs. A photo of the Minister heads the file. It's the complete that interrogated me on Oasis. Orlando Wolfe.

I leap into the air, let out a massive 'Yes!' and throw my arms above my head. Success!

I recall the conversation Wolfe and I had. Even in the interrogation room I recognised that he and I had a lot in common. I remember how intently he listened as I told him about my dream to build a city for mutant humanoids on a satellite. He was adamant that could never happen, making it clear that the satellites were only for completes.

Now I have an available site to build a new city on Earth, Orlando Wolfe could prove the man to help me. I settle down at the console and begin to read Wolfe's auto-mail and files. As I suspected, Orlando Wolfe is a powerful member of the Symposium. He's on the sub-committee looking into the possibility of the integration of mutant humanoids on Oasis. That surprises me. He seemed so adamant the day I met him that Oasis was only for completes. Of course he may have got himself on to the committee to act as a subversive, ready to undermine any proposals that those in favour of integration might suggest.

There certainly appear to be problems with the migrants from C1 – complaints from employers about their work not being up to scratch and from residents who don't appreciate living next door to them. I understand that. I wouldn't want to live next door to those cretins either.

Orlando Wolfe doesn't do much about these complaints, but he doesn't trash them. I suspect he's collecting evidence, biding his time before taking action.

As I trawl through file after file, I come across a series of fotograms, head and shoulder shots of members of the Symposium, with their names and the posts they hold. I sift through them. Typical politicians, men in suits, some more shifty-looking than others but all trying to look serious and powerful. What a joke. Women too, power-dressed to kill, but not as many as I would have expected from completes attempting to build an ideal society.

I select one fotogram at random: Harold Smythe, Minister for Education, is the caption. The folder opens to reveal a further series of files. Each one contains notes on Smythe's opinions on various issues and how he voted on them. Yawn, yawn. There's another file marked personal and when I open it, I see fotograms of his family, a rather severe-looking woman and three children. I open more folders containing similar notes on other Symposium members, both personal and official.

All the politicians seem to have children. Obviously no problem with propagating the species as far as completes are concerned.

I wonder what it would be like to have children. I think of Isis now on a satellite called Hos-sat waiting to give birth. I had a little fling with her once. That could have been my baby. It isn't, of course. The timing is way off, but how would I feel if I were the father? Heracles, a father! What a laugh. Nah. Not my bag this family lark, although from these fotograms the families look happy enough.

One folder seems to be missing, that of Orlando Wolfe. I soon deduce why.

These files contain information about Wolfe's colleagues that he has compiled himself. The devious bastard.

I grin. It takes one to recognise one. He's made of the same stuff as I am.

Another image catches my eye. It's the man who came to Headculturedome, the day little Mercury disappeared, the first complete I'd ever seen. Mercury called him Mr. Suit. Yes, that's him all right, a thin-faced, rather intense man. Not as cocky looking as Orlando Wolfe. The caption informs me that his name is Alexander Court, the Minister for Culture. I click open the folder, go straight to the personal file and find another fotogram of him with a rather frail-looking female at his side. In tiny letters at the bottom, it says, First wife, Lisa, died in childbirth. I open the next page. There is Alexander Court with another female and two children, a boy and a girl, named Stuart and Bella.

I don't believe it. His new wife is Stella Jameson, the bitch who chose Athene as the new CEO instead of me. I slap my hand down on the desktop. Shit. My old agro about her builds up. Why the hell should she, a complete, choose our leaders? I glare at the fotogram. Her steady blue eyes stare back at me. Blond hair frames her serene face. She's very sure of herself. And beautiful – if you like that type. I have to admit I wouldn't kick her out of bed.

I scroll down and sure enough there is quite a long article about Stella Jameson's ancestors, the originators of Worldwideculture, and an update about her current position as owner and managing director.

Among her many duties, I read, *is the appointment of the mutant humanoid CEO in charge of all the English speaking compounds.*

It's not fair. Why should this female complete have so much power over us?

I scroll up to the fotogram again. She is holding Alexander Court's arm and looking up at him with a self-satisfied smile. The smug bitch. There's no doubt she wears the trousers in that relationship.

I scroll down and am in for another shock. There's another fotogram of Alexander and Stella, this time with a young male. Printed underneath it says that the young man's name is Michael Court. But that can't be right. It's little Mercury from C55, I knew him when he was a child. Shit. Somehow or other he's inveigled himself into that family and changed his name to Michael Court.

I think back to that interrogation with Wolfe. When he told me the satellites were only for completes. I blurted out that if that was the case why had I seen a mutant humanoid coming out of the university? I remember the way Wolfe's eyes narrowed as he asked me to write down the name of the humanoid I thought I'd seen and any other details I knew about him to give him the next day. Before I could decide how much to tell him, I was returned to Earth.

Wolfe was very interested in the identity of that migrant from Earth. No doubt he will still be interested. I had seen Mercury online coming out of Oasis University and again in real life through the transparent walls of that prison cell. He saw me too. The glass was obviously soundproof so we couldn't speak but he recognised me all right and I him.

Could it have been Mercury who was instrumental in getting me released the next morning? I'm confused. Is he friend or foe? What the hell is he doing on Oasis?

I scroll down and there is a picture of the whole family, Alexander, Stella, Michael, Stuart and Bella. Michael Court looks a little uncomfortable. I'm not at all sure he likes being a member of that family. Perhaps they kidnapped him. Perhaps I could be his rescuer.

If I have anything to do with it, Michael Court will soon be little Mercury again and back with Kali in C55. At least she will be happy to see him again.

I write a coded message to Orlando Wolfe, reminding him who I am and saying that I would grateful for his help with resources from Oasis to build a city on Earth.

In return, I could help you find the mutant humanoid I saw on Oasis. I suggest that you investigate Michael Court, the adopted son of Alexander Court, the Minister for Culture. Michael Court is a mutant humanoid masquerading as a complete. He was brought up on Earth and disappeared four years ago. A close examination should reveal his mutations.

Wolfe replies immediately and says he will look into the matter. To be honest, I do have a twinge of conscience about betraying little Mercury; but the next day the first delivery of building materials arrives so I dismiss my qualms. His problems are the last things on my mind.

Time to call a general meeting of every member of Compound Creative.

I send for Thor and ask him to come to Compound Creative with twenty loyal male colleagues from C99. Naturally I mean loyal to me. Not to Athene. They've been working for me for some time, designing the proposed city. Now I need them to lend a bit of weight to my speech.

Thor and Sati draw up notices and pin them up all over the compound. They announce a meeting in the theatre at 8.0 p.m. staying that attendance is compulsory. They're snazzy posters in primary colours. No one can miss them.

My colleagues from C99, dressed in their usual jogging suits in dark colours (did I really wear such things?) line up at the back of the stage. I sense an air of excitement in the audience. Everyone is intrigued by the appearance of these stern-faced strangers.

In contrast to the dark overalls of my erstwhile colleagues, I'm decked out in a suit made of bright coloured fabric.

'We'll show them we have a sense of theatre too,' Sati says. She hovers in the wings, making sure everything goes smoothly. 'Go on. This is your big moment, Heracles! On you go.' She gives me a little shove and I stride on to the stage and stand with my three legs apart.

I'm rewarded by a gasp of admiration and some applause. The faces in front of me are raised in anticipation. There's no music. No razzamatazz. I launch straight into my speech.

'I, Heracles, am your new leader. I'm not a temporary replacement for Kata-Mbula. I have complete power over the sectoid. You may find my style of leadership somewhat different from Kat's, but, as long as you conform to my rules, you will find me fair.'

I look at the faces in front of me. They have no idea what I am about to say. No clue about the change in their daily lives that I'm about to initiate.

'Humanoids have lived in compounds for over two hundred years, but now that the Earth is no longer toxic we can begin to live outside again, as human beings did in the past. My plan is to build a city on the waste ground outside Compound Creative. It may be that migrants from other sectoids will come to share it with us – but, naturally, you will have the first option to live in the houses or flats that will be built. I am building it primarily for you.'

A stir of excitement.

'Suppose we don't want to live there?' pipes up the actor who plays Romeo.

'Then you can stay in the compound. No problem. The move is not obligatory.'

A communal sigh of relief.

These stick-in-the-muds are so used to communal living they're resistant to change. Ah well, little by little, they'll begin to see the advantages of city life.

I begin to paint them a picture of rows of streets with painted signs over shops, sports centres and theatres, offices and factories, images that create an idea of the energy of a city.

'I would like to introduce you to the stage party, humanoids from C99, the flagship compound. They are the architects, draughtsmen, engineers and general overseers of the city project.

'First we will build a tower, to be known as The Heracles Tower, a powerful symbol of our city that will seen for miles around. As soon as that is finished we will start constructing the city. From now on you are to have a new work schedule. You will be builders as well as actors, dancers and stagehands.'

Consternation. A buzz of protest.

I pause and try to soften my message a little by saying. 'I note that every morning you have been doing warm-up exercises before starting rehearsals. In future, rehearsals will not begin until 2.0 p.m. The mornings will be spent building.'

A ripple of shock runs through the assembly.

'Yes. Building. This will warm up your muscles and provide a workout that will increase your strength and stamina. You will then be free to rehearse in the afternoons and evenings. We shall start the new schedule tomorrow morning at eight o'clock.'

Lots of chatter but I override it with ease. 'I want you to understand that every member of the sectoid – with very few exceptions – will take part in the physical labour demanded by this project. Male and female. This is your city, your project, and you will share the work required to bring it to fruition. Keep an eye on the notice-boards for instructions about which work group you are to join.'

I signal to Thor to step forward and he stands legs apart, a veritable colossus. 'You will all report to Thor, the foreman. He will be in charge of the day-to-day work. You will work to his orders.'

He grins with his two mouths, but there is something in the solidity of his stance and the fixed look of his steel-grey eyes that suggests it would be wise not to cross him.

Another burst of anxious chattering, but once more I have no trouble in restoring order. 'One last reminder. Tomorrow morning, eight o'clock sharp, you must all report to Thor, outside the door of the compound. I wish you a good night's sleep and a productive day's work.'

Not surprisingly Bathsheba is waiting to see me after the meeting, her face dark with anger.

'You can't do this,' she says. 'You can't cut down the rehearsal time and you can't expect actors to do manual labour.

'Oh but I can,' I assure her. 'Just watch me.'

I don't have to explain myself to her. I'm not her precious Kat. I do, however, assure her that she will not be expected to join in the physical work of the building. She's not sure whether she's exempt because I regard her as Kata-Mbula's deputy or because I consider her too old. I note with a certain satisfaction that, however egalitarian her beliefs, she does accept her exemption from manual work. Like all idealists, her beliefs are only skin-deep.

The members of the council are hovering around waiting to talk to me too, but I march straight past them without a glance in their direction.

I thank my colleagues from C99 for their continued work on my behalf and for their supportive presence, before escorting them to the transporter.

Apart from Thor. He stays, of course. It's good to have my mate, Thor, here. I have a feeling he's going to prove indispensable to me.

We go to the bar for a celebratory beer.

'Went well,' I tell him. 'I doubt Athene even noticed twenty males from her sectoid were missing for an hour or two today.'

'Just shows how easy a takeover would be,' quips Thor, raising his glass. There's something about the tone of his voice that tells me he's not totally joking.

'It's not time yet,' I tell him. 'I have to build my tower and city first.'

Thor takes a gulp of his beer. 'Maybe we – you – could plan the coup to take place at The Big Event.'

'Maybe,' I say. It is something I've already been considering. 'When I decide to make my move, I promise you will be the first to know.'

Chapter Six
Police State
(according to Michael)

Journal

A frantic text from Lizzy, 'Come quickly.'

Nothing else. Really, she is too reliant on me. She expects me to rush over and rescue her from some imagined catastrophe any time she chooses.

I have an essay to complete on the difference between the theories of Freud and Lacan, so I can't go yet. It's due tomorrow morning, the day Father has arranged for me to leave for Hos-sat. I stick at it, tapping away on the computer until I've finished it – more or less, although I'll have to do a quick check in the morning before sending it to the tutor.

I call Lizzy. No reply. I leave a message asking what's up. No reply. I'm not sure how long I'll be staying in Hos-sat, so decide I'd better go the Project now. I leave yet another message asking her to meet me at the Obelisk and dash off.

She's not there. I take a risk and weave my way through the narrow streets to her house. It looks deserted.

The neighbours she told me about are lounging on the steps of the house next door, munching. They are not prepossessing specimens. Their wide square faces and small eyes make them look quite simian. All the males are bare-chested and both males and females have their arms and legs exposed, as if keen to soak up every bit of fresh air they can. Their mutations are very obvious. Two heads, extra limbs and eyes are not exceptional for humanoids but ugly protrusions such as carbuncles on faces limbs and bodies are rare. They have a preponderance of these ugly lumps. I'd been told that the members of C1 have very basic intelligence, but had no idea they were so physically challenged.

For the first time I understand exactly how Lizzy and other completes must have felt when confronted with such mutants for the first time.

I nod at them but they don't reply. I knock on Lizzy's door but it is clear that there's no one there. The window shutters are down and the front door closed. Further down the street, at intervals, I see more mutant humanoids sitting on the steps of the houses they have been allocated.

As I start to move off, a huge mutant humanoid with a sweaty protuberance on his chest the size of a melon, stands up, points at Lizzy's house and shouts, 'Gone!' Others take up the chant, 'Gone, gone, gone.'

There is no mistaking what they mean by 'Gone.' I'm too late. Lizzy and her family have been evicted and I doubt there's much I can do about it but I'll go the Rehabilitation Centre straightaway and find out if Lizzy and her family are there.

As I leave the Project, two uniformed men step out in front of me. Police? I'm not sure, but something tells me I'm being arrested for being in the Project without permission. I decide to make a run for it.

'Michael Court?' one of the men shouts after me.

I stop and turn round, an automatic response when someone says your name. Big mistake. I've just confirmed my identity and immediately I understand that this is not a random encounter.

'Who wants to know?' I ask.

They don't answer but approach me, twist my arms behind my back and handcuff me.

No matter how much I struggle it does no good. There are two of them and they are tall, well built and strong. I look around seeking help but the one or two passers-by look away, not willing to get involved. The men look like officials. They take out some sort of bandage and proceed to blindfold me.

'What the hell do you think you're doing?' I yell at them.

This results in a wide piece of tape being stuck over my mouth. They grab the top of my arms and, in spite of my resistance frogmarch me along. We seem to be going in the wrong direction for the police station.

A few minutes later we arrive at our destination. There's the sound of doors opening and shutting. They take off the blindfold, but not the tape on my mouth, or the handcuffs and push me into a small room with no furniture or amenities, apart from a bucket.

I hear the key turn in the lock. I've been banged up and there's nothing I can do about it.

I'm left alone for about half an hour until the same men return. They untie my hands but not my mouth and start to strip me. I lash out at them now that my arms are free. No use. I'm short and skinny and they are tall and brawny. They handcuff me again and walk out, taking my clothes with them, leaving me naked. It's freezing.

The thing Father has dreaded all along has happened. Someone suspects that I'm a mutant humanoid and is determined to find out for sure.

Good job the surgeon and the therapists did such first-class work removing my mutations. There should be no evidence of my former status. Or will there? It's quite recent surgery after all. Less than two years. I think of Father's tiny scars where his wings had been removed as a baby and find myself wondering if there could be any sign at all that I have been operated on. I shiver and not just because of the cold.

I start to consider what my reaction would be if I were a born complete who'd been wrongly arrested, stripped and humiliated in this way. I wouldn't be afraid. I'd be furious, indignant and demand my rights. That is how I must respond.

I must psyche myself up and make it clear to anyone who comes through that door that they cannot treat me like this. But it's difficult to keep my dignity naked, my mouth taped up and my wrists cuffed behind my back, let alone protest.

Two men in white coats enter the cell. I've never seen either of them before. One of them holds something in his hand. It looks like a torch, but when it's shone on my skin it gives out a red light. Infrared. Now I really am scared. Can this instrument reveal deep scars under the skin from the operation that transformed me from mutant to complete? I don't know. Keep your cool, I tell myself. Don't let them see your fear. Be outraged, offended, shocked at the way they are behaving towards you but, whatever you do, don't look afraid. There isn't much I can do, naked and deprived of speech but I do what I can. My eyes flame with fury. I twist and turn, determined not to make life easy for them. I need to make it clear that their behaviour towards me, a legitimate citizen of Planet Oasis, is unacceptable.

The scrutiny of my body is thorough and I hear little clicks as if there is a camera in the torch taking photographs. X-rays. They examine every little bit of me. When they point the X-ray camera on my back and shoulders I feel a twinge of fear. Will there be any indication that I once sprouted wings? I manage to control the tension and the torch soon passes on to other parts of my body. Whoever tipped these men off about me doesn't know the particular location of my mutations. Not surprising. The only people who know about them are Kali, Father and the specialist staff at Hos-sat. Possibly Stella. None of them would have any reason to betray me. Not even Stella. She wouldn't do anything to damage Father's reputation. Unless of course.... But that doesn't bear thinking about.

It does occur to me that this is a funny way of going about things. What about taking a sample of my DNA? I've read about how useful it was to solve crimes. Surely that would reveal if I had any mutant genes; but maybe that technology has been lost or discredited. Maybe there are people who have their own reasons for wanting it to fall out of use. Criminals or completes like me who were once mutants.

My other peculiarities would be recognised by everyone who knew me as a mutant, my jerky walk and high-pitched voice.

The men in suits decide to test out these characteristics. I resist at first as a complete would do and refuse to move, but when they prod me I take pride in demonstrating my manly walk and stride about.

Once satisfied with my movements, they rip off the tape from my mouth. It really hurts but I don't even flinch. Don't want to give them the satisfaction. I make my voice as deep and masculine as I can and rent my fury on them.

'How dare you do this to me? I'll have you punished for your treatment of me. It's against the law to arrest a complete human being and subject him to such humiliation. An infringement of human rights.... ' My rant seems to go on forever. There is no sign of squeakiness in my vocal chords. Good old Moira, speech therapist extraordinary. If she could hear me now she'd be proud of me.

The two men have had enough of my tirade and tape up my mouth again. They exchange looks, nod at each other and knock on the door to be let out. I wait. I suppose they are checking the X-rays. After what seems like hours, the door opens and my clothes are thrown in. A man steps inside, takes off my handcuffs and goes out again quickly. I rip off the gag and put my clothes on. I continue to wait. The door opens, the men who brought me here enter, blindfold and gag me again and push me outside. They take me for a long walk, marching me round in circles, trying to disorientate me most likely. They stop and take off my blindfold. We're back where they found me. They rip off the tape over my mouth and give me a shove towards the Project as if they think that is where I belong.

I watch them as they storm off. They are only minions, obeying orders. There is something about them that makes me doubt they are policemen. They appear more like common thugs. But what do I know? I have little experience of either the police or thugs.

As soon as they're out of sight, I find myself shaking uncontrollably. I want to sit down there on the edge of the Project and howl my eyes out; but know I mustn't do that. I begin to stagger home. It takes me a long time. Every landmark looks different. Surreal. The more I hurry the slower I seem to go. I lurch from side to side unable to control my movements. I'm in one of those nightmares I suffered from as a child.

Back at Home-Court-Jameson at last, I let myself in, stumble to my room, throw myself on my bed and burst into tears.

'Supper's ready!' Stella sings out.

But I can't sit down to eat with the family. There's no way I could eat a thing and no way I could face the children's questions about why I'm upset.

Father knocks on my door. 'Michael. Can I come in?'

In he comes and sits beside me on the bed and, between sobs, I pour out my story. He listens without interrupting, taking in every detail of my account.

'It was the most dreadful, humiliating day of my life,' I tell him. 'Who would do such a thing, Father? Where do you think they took me? It was like a cell, but I don't think it was the police station. I know I was blindfolded, but it didn't seem as if we were walking in that direction. And they knew my name, Father. They knew who I was. Can you believe that?'

Father sits for minute, his arm round my shoulders, thinking about what I've told him.

'It's my guess that they took you to the interrogation room in the Symposium,' he says eventually.

I stare at him, unable to believe my ears. 'An interrogation room? I thought this was a democratic state.'

'Sometimes it is necessary to….' He stops. 'Look, Michael. Don't worry. I'm on the case now. How dare they arrest my son and treat him like that?'

His response matches the way I felt in that cell. Indignant. Furious. The difference is that I was powerless. I could only rave. Father can do something about it.

'And Father, I was dragged through the streets and no one commented or protested. Not one person tried to help me. Is this normal procedure in Oasis to arrest someone, handcuff him, blindfold him and drag him through the streets? I thought we lived in a civilised city, but the words police-state spring to mind.'

'Oh don't say that, Michael.' Father grips my shoulders. 'In any place, however civilised, there is always a section of the community who think they are above the law and others who are afraid of them.'

'Bullies,' I say. 'I wouldn't be surprised if these bullies torture people too.'

Father looks a little uncomfortable. 'I think it would be best, Michael, if you feel up to it, to go to Hos-sat as planned tomorrow morning. With you safely out of the way, I will deal with the situation here. I intend to find out who is behind this travesty of justice. I have my suspicions who is responsible and intend to find out for certain.'

He pauses for a moment. I see a nerve working in his neck. In spite of his seeming control, he is very upset. And angry. 'I want this person arrested, strip-searched, and humiliated, yes and tortured if necessary and sent to Prison-sat.'

'But if you did that, you'd be behaving just like them.' I'm pleased he feels so strongly about the way I've been treated but behaving the same way is surely not the answer.

Father takes a deep breath. 'You're right, as usual, Michael. But when something like this happens to my son I find I don't just want justice. I want revenge.'

I have never heard Father speak so strongly before. It's gratifying but I do hope he doesn't do anything he will regret. After a while he calms down and gives me a wry smile. 'Life does not always run smoothly, Michael, and it's not always easy to play by the rules. Don't worry, I won't do anything unethical. But I would like to see that man punished properly for what he did to my son.'

Journal Entry

Before I leave in the morning, Father comes to my room. 'I understand you were picked up near the Project. What the hell were you doing there?'

He's already discovered the details of my arrest and is not well pleased. His face is taut, pinched with fury.

'I needed to see for myself what was happening there.'

'Why would you want to do that?'

'I told you the other day that my friend's cousins have been evicted, seemingly to make room for the mutant humanoids. As a student of politics it is vital for me to see for myself what's going on.'

He shakes his head. 'Michael, you can't take on the problems of the whole world. You're becoming too involved in such matters.'

I shrug. 'That's just how I am. I can't help but be involved.'

'Did you talk to any of the mutants?'

'No.'

'Did you recognise any of them?'

'No.'

'Was there anyway that they could recognise you?'

'No. Why do you ask me that? These humanoids are from C1. There is no way they could know me.'

'I'm just trying to get the bottom of why you were arrested.'

'I don't know why.'

'Stella thinks the reason you were there was because you were trying to make contact with the mutants, that you regret becoming a complete and coming to Oasis to live with us. Is that true?'

'Stella. What does she know?'

'She told me she had lunch with you the other day and that you said some pretty outlandish things that led her to think that you're not completely happy here.'

'She's nuts.'

Father faces me. His face is stern. 'Michael, Stella is concerned about you. We both are. You must realise that any contact you have with mutants is likely to be perceived as suspicious. You must not return to that district. I forbid it.'

I can't believe he said that. 'You forbid it?'

'I do. You must never go near the Project again.'

'You can't forbid me to do anything.'

'Actually I can.'

I feel my temper rising and turn away to finish packing my rucksack to take to Hos-sat.

I have no reason to go to the Project again now Lizzy is not there, but it sticks in my throat that Father thinks he can tell me what to do.

'Michael, I have no wish to play the heavy-handed father, but in this matter you must obey me. For all our sakes.'

If I wanted to communicate with mutants on my own behalf it wouldn't be with those poor creatures in the Project. It would be with Kali and Isis and Odysseus, humanoids I already know and respect. The fact that I have resisted contacting them all this time shows how much I respect my father. But now he has shown how little he respects me.

We kind of make it up before I leave, but I'm still seething inside.

He gives me the Hos-sat code for the teleporter and he and Stella stand smiling together at the front door and wish me well with the operation.

If they knew that the real purpose of my visit to Hos-sat is not to have a vasectomy but to make contact with a mutant humanoid they would not look so smug.

Journal Entry

I call into uni on my way to the teleporter as planned, read through the essay, make a few alterations and send it off to the Prof.

I put my head round the divider that separates Jonathan's workspace from mine and tell him I'll be away for a few days. 'I have to go to Hos-sat.'

'You're not ill, man?' His usual relaxed manner has changed to concern.

'No, just visiting a friend. Someone from the satellite I was on before.'

I don't mention what happened yesterday. I've never told Jonathan about my past. It wouldn't be wise. I do tell him about Father banning me from visiting the Project and how angry I feel.

'Typical,' says Jonathan. 'Fathers think they own us and can tell us what to do. Usual teenage versus parent stuff.'

Is it? I didn't know that. Makes me feel a bit better.

'It's not as if I want to go the Project anymore. Lizzy has left.'

'Good for her. Has she got a job?'

'Not as far as I know. I think the whole family have been evicted.'

'That's bad news, man.'

'When I come back I'll go the Re-hab Centre and ask a few questions.'

'They won't tell you anything. More likely to drag you inside and brainwash you as well.'

'Ha, ha,' I say grinning, before realising the implications of what he's said. 'Is that what they do there? Brainwash people?'

'I tell you man, by the time they've finished with you in there, you don't know who you are. I had a mate once who.... Never mind. What I'm saying is, if she's landed up there that's real bad news. If she ever comes out you probably won't recognise her. She won't be the girl you fell in love with, that's for sure.'

'I'm not in love with her. She's a sweet girl, but I don't love her. As a matter of fact, Lizzy and I are more or less finished. I mean we're still friends but there's no future in it.'

'I told you that ages ago. People like us shouldn't get involved with Project folk.'

I feel a little uncomfortable. This conversation is not so different from that with my father.

'Anyway,' continues Jonathan, 'no need to think of the future. Lighten up, man. Start enjoying yourself now. When you come back we'll go out sharking.'

'Sharking?'

'Looking for talent.' He must see I still haven't caught on. 'Girls. For someone so clever you're not very street-wise.'

He's right. I'm not.

He gives me a friendly push on the shoulder. 'See you, man.'

'See you,' I say back.

As I walk to the teleporter that will take me to Hos-sat I think what a good friend Jonathan is and that my father is apparently only behaving like every other father of teenage boys. I send Father a text, apologising for my rude behaviour and tell him that I look forward to seeing him when I come home.

Chapter Seven
Swords into Ploughshares
(according to Odysseus)

I have achieved my ambition at last: I am now curator of the largest museum on Earth. But I don't feel like celebrating.

My friend and former adversary, Brahmin, is suffering from an illness that they say is terminal. I sit at the side of his bunku, wipe his wrinkled foreheads with wet cloths or lift a drink to one of his withered mouths. He swallows with great difficulty, dribbling half of it down the folds in his neck. I endeavour to mop it up. The drink is usually water but today I give him a drop of brandy and am rewarded by seeing a glint of pleasure in his pink-rimmed eyes. Anything I can do to make his final days bearable I will do.

Before his illness, we spent most of our time arguing about the authenticity of some artefact or other or about how the museum should be organised. These disputes were all too often acrimonious. We attacked each other's suggestions in the most hostile language we could summon up. Isis would raise her eyebrows and open her moon-shaped eyes in mock despair at what she considered our childish squabbles.

'You two crinkly-crumblies should know better,' she would tell us and stalk off to pursue some project of her own she considered more important. She saw us both as old. Brahmin is, of course, much older than me. But Isis was right. Brahmin and I should have known better than to spend our time quibbling. Rivals for the job of curator, we sought to disparage each other's intellectual prowess at every opportunity. With his imminent demise I realise how much I shall miss him.

Who else in C98 can I engage in academic conversation? Who else has a comparable level of acumen to mine? Who else appreciates the importance of preserving these paintings, icons and sculptures for posterity?

Brahmin gasps for air. A tear creeps down my cheek. My friend seems intent on leaving me and I shall be bereft, a lone relic in a building full of relics.

For the past few months, since Athene became CEO, day after day, week after week, packoids of artefacts have been arriving from Museum Oasis. Brahmin and I have fought over them with bitter glee: who should open them, who should take possession of the treasures and where they should be displayed? Another tear appears. I'm going to miss the old bugger when he's gone.

Our previous sectoid leader, Durga, delayed her decision about which of us should be curator. What seemed like hesitancy on her part was perhaps her way of ensuring that constant competition would produce the best work from both of us. Without sounding too arrogant I would like to make it clear that for some time I have been convinced that she would choose me. Brahmin was here first, the sitting tenant so to speak, but I truly believe I have proved myself the better manager and warrant the appointment.

Due to Brahmin's illness, it may seem to others that the position has been awarded me by default. He is dying. The job has become mine. Not one humanoid in the compound has bothered to congratulate me even though I've made a point of gliding round the public areas to make my presence felt. Isis would have congratulated me if she'd been here, but she's in Hos-sat with biological matters on her mind.

The continued delay of my appointment was partly due to the change in leadership. Durga became a prisoner after that failed attack on C99 and our new chief, Jagadgauri, has shown little interest in the museum, too busy instigating her own plans. The confirmation of my appointment came directly from Athene.

As I sit by Brahmin's bunku, running the wet cloth over his face, neck and shoulders I hear strains of that wretched song, "Lay down your arms."

The song, written by Doron Levison in the aftermath of the Yom Kippur war, back in 1973, is being transmitted almost constantly throughout the compound. Levinson lost many colleagues in that war as well as his own eyesight and the composition was a plea for peace and an end to military conflict. Originally written in Hebrew, the lyrics were translated into many languages and became a popular anthem advocating peace. This version is in English. I'm a little wary of music deliberately composed to work on the emotions. Any piece, however perfect, played over and over again becomes tiresome. In this case, the message portrayed is pure propaganda.

Jaga has resurrected the song to promote acceptance of the radical transformations she is making. She has a vision of the future that she's determined to impose on her workforce. I'm not sure if the song will achieve its objective or not. I doubt it.

The words of the song reflect the passage from Isaiah 2.4: *They shall beat their swords into ploughshares and their spears into pruning hooks. Nation shall no longer raise up arms against nation, neither shall they learn war any more.* I doubt anyone notes the biblical reference apart from myself. Brahmin would, but he's not capable of registering what is going on.

C98 has always been famous for its army, but after its abortive attempt to invade Oasis and its pitiful efforts in more local forays, the days of the golden warriors seem to be numbered. Jaga has decided to disband the army, retaining a token force for ceremonial purposes. She uses its manpower to cultivate the land.

Huge banners have appeared all over the compound stating THE FUTURE IS AGRICULTURE and LAY DOWN YOUR ARMS AND PICK UP A SPADE and other similar slogans. Laudable sentiments in their way, but like many new leaders, Jaga has rushed headlong into the reformations without due thought.

At the moment those detailed to work in the fields, breaking up rocks and trying to dig the hard baked ground are complying with her demands, but I note the dour looks on their faces and wonder how long their compliance will last.

This morning, several of the workers fail to turn up for work on time. Jaga storms down to their dormo-cubes, accompanied by the ten warriors who form her personal guard. Under her direction, they kick open every single door of the cubes. Jaga stands in the passage, corn-coloured hair a halo round her head, her face flushed with rage, and delivers her command.

'Get out here this minute and line up, ready for work.'

She exerts her authority from the sheer strength of her will, like a teacher. The reluctant field workers emerge and line up as instructed. I can hear her voice over the music – scoffing at their complaints, their bad backs, their petty coughs and colds. 'Are you children? Grow up. Act like responsible adults. Fulfil your duties. You will work two hours longer today. That should remind you to be on time tomorrow.'

Jaga and the guards accompany the workers outside. It must be demoralising to be prodded and ordered to move along by these privileged warriors, who were once their colleagues. I understand their reluctance to exchange “arms for ploughshares” and their glorious uniforms for drab labourers’ garb – rough trousers topped by T-shirts stamped with the motif of a dove.

Jaga has won this round, but how long will it be before the resentment her regime is creating leads to a full-blown rebellion? She longs for them to share her vision, but when inspiration fails she resorts to the usual dictator’s tactics: threats and punishment.

Brahmin slips into sleep. After a moment or two, I check his pulse, a slow, steady pattern. I creep out of his dormo-cube and slide the door shut to block out the dreaded song.

I start my circuit of the compound, coasting along smoothly without the usual jerky movements of many of my fellow mutant humanoids.

There are very few warriors left inside the compound today. Those that remain, lounge about looking jaded. No longer allowed to play compu war games or practise martial arts, they have been detailed to research the plants and vegetables appropriate for an arid climate. An arid way of passing their time.

A group huddled together in the corner of the Recreation Room look up as I pass and stop their low pitched muttering. I note that the dark-skinned Indira with the dreadlocks is one of them. Are these erstwhile warriors plotting something? I know enough about conspiracy theories to suspect that they are. I am one of the managers and they would naturally be wary of me. I raise a questioning eyebrow. Indira gives me a quick nod of recognition. I glide on.

Outside Jaga’s office stand four warriors in full dress uniform. Dionysus – or Osiris as Isis calls him because of the myth associated with their names – is one of them. My son-in-law. I nod at him but he makes no sign that has seen me. All four warriors stare straight ahead, faces impassive.

Imposing in their red uniforms with gold fringes and trims, they must be proud to have been chosen as Jaga's personal guards. I wonder if their colleagues huddled in the corner are envious of their status.

I must have a word with Dionysus later when he's off duty and find out if he has heard from Isis. They parted on bad terms. Isis was adamant that she should go to Hos-sat to make sure their baby had a perfect birth.

Dionysus said that if she went he wouldn't visit her there. As far as I know, he has kept his threat.

Perhaps he's afraid that if he goes to Hos-sat he'll be arrested again. Not surprising that he doesn't trust completes when you think what he and his colleagues were subjected to on Oasis: put on show in the museum and expected to march up and down like robots to entertain the visitors. Appalling.

But, in my opinion, there are good and bad completes just as there are good and bad mutant humanoids. All of us are flawed. There is no reason to believe that Isis will be treated badly. She has permission to be there. The warriors hadn't. Giving birth at Hos-sat with its state-of-the art facilities and highly trained staff must be the best chance for her and the baby. I don't think Dionysus has forgiven me for encouraging Isis to go. When I feel Brahmin can be safely left I will go and visit her, even though I know it is not me she wishes to see.

The truth is, I miss Isis. Not for her intellect, which is nominal, but for the person she has grown up to be. For her bright personality, her sense of humour and, yes, for the way she cares about me. I brought her up as my child and later, discovered that she was in truth my daughter. Now I am to be grandfather to the first baby born to a mutant humanoid for twenty years.

It seems the danger of Earth's contamination has passed. The ground is becoming fertile again and the humanoids too. What exciting times we live in. How fortunate I am to be part of this change.

The big doors to the compound are open wide to the outside world. No cold wind assails us. Jaga is standing on the step, her blue-green eyes searching the horizon. In the foreground members of her workforce, male and female, backs bent, are breaking up hard-baked soil and rocks in the hope that the barren land will soon be transformed to the fertile.

Aware of me beside her, Jaga says, 'Imagine it, Odysseus, field after field of golden wheat shimmering in the sun under a blue sky. The future is agriculture.'

'It will take time,' I warn her.

'Not so long if everyone works hard,' she says. 'No more living shut up in compounds. We'll be a rural community, living in stone cottages with thatched roofs. No cities or towns. No pollution. Village life is the answer. We will work the land. No need for industry. No need for factories. We will be self-sufficient.'

This is Jaga's vision. But can't she see that turning proud warriors into peasants is a recipe for disaster? I think of Indra and the group I heard whispering together in the RR. Are they plotting a mutiny? I have no proof of this but history tells me that dictators who oppress their countrymen are destined to fall. I fear for Jaga. Maybe I should warn her of the likely consequences of her actions.

She turns to me and gives me a penetrating look with her hazel eyes. 'Tell me, Odysseus. How is Brahmin?'

'Sleeping at the moment, but he's very frail. I don't think….'

The lump in my throat prevents me completing the sentence. Jaga understands and touches my arm lightly.

'When he finally leaves us, I have something I would like you to do for me.'

I have no idea what it could be. I do hope she doesn't want me to pick up a spade and help with the digging. I don't feel up to that.

'I want you to make sure the museum is ready to be open to the public as soon as possible.'

It's the moment I've been waiting for: to open the museum and allow others to view our treasures.

'I'd like a big opening. A proper ceremony. Crowds of humanoids from other sectoids making their way to see it through the fields.'

She screws up her eyes and looks out at the horizon again. 'Wouldn't it be wonderful, Odysseus, if the wheat was ready by then? We could cut a way through for our visitors and they could arrive singing and dancing.'

'I think it will take time for the corn to grow….'

She's not listening to me, lost in her dream of a sea of golden wheat and humanoids from other compounds arriving on foot. Her straw-coloured hair and golden-skinned face glow in the sunlight.

She turns her eyes on to her workforce. 'Life in the open air is good for us. No longer enclosed in compounds we will grow healthy and strong. You too, Odysseus, must spend part of each day outside. A little walk gives you thinking time. Brahmin believed in that.'

Brahmin insisted on going outside, breathing in the "fresh air" as he called it. I can't help thinking that these excursions did not help his health. Maybe the air was too strong for him, too much of a shock to the system after years of breathing the artificial air from neo-air-conditioning units.

I'm not as old as Brahmin but I'm taking no chances. I shall not be spending much time outside. Besides if the museum is to open to the public I will have plenty of work to do inside.

Jaga is talking again. 'You see that dome in the distance?

That's C97 known as Compound Creative. The members of their workforce could well be our first visitors. By the way, Odysseus, did you know that your previous colleague, Heracles, is now head of that sectoid? I'm sure he'll be interested in the museum. Why not contact him and offer him a preview?'

I'm not sure it would be politic to do that in view of our somewhat chequered history, but I nod at Jaga as if I agree with her. Cunning Odysseus must be circumspect.

Brahmin dies in his sleep. A good way to go, a happy release: all the old clichés come to mind.

Jaga is outside overseeing the progress of her workforce as usual. I inform her of Brahmin's demise and she says he should be buried in a special plot she has designated as a cemetery.

'His passing will be marked by a religious service with a procession and music,' she tells me.

I have no doubt that the song that has been haunting us for weeks will be included, along with other renderings of pleas for peace.

I peep into Brahmin's cube where two females are attending to his body. I nod at them, but avert my eyes from his emaciated corpse. I leave them to their task and return to the museum. I need something to distract me, to stop me dwelling on his death.

I glide round looking at the exhibits. Everything is grouped in chronological order from medieval to contemporary. There are too many gaps. I need more paintings, more sculpture and more pottery before I can consider opening the museum to the public. The packoids of artefacts received from Oasis are welcome, but the selection is haphazard, usually only one example from each period or school of art, which gives little opportunity to show the development in style. Little thought seems to have been given to these gifts. It's almost as if they've been selected at random. The problem is there is no direct communication between the two museums. This is something that, as the newly created curator of Museum Earth, I hope to change.

Raised voices disturb my thoughts and I follow the noise to the dino-cube, skating swiftly along. Dionysus is marching at the head of ten warriors, all in full dress uniform. Practising for the funeral, I assume.

Their heads, topped by their plumed animal helmets, are held high. Superb. Colleagues at the tables taking their nutri-rations stop eating and look up in wonder.

Dionysus calls 'Halt!' and the warriors pull up sharply. He turns and addresses everyone in the dino-cube. 'Are you peasants or warriors?' he asks in a formidable voice.

'Warriors!' cries a young humanoid near me and jumps to his feet, raising his arm, his hand a fist above his head, a mixture of the Nazi salute and Freddie Mercury's gesture of power.

The cry is taken up by others, 'Warriors! Warriors!'

'Then follow us!' Dionysus orders and I watch bemused as, food and drink forgotten, the diners stand and march behind the cohort, trying to keep in step.

Everyone ignores me, but I follow too, keeping close to the walls, sliding smoothly along, hoping that no one will notice me, on the periphery, but near enough to see what will happen next.

They march into the Recreation Room and I slip in after them.

From the corner of the room, Indra and his group look up warily.

'Follow!' yells Dionysus.

Indra tosses back his dreadlocks and whispers to his fellow conspirators. Is this to be a confrontation? I can't hear what they're saying but it seems they've come to a decision. To my surprise, they stand as one and join the mini-regiment that has formed behind Dionysus and his warriors.

A cheer goes up. 'Warriors unite!' This is a united front for what I'm now sure will lead to the army's attempt to take control of the sectoid. A military coup.

I must go to Jaga and warn her.

The warriors continue to march through the compound. In the compu-centre, those sitting at their workstations are exhorted to 'Follow!' and they too join the ever-growing regiment until there is a fair number of warriors marching in step, or at least trying to. It's a while now since they've practised marching.

While they continue recruiting and marching, I go to Jaga's office. No guards to stop me, I knock on the door, open it and look inside. She's not there.

I hear cries of 'Are you with us or against us?' and always the reply is the same. 'With you. With you.'

'Then follow!' Dionysus commands and a chant goes up, 'Follow, follow, follow,' as more rebels join them and make for the outside door.

I weave my way though the phalanx of warriors in an effort to reach the door before them. The pace of their marching is consistent and I manage to slip through. I stop in the doorway and scan the scene. The field workers are busy, breaking up stones and attempting to dig the hard earth.

There's no sign of Jaga.

I'm almost bowled over by the golden warriors who march on towards the workforce in the fields. I steady myself and stand to one side, looking as unobtrusive as possible. I find myself trembling. I have reason to be afraid. After all, I am part of the management they are seeking to overthrow. They ignore me and march on. Too old and weak in their eyes to be a threat, I assume.

Suddenly Indra and his group break through the ranks shouting, 'Mutiny, rebel, rise up my brothers and sisters! Are you peasants or warriors?'

The workers hesitate. For a moment I think they are going to fight their erstwhile colleagues who are outshining them in their glittering uniforms; but I've misjudged the situation. They raise their axes or spades in a symbolic gesture high above their heads, step out and join the circle of their uniformed colleagues as they march round the field. They clap and beat out a rhythm on their gardening implements, determined to keep in unison.

Jaga, straw-hair awry, a scythe in her hand appears, pushing her way through the few stragglers left inside. They fall back and allow her to pass. She stands in the doorway and takes in the scene.

'Oh Odysseus,' she says when she sees me. 'What is happening?' Without waiting for an answer, she strides out to confront the rebels.

She stops, scythe held high, calls out 'Halt' and, for a moment the warriors do stop, so used are they to obeying her orders.

A moment later, Dionysus yells 'Forward march!' and they obey him, marching in a wide circle to the beat of the makeshift timpani.

I have no idea what will happen next. It looks as if the warriors and workforce, some in uniform, some not, will go on marching round the field forever.

Jaga sees her dream collapse. The very warriors she chose as her personal guard are leading the revolt, their loyalty to their colleagues more important than their loyalty to her.

I feel sorry for Jaga and consider helping her, but what can I do apart from lending her moral support? In the back of my mind I am already thinking that she brought this on herself with her insistence on forcing the warriors to till the land. Which side should I be on?

History tells me that a military takeover is the most likely outcome and that it would be politic to align oneself with the winning side. Or at least not do anything to make them arrest me. On the other hand, I have always been loyal to my leader and don't like to see her friendless.

While I'm debating what position I should take, Indra and his group break away from the other marchers and approach Jaga. She raises her scythe. They take a step back.

At that very moment, a chariot appears in the distance, drawn by two golden mechanical calves, and in the chariot is a warrior with a burnished gold helmet in the shape of a bull, long red hair flowing out behind her in the breeze.

Jaga gives a little cry as she realises that her sister-wife, Durga, has returned to reclaim her sectoid: the power behind the coup.

Indra and one of his colleagues attempt to take Jaga by the arms to take her into custody, but she shakes them off and makes her own way back to the compound, the arresting party following behind her. Jaga doesn't look at me as she passes but re-enters the compound with a fair degree of dignity.

Indra and his group follow her inside. I'm sure they've been detailed to lock her up but there is little I can do to help her without getting myself arrested as well.

As Durga approaches, Dionysus instructs his warriors to 'Forward March' and draw up in formation to greet her. Durga's chariot pulls up to face them.

Captain Dionysus moves briskly to the side of her chariot. Durga gives him instructions and he addresses the warriors. I hear enough words and phrases to get the gist. 'Full dress uniforms or choir robes, Great Hall, Ten minutes,' and off they go to fulfil those commands, a unified force under Durga's control once more.

Everything has happened so quickly I don't what to

think. A coup has certainly taken place, the result of some careful planning. If not, how could Durga have made such an opportune entrance?

I remember thinking that Indra and his colleagues were plotting something in the corner of the RR, but had no idea their plan was masterminded by Durga. As far as I knew, she was still a prisoner in C99.

The coup has been carried out without bloodshed. That's one good thing. Jaga has been replaced with Durga. I'm not sure what I think about that. Again I think how quickly the change has occurred.

Durga stops her chariot next to me.

'Good to see one intelligent face here, Odysseus,' she says. 'Will you join us in the Great Hall?' She narrows her eyes and gives me a shrewd look. 'We'll have a private chat later and you can tell me exactly that stupid sister-wife of mine has been up to.'

Chapter Eight
Funeral Games
(according to Odysseus)

It's like old times. Here we are, assembled in the Great Hall, the golden warriors reinstated.

I imagine that the coup was fairly easy for Durga to arrange. The warriors would have needed little persuasion to lead the revolt. Who would not want to replace hard labour with mock fights and exchange grubby trousers and T-shirts for elegant uniforms? The members of the choir look equally delighted to have cast off their peasant clothes for those long blue robes.

Trumpets blare. The arena is flooded with golden light from the glass dome. Durga crosses the threshold in her chariot. Those of us who line the curved walls step back out of her way as she storms by. Her bull's helmet with its massive horns, her breastplate, sword and spear shine out in triumph, red hair streams out behind her. She makes two circuits of the hall, wheels round and pulls up short, flanked by the warriors, resplendent in their red and gold uniforms and animal-headed helmets of wild animals – lions, tigers, wolves, leopards and hyenas. But the warriors look far from wild. They are controlled, at ease, in their rightful place again.

Durga has always prided herself on her expertise in public speaking and she makes the most of this occasion to demonstrate it. She doesn't speak of the coup itself, but of reparation, of creating order out of chaos, of restoring the army to its former glory.

She deepens her voice and starts to talk about Brahmin. She calls him "our beloved spiritual leader" as she informs the workforce of his demise.

'He was a good man, very knowledgeable and clever. He might well have been the new curator of our museum – if he had lived long enough.'

My heart sinks. I do hope she's going to be as supportive of me as Jaga promised to be.

Durga tells us that Brahmin's funeral will take place later today. 'Let's make it a celebration of his life with the golden warriors on parade and the choir singing.'

I can't help thinking that the funeral provides a propitious opportunity for Durga to consolidate her takeover.

I am not religious myself. My study of history reveals too many wars, too much devastation executed in the name of religion for me to believe in a benevolent deity. But Brahmin was a believer and should be given such a ceremony.

The warriors spend most of the day rehearsing for the funeral. It is so long since they've marched formally together that they need to make sure their steps are synchronized. There's no problem about their fitness. Jaga insisted they attended the gymnasium every morning before starting work. But being part of a formal parade means that they have to be co-ordinated, their marching synchronised, but they are out of practice.

The members of the choir are busy practising the hymns and anthems they used to sing when Brahmin was choirmaster. Appropriate.

Durga is busy for most of the morning, organising the pulling down of what she calls 'those ridiculous banners' and collecting the piles of pamphlets on peace scattered around the compound. All this propaganda is to be burnt.

Durga does find time to come and see me in the museum. She bursts in without ceremony and strides round the vestibule.

'How could my sister-wife come up with such a ridiculous scheme? "The future is agriculture!" What next? What a travesty to turn my beautiful warriors into manual labourers. Couldn't you do anything to curb her enthusiasm for this ill-conceived scheme, Odysseus?'

I feel like saying that it was Durga's fault for leaving Jaga in charge while she careered off to that fiasco of a raid on C99; but I decide it is more politic to keep my mouth shut.

I do say, 'Once Jaga had made up her mind there was little I could do to get her to change course. I did try to tone down some of her – what shall I say – wilder ideas.'

'Wild is about right. She did it to spite me, to ruin my empire. Her appointment was only ever meant to be temporary.'

'I don't think she saw it like that. She had a vision of field upon field of wheat, of the sectoid growing its own fruit and vegetables and being self-sufficient.'

'She let the myth of her name go to her head. Jagadgauri, Harvest bride of Shiva indeed.' Durga narrows her green eyes. 'I see you have some new acquisitions.'

'Indeed. From Museum Oasis.' I hesitate. Is this the moment to ask for her help? 'It was part of the agreement in the treaty that we should share their resources. They have sent some items and I'm very grateful for that, but I would like to have some say in the artefacts selected.'

She considers this. 'Leave it with me. I'll see what I can do.'

I have the feeling that once she's back in her office that promise will be forgotten. I must try another strategy.

I think of the myth that gave me my name. Odysseus was known for his cunning and I have my share of that quality.

'Durga, you must realise that a fully equipped museum could bring you and your sectoid considerable prestige. Trips could be arranged from other compounds to view our treasures. It would demonstrate that you are a leader, not only interested in warfare but in history and culture as well.'

She narrows her eyes. 'Interesting,' she says. 'That's exactly what Brahmin told me.'

'We thought the same way about most things.'

'I thought you were always arguing.' She smiles with a hint of malice.

'We had disagreements about the best way to exhibit the paintings or statues, but both of us were intent on making the museum perfect. Sometimes we differed on how to achieve that perfection, but on important matters we thought the same way, both working towards what was best for the museum, best for the sectoid, best for you.'

She laughs and turns away. 'You have quite a way with words, Odysseus.'

'I've had a good teacher,' I tell her, letting her decide if I refer to Brahmin or to her.

She continues to pace around the vestibule.

'Would you like to have a more detailed inspection of what we have done?' I ask, trying to guide her into the scooped out cave where the Renaissance paintings hang.

'I would, but not today. I have lots to do to prepare for the funeral.' She moves swiftly away. In spite of what she must have suffered over the past few months she is very sure of herself.

I give a little bow. 'Of course.'

She stops pacing and confronts me. 'Would you like to make a speech at the funeral, Odysseus? A eulogy. I was going to do it myself, but I really think it would be better coming from you.'

'I'd be delighted,' I say.

She actually leans forward and lays her hand on mine. 'You did say just now that you and Brahmin thought the same way about the major things.'

'That's right.'

'He was very dear to me. I understand you have been at his side throughout his final illness. I appreciate that. I really do. I'm just sorry that I didn't return sooner, in time to say goodbye.'

I swear there is a tear in the eye of this formidable woman, the renowned leader of the golden warriors. I feel honoured to have seen this softer side of Durga.

'I will spend the rest of today writing a speech worthy of him,' I promise her.

'No need for that, just speak from the heart.' She presses my hand, releases it and strides away.

At the door she turns, her face composed and gives her parting shot. 'Not too long-winded though, eh Odysseus? We don't want to bore everyone.'

It isn't until I'm sitting at my workstation thinking of few well-chosen phrases to start my speech that I remember that I should have asked Durga what has happened to Jaga. Perhaps it's just as well. I have to be loyal to the present leader and Jaga's location is not my concern.

It occurs to me that the warriors are virtually redundant now, apart from taking part in ceremonial events. Another war would be as ill conceived as Jaga's dreams of a golden harvest. A token, ceremonial army is the only answer. But will that satisfy the warriors? Or Durga?

Late afternoon comes the call for everyone to go outside for the ceremony. The entire sectoid assembles once more. A few surprises await us. A funeral pyre has been erected. Six golden warriors carry the white shrouded body of Brahmin and place it on a platform above the twigs and branches that the workforce have managed to scavenge from the newly sprouting countryside. I note that Jaga's banners and pamphlets are also being used as fuel.

At the sound of singing everyone looks up. In the distance what looks like a motley troupe of travelling players is moving towards us to the beat of drums and voices raised in harmony.

Our neighbours from Compound Creative are coming to pay their respects to Brahmin.

I had no idea he was held in such high esteem.

It must be Durga's idea to make a grand occasion of this funeral in order to consolidate her return to power.

What a cynical old humanoid I have become. I find I am annoyed by the excessive attention being paid to my ex-colleague. Even in death he is up-staging me. All this ballyhoo tends to support the view that my appointment as curator is merely expediency, not a deserved choice, and this rankles somewhat. Not only cynical then but disgruntled, jealous of a deceased humanoid. That's the depths to which I've sunk.

The travelling players stop before reaching the pyre and I can see it is a multi-ethnic group with skins of various shades from white to brown to black. Their colourful costumes have been chosen to celebrate a life, not to mourn a death. Their faces greet us with wide smiles as they line up and begin to clap in time with the rhythm of the drum and their ever-moving feet. Our choir begins to clap in time with them and the warriors march on the spot, a mutual act of greeting from the two sectoids.

Durga is clapping and smiling too. As the dancers approach our visitors, they file off into two columns, as I've seen our warriors do. They turn to face each other and continue clapping and smiling.

Through the space between the two lines of humanoids strides a figure dressed in a long white robe trimmed with blue, wearing a turban. Under the turban is the huge square, three-eyed face of the new head of Compound Creative: Heracles. Durga looks disconcerted. He was her captor, she, his prisoner. She stops clapping and glares at him.

Heracles looks over his shoulder, holds out a hand to someone behind him and along trips one of Durga's sister-wives, the two-headed Sati, looking as sweet and deadly as ever.

For a moment I think Durga is going to call over her warriors and arrest both of them, before they have a chance to speak.

After all, Sati did leave her warrior sister-wife for dead in the wilderness after the raid on C55 and Heracles kept both Sati and Durga incarcerated in cells in C99 for months.

Heracles treats Durga to a wide grin and Sati giggles.

A pause. We wait for Durga's reaction. She takes a deep breath.

'Heracles, Sati,' she says smoothly. 'We are delighted that you could attend this memorial service to our beloved Brahmin. I invite you sit beside me to witness the occasion.' She guides them to a structure where those of us of high rank are to sit. Maybe there won't enough room for me now, but yes, Durga beckons me and I duly follow them to the temporary royal box.

'Where is Bathsheba?' Durga asks Heracles. 'My invitation earlier today was to her.'

'Bathsheba is not in charge of Compound Creative,' says Heracles. 'I am.'

'Since when?'

'We've been there several days now, Sati and I.'

'Athene appointed you?'

'She did indeed. Did she appoint you leader of this sectoid?'

'Athene told me I was free to make my own choices.'

'So you decided to reclaim your sectoid for yourself. A bold plan. Where's Jaga?'

'Where she deserves to be. Where I didn't deserve to be.'

'You've locked her up?'

'It's quite a comfortable cell. You don't need to worry about her.'

'I'm not worried. I was interested in her project though. She wanted to work the land, build little villages and move everyone out of the compound.'

'You think that was a good idea?'

'To move out of the compounds, yes. To live in rural communities no.'

'Have you another plan?'

'As a matter of fact I have.'

'And what's that?'

'Let's just say I'm more of a city boy myself.'

Durga gives a short laugh. 'I can believe that.' She pauses. 'You're not thinking of trying to rescue Jaga, are you?'

It's Heracles's turn to laugh. 'Why would I do that? Or more important how could I do that? You're the one with the army, Durga. My sectoid consists of dancers, singers, actors, artists and crafters. They are hardly equipped to carry out a rescue mission.'

'And that appeals to you – all this namby-pamby dancing?'

'Wait until you see them perform. I think you'll be impressed.'

Durga stares at Sati. 'I see you brought your concubine with you, my darling sister-wife.'

No chance for a reply. A blowing of bugles and the golden warriors are about to start the ceremonial parade. But our party is not yet complete.

Like a *deus ex machina* in a Greek tragedy, Athene appears. She doesn't exactly fly in but drives through the wide doors from the Great Hall in Durga's motorised chariot. Durga frowns so I know Athene is not an expected guest.

The coup has been carried out without her permission and Athene has appropriated the chariot to make some sort of point.

Athene pulls the chariot to a halt. She looks as serene as ever in her long white robe. She gazes around the assembled company through her one deep blue eye. She makes a speech about Brahmin. It's formal, not in the least sentimental, an appreciation of his hard work, his religious beliefs and his work with the choir, but she doesn't list his qualities. That is left for me to do. Her voice carries well in the open air but is subdued and sincere. The speech is short. Very short. I have no idea what she really thinks of Brahmin or of the takeover.

I step forward, clear my throat and list my ex-colleague's qualities. He was erudite, knowledgeable and dedicated. I repeat what I said to Durga earlier – that he and I might not have always agreed on the little everyday details (a few amused exchanged looks and nods here) but that when it came to the future success of the museum we were "on the same page." I read the latter phrase online recently and believe it makes me sound progressive or at least in touch with modern life. I imagine Isis rolling her eyes. My speech is not as short as Athene's but only a few coughs towards the end, advise me politely that enough is enough. Durga gives me a nod. I think she is pleased with the generosity of my effort.

The choir sings. The warriors strut their stuff more or less in unison. I see Durga wince a couple of times as someone misses a beat. In my eyes they are splendid, a welcome addition to any formal occasion.

It's the turn of Compound Creative. They have prepared a dance in Brahmin's honour. I find it incredibly moving. I find a tear escaping and am obliged to blow my nose. Silly old fool that I am. I'm going to miss the old bugger.

The dance is to be followed by the burning of the body.

I can't watch that. I imagine the old man's flabby flesh hanging off the bones and catching fire. I am also aware from my reading of history that the burning of human flesh smells. I've no desire to breath in the putrid stink of death.

I slip back to the museum and try to take my mind off what is happening outside by studying some of our newest acquisitions. One of them is a tiny silver icon of Saint Sebastian. Brahmin would have loved it. I glide into the inner cave, his inner sanctum as we called it, and choose an appropriate niche for it. Perfect. Satisfied with this little ritual, I return to my workstation and start to make a list of the sections of the museum that could do with additional pieces.

I have only just started on the list when Dionysus appears. At first I think he has news of Isis and, because of the mood I'm in, I believe it to be bad news. I look up and frown.

'How is she?' I ask.

'She wants to see you,'

'Really? When?'

'Now. She's in Durga's office.'

It takes me a moment to realise that he's not talking about Isis, but Athene.

I pull myself together and accompany him along the passage that links the museum to Durga's office.

'Any news of Isis?' I ask Dionysus, the handsome young man beside me.

'Not yet but the baby is due any day now.'

I put my hand on his arm. 'Are you going to see her?'

'I don't see how I can at the moment. With Durga back and everything.' He looks down at me. 'Don't worry, Sir. We're in touch. She seems to be fine, but….' He hesitates. 'Maybe you could go. She'd like to see you.'

'It's you she wants, Dionysus. You know that.'

'I really can't get away at the moment, but I am worried –

not so much about Isis – but about the baby. Do you think they will let her keep it?'

'What do you mean? Why shouldn't they?'

'They might kill him and tell us he died of natural causes soon after he was born.'

'Why would they do that?'

'Completes don't like mutants. They don't want any more of us. They might put him in a bottle in the museum labelled, "The last mutant humanoid."'

I glance at his face to see if he's joking but he looks as serious as ever. 'Or perhaps they'll keep him alive to study him – put him in a cage so that they can monitor every stage of his development.'

'You don't really believe that,' I say.

'I wouldn't put it past them. They seem fascinated by us mutants.'

There's bitterness in his voice. The time he spent in Museum Oasis on show is playing tricks with his mind. Post-traumatic stress. Battle fatigue, although there was no battle. I must spend time with him and try to help him. After all he is my son-in-law.

Athene is on her own in Durga's office. She smiles, stands up, walks round the desk and holds out her hand to shake mine. 'Good to see you again, Odysseus. We need to chat.'

'Delighted,' I tell her.

She takes a seat on a shaper and signals for me to sit on the one beside her. An informal chat then. 'Now, Odysseus, some strange things have been going on here. I'd be glad to have your view on what's been happening.'

I'm not sure what to say. I tend to keep out of anything political, things that do not concern my day-to-day work in the museum.

She senses my hesitation. 'What did you think of Jaga's scheme to turn the warriors into agricultural workers?'

I summarise my thoughts on the matter, making sure I'm not over-critical of Jaga, just in case Athene is thinking of reinstating her.

I tell her that Jaga's idea of turning swords into ploughshares has precedents in history but that in my opinion she didn't prepare the sectoid sufficiently for such a drastic change. This sudden switch to a new direction led to resentment. Once Durga was on the scene again a revolt was inevitable.

Athene considers this. 'You and I both know that the golden warriors are an anachronism, little more than a token force. Their study and practice of military procedures are their way of fulfilling their creative targets.'

She looks at me carefully trying to judge my reaction to this.

I can't help wondering why she wants confirmation from me, but am nevertheless flattered by her respect for my opinion.

'Working towards creative targets is all very well,' I tell her, 'but historical studies show that the building up and training of armies usually culminates in action of some sort. Soldiers expect to fight. An attack on some enemy, real or invented is likely, especially if the leader has a warlike disposition.'

'Plus a desire for power.' Athene sighs. 'The sister-wives of Shiva – Jaga, Durga, Sati and even Kali – are all ambitious. And ruthless. They could cause me problems in the future. I can see that.'

I nod but privately believe that no leader's position can ever be safe. It's not just Shiva's wives who are a threat. I am pretty sure that Heracles is waiting for his chance to grab power too. As the new leader of Compound Creative he will have more freedom to plot against Athene.

Athene turns to me. 'Odysseus – how committed are you to your work here in the museum?'

It's an odd question. How could she not know how dedicated I am to my work? 'Completely committed,' I answer without further thought. 'In fact I wanted to talk to you about that….'

'And yet you came to the meeting I called about the possible leadership of Worldwideculture. And you agreed to be interviewed by Stella Jameson when she was considering who to appoint as leader.'

Athene must think I'm interested in unseating her too. I can't believe it. I'm probably her most loyal supporter.

'As Chief Chronicler I am naturally interested in the process of the selection of leader. I've never had any aspirations in that direction myself. To be curator of the museum is the height of my ambition I assure you.'

'To be honest, I'd like you to be a little more ambitious than that. I respect your opinions, based as they are on an intelligent analysis of the past.'

Her blue eye deepens in intensity. 'What I am hoping, Odysseus, is that you will agree to be my second-in-command. I need someone to consult whom I can trust. Someone wise. Someone who would be a worthy successor if something happens to me.'

'I'm very honoured that you should think of me, but what could possibly happen to you? You are young and have many years of leadership ahead.'

That's my automatic response, but I know, as she does, that a leader can fall at any time.

My mind is in a whirl. She's offering me a chance to be her chief adviser with the possibility of succeeding her. 'But I understood that Heracles was your deputy?'

'Yes and I will permit him to retain that position – at least in name. We'll invent a new title for you. Chief Consultant perhaps.'

I'm already Curator of the Museum and Chief Chronicler.

Do I want this extra responsibility? The turmoil in my stomach tells me I do. I'm more ambitious than I thought.

'Will I still be Curator of the Museum?' I ask.

'I know it's a project close to your heart but you must learn to delegate. Think of yourself as in charge of policy, but find someone you trust to be in charge of every day affairs. Eventually I'd like you to move to C99 to be at my side. But at the moment I need you here to keep an eye on Durga.'

I can't believe what is happening. I've never had such a day in my life: the rebellion, Durga's coup, Brahmin's funeral and now this offer that I don't seem able to refuse.

Athene continues, 'I have to accept Durga's coup. I don't have much choice. The warriors are glad to have her back in charge.'

She's right. It's a done deed.

'If she has ideas of attacks on other compounds or even, Zeus forbid, on Planet Oasis, you must let me know immediately.'

'As for Jaga,' Athene continues, 'I can't allow her to remain captive here. Have you any ideas about her future?' Athene is already treating me as her consultant.

'Jaga's vision of reclaiming the land, of getting us out of the compounds to live and work in villages is not a bad idea in principle. It is time for us to think about moving out of the compounds to live in daylight as people did in the past. We've been shut up long enough. Is there a compound where Jaga could go that would be open to such a experiment?'

'I'll give it some thought, do some research. I'm sure there's somewhere she could use her skills. For the moment I'm going to take her back with me to C99. As far as Durga is concerned I'm taking Jaga back as a prisoner. This will allow Durga to save face and not undermine her authority. I will spend some time talking to Jaga about her ideas for the future. I may want further advice from you about this. After all, you have experienced some of the highs and lows of her plan in action.'

I find myself flushing with pleasure.

Athene stands and shakes my hand. 'I look forward to us working more closely together, Odysseus.'

Still feeling a bit bemused I say, 'Me too' and find that I mean it.

'I must go to Durga now. She's kept her spirits up very well during the funeral, but I know she's upset. The loss of her father must have been a big shock to her.'

It takes me a moment to grasp the significance of what she is saying. Once more I've been lacking in perception. I had no idea that Brahmin was Durga's father.

That explains why Durga couldn't bring herself to appoint me as curator over him. All that procrastination makes sense now.

I wonder yet again how I can see things of the intellect so clearly yet fail to see what is going on in front of my eyes. I shall have to be wary about jumping to conclusions when offering advice to Athene. Ironic really that she sees me as a suitable counsellor.

Chapter Nine
New Friends
(according to Isis)

It's not so bad in here. It's a hospital but that doesn't mean I have to stay in bed all the time. In fact they encourage me to get up and do things. Once they find out that I like making things, they send in someone they call an occupational something-or-other to help me. I tell her what I'd like to make and she provides the materials. Her name is Bridie. She's real friendly and helpful.

She teaches me things I didn't know before.

For one thing, she teaches me to knit. She gives me three knitting needles so that I can use my fingers on all three hands. She giggles as she tries to work out how to do this. I'm the only mutant humanoid she's ever had as a patient. The others are completes like her and only have two hands and ten fingers.

'Once you've got the hang of it, you'll be able to knit much quicker than everyone else.' she tells me. 'I'll download some patterns and you can make clothes for your baby.'

On the compu she shows me pictures of babies wearing little woollen jackets, hats and bootees. Cute.

She brings in a sewing machine. I've never seen one before, let alone used one, mainly because there wasn't such a thing in the compounds, not even in C98.

'You should have asked for one,' says Bridie. Apparently,

we humanoids in the compounds can ask for anything we want. Completes will consider our request and, if approved, supply us with it. I didn't know that.

'How could I ask for it, when I didn't even know what a sewing machine was?'

She seems surprised. 'Haven't you seen one on the Internet?'

That's when I come clean and tell her I'm not that brilliant on compus.

'I've nothing against them. Just not interested in looking things up and that. Seems a waste of time to me. I'd rather be doing things like making clothes and pretty things for our dormo-cube or doing beauty treatments.'

Bridie shows me how to use the sewing machine and I catch on real quick. Not totally stupid then.

'You've got the hang of it straightaway,' she says, echoing my thought. She's a sweet little thing with rosy cheeks and a shy smile.

I like all the completes I've met so far, Bridie and the nurses and doctors and that. All totally kind. I suppose you have to be a caring humanoid – or rather human being as they call themselves – to work in a hospital.

Today Nurse Gemma comes in to check what she calls my vital signs and to chat to Bridie. They tell me they're "best friends" which means they go out together in the evenings. I wonder where they go. It must be great to have a best friend, another female I mean. I've never known what that's like. Must be brilliant to have someone to talk to about make-up and clothes and that. Males don't understand how totally important these things are. Not even Osiris. And certainly not Odysseus.

Bridie and Gemma and all the other nurses seem quite fascinated by me and ask me all kinds of questions about my life on Earth and about the mutations of other humanoids. I answer as best I can. I tell them life was pretty shitty in C55 with the snake woman as boss. We were treated like slaves. That's probably where my dislike of compus comes from. We were supposed to sit at them all day and all evening too sometimes.

They ask me to describe Kali and are amazed when I tell them that the snakes round her neck and wrists are actually part of her body.

'But are they real snakes?' Gemma asks.

'Totally real,' I tell her. 'One of them bit Sati – you know the two-headed nympho I told you about yesterday. Poisoned her. She didn't die, but she could have done, if Kali hadn't given her an anti something or other.'

'Antidote,' Gemma says.

Gemma is real pretty. Her skin is darker than Bridie's and her hair is dark too. I think it's quite long, but she wears it tucked up under a white cap for work so I'm not too sure.

'It must be awful to be locked up in compounds and not allowed out,' Gemma says, her big brown eyes wide.

'I've never known anything different,' I tell her. 'Outside is the wilderness. Nothing grows there and it's freezing cold. I did go out once but that was a mistake. Never again.'

'But surely that was in the past,' says Bridie. 'The Earth is not contaminated now. Things have started to grow again.'

'Dunno. I've not been outside again and don't want to.'

'Stockholm syndrome,' says Bridie with a knowing nod at Gemma.

'No,' says Gemma, shaking the thermometer and popping it under my tongue. 'That's when you bond with your kidnappers. "Institutionalised." That's the word you're looking for. Applied to people who have grown accustomed to being in prison or a children's home or in any kind of institution. They prefer to keep to the status quo, rather than venture into the outside world. It's fear of the unknown.'

I haven't a clue what they're on about. I'm not afraid, just happy in C98. When Gemma takes the thermometer out of my mouth, I try to tell them how I feel.

'I'm happy in our compound, especially now Osiris is back from the war. We've got a lovely dormo-cube, which I've decorated with things from the museum.'

I wish they could see it. 'Maybe you could come and visit us one day, after I've had the baby.'

Bridie and Gemma exchange looks. They often do that. 'But wouldn't you rather live in a proper house rather than a compound? If it were possible, I mean,' asks Bridie.

I shrug. 'Now I'm with Osiris my whole life has changed for the better. I don't want to leave C98. Ever.'

I tell them about the golden warriors and how magnificent they look in red and gold and about the pretend wars they play on the compus, how they have mock fights with each other with blunt swords but how Osiris really did march off to war.

'He was away for ages, but, thank Zeus, he came back. I don't know what I would have done if he hadn't.'

'Isn't he allowed to come and see you here?'

'Of course, but he's very busy, you know.'

He should come. He should make time to see me. I sniff, blow my nose and change the subject. I don't want them to see that I'm upset. I don't want them to be critical of Osiris.

'Mind you, I wasn't happy in my previous compound, C55. Kali, the snake woman, was in charge. She was the one that made us sit at compus all day to reach our targets. Dead boring. Put me off compus for life. Luckily I spent most of my time in the histo-lab with Odysseus and he let me do what I liked – more or less.'

'Who's Odysseus?'

'Odysseus is the sort of head-history-person. There's nothing he doesn't know about the past. Actually he's my father. He brought me up.'

'What happened to your mother, if you don't mind me asking?' Gemma asks, her eyes wide.

'She died years ago. I don't think about her much. At least I didn't before I found I was expecting. Now I think of her quite a lot. I wish she could have lived to see her grandson.'

Another exchanged look. 'What makes you think you're going to have a boy?' Bridie asks.

'I always think of my baby as male.'

'But surely the doctor has told you….'

'He hasn't told me anything.'

'Well, remember you had those scans?'

'Scans?'

'When you went in the other room and they took X-rays of the baby inside you?'

'Yes, I remember that.'

'Didn't he show you the result? The scan? A little photo of the baby inside you. Didn't he tell you the sex of the baby?'

'No. He just said everything was all right. No worries.'

'I'll find out for you. Be back in a minute.'

While Gemma's away, Bridie returns to the subject of compus.

'Didn't you learn how to use computers at school?'

'We don't have school in the compounds. Everyone is given a compu to help us reach the targets. I'm quite good at typing things – lists, labels for the museum, things like that. But they don't count. They're not creative. The rest of the compu stuff is sooooo difficult. Odysseus lets me do what I want – make-up my face and nails, sew, things like that. Says that can count as creative work for the targets.'

'Targets?' Bridie frowns. 'What are these targets for?'

I shrug. 'Dunno. Never asked that. We just do them.'

'Tell you what,' Bridie says. 'We'll do fifteen minutes on the computer every morning, but only to give us ideas or techniques for making things. Motivation is all.'

I'm not sure what she means, but she's so nice that I agree. Fifteen minutes is nothing.

'We'll get lots of ideas for making clothes and other things from the Internet,' she tells me.

I tell Bridie that I get the ideas for making clothes from looking at old paintings. Especially since I've been expecting.

'One of them is a lady in a long blue cloak and hood thing with a long white dress underneath and she's holding a baby, a plump male. He's naked and totally gorgeous and the lady looks so loving as she looks down at him. Serene. Odysseus taught me that word. Serene. That's how I want to be with my baby.'

'The Virgin Mary and Child,' says Bridie.

'Oh no, she can't be a virgin. She's the baby's mother,' I tell her.

Bridie giggles, but I don't know why. What I've said is the truth.

'Odysseus did tell me the name of the painting, but I can't remember. He's always telling me things, trying to teach me about the past but I can never remember a thing.'

'You remembered the word serene,' says Bridie, but can't help adding, 'the good thing about computers is that you don't have to remember. The computer does that for you. You can have a list of favourite things. One click and it comes up and reminds you.'

She's determined to get me on that compu.

Gemma comes back holding a little fotogram. It's my baby. Tiny, curled up. A bit blurred.

'Look,' she says. 'No penis. It's a girl. Isn't she just perfect?'

'Perfect,' I say. I tell myself I'm not disappointed. It would be nice to have a boy, a little Osiris, but on the other hand a female would be good too. I can dress her up in pretty clothes and when she's older teach her all about make-up and all that. Maybe next time I'll have a boy like the lady in the painting.

'You'll have to think of a name for her?' Bridie says.

I look at the tiny curled up creature in the fotogram. I can see her back and two tiny feet and her shoulders and the beginning of her arms, but I can't tell how many. It's a bit blurred.

'I'll have to see her face before I know what to call her. Osiris may have ideas too. Can I keep this?'

'Of course you can,' says Gemma.

'You won't get into trouble for giving it to me?'

'Not at all. Sometimes the doctors prefer the nurses to give it to the patient.'

She and Bridie stay a bit longer chatting to me before going to change their clothes. They're going out together this evening.

'We'll pop in and see you before we go,' Gemma promises.

I sit studying the tiny creature in the fotogram. It doesn't seem possible that this little creature is nestled warm inside me.

Out of her nurse's uniform Gemma looks quite different. She wears a short red skirt and black top. She does have long hair. It's shiny black and dead straight, reaching all the way down her back. Amazing.

'You look divine,' I tell her. 'Totally divine.'

She blushes and laughs.

Bridie comes in. She's wearing white trousers and a loose blue top.

'Where are you going?' I ask them.

'To the cinema and pizza parlour,' says Bridie.

'And afterwards to a disco,' says Gemma. 'To see if there's anyone worth picking up.'

I wrinkle my forehead. Sometimes I have difficulty understanding what they're talking about. Yet we all speak English.

'To look for sexy men,' Bridie explains. 'Have a bit of fun.'

I roll my eyes until the whites show. 'Good luck! But be careful.'

'Talk about pot and kettle,' says Gemma.

'See you tomorrow!' calls Bridie and off they trot to a life and world I know nothing about.

A few minutes later tall Janey arrives and makes me do some pre-natal exercises. Just a bit of stretching. Nothing too exhausting, thank Zeus. I show her the picture of my baby.

'A girl,' she says. 'Lovely.'

Janey leaves and short, plump Moira takes over. She makes me do breathing exercises.

'It will help with the birth,' she informs me. I lie on my back and take deep breaths. 'In…. and out….' Moira chants and I obey. It's quite relaxing. I nearly fall asleep.

I'm still clutching the photo. I show it to her as well.

'She's beautiful,' she tells me. 'Perfect.'

I have to admit I'm well looked after. In the morning, the doctor will examine me as usual and make sure everything is going according to plan. It shouldn't be long now before I have my baby. I can't wait to see her and hold her and cover her face and body with little kisses. I'm getting used to the idea she's female.

Janey rushes back in, looking flushed and out of breath, her eyes bright. 'Surprise! You've got a visitor.'

'Just a tick.' I sit up, get out my makeup bag from under the pillow and put on some lipstick. He's been a long time coming. He can wait a minute or two longer. I'll play it cool.

Janey and Moira are standing close together just outside the door, chatting, excited. I wonder why. I know Osiris is good looking but I didn't know he could have this effect on other females. Thing is they're both so old. Must be at least thirty. If only they knew how stupid they look with their red faces. They should calm down and act more dignified-like.

Janey sings, 'Walk like a man,' in a silly high voice and Moira calls out, 'Don't forget to breathe.'

They are almost smothering him. Reminds me of a scene outside a pop concert I once saw on the tele-screen. A group of young females burst through a barrier thing and threw themselves on the singer, screaming and shouting out his name. Ridiculous.

As for these two, what fools they are making of themselves. I look away and pretend to take no notice, but I can't help the occasional peep. I can't see him, only the backs of these two bulky females. Their silly squawks of delight fill the room.

At last they stand back and I see him properly for the first time. It's not Osiris. It's a stranger who stands there grinning at me. No. Not a stranger. It's my mate, little Mercury. I don't believe it.

'Mercury! It's great to see you. How long is it now? Years and years. Grab a shaper and come and sit by me,' I tell him, although this hard backed, rigid thingammy-whats-it can hardly be called a shaper. No body could ever fit that shape.

He skips across the room and sits astride it, his arms and hands resting on the back.

'Let's look at you,' I say. 'You've changed a bit. Older I suppose. Not much taller though.'

'You've changed too,' he says. 'More grown up. And fatter.'

'There's a reason for that,' I tell him rolling my eyes.

He grins. 'I realise that.'

'Well, we'll leave you to it,' Janey says, reluctantly.

'Enjoy your reunion,' says Moira.

They wave at us and walk off, giggling.

'Silly old cows,' I tell him. 'I'm glad they've gone. Now we can talk properly.'

But we are not quite at ease with each other.

'Well, Merc,' I say, 'What have you been up to?'

'Same old, same old,' he says.

'Still the same old clever clogs, sitting at a compu all day, learning things?'

'You've got it.' He gives a nod at my large tum. 'I don't need to ask what you've been up to.'

'My life has taken a turn for the better. I fell in love and this is the result. Take a look at this.'

I hand him the fotogram and watch his face as he stares at it. He seems to be totally scrutinising it. I'm amazed he's so interested.

'I'm trying to get used to the idea,' I tell him.

'That your baby is a complete?'

'That's she's female. I'd so got it in my head that I would have a son.'

'The main thing is that she's healthy,' says Mercury, sounding more like the old nurse who looks in on me from time to time; the one in charge. Gertie. 'The gender is unimportant.'

'You're right. It's just taking me time to get used to the idea.'

'Some people take longer than others to process things,' he says.

'Well, you know me. I've never been that quick.'

'You'll love your baby whatever. Nothing to worry about.' Now he sounds like Odysseus. They're both know-it-alls.

'What did the doctor say about the scan?' Mercury asks.

'Nothing. He didn't show it to me. The nurse did. Gemma. She's real cute Gemma is. She was a bit surprised the doctor hadn't shown it me, so she took herself off to the lab and found it for me herself.'

'She got it from the lab, you say? Just a minute. I'll go and check. There may be more images, taken from different angles.' And he's off, moving quickly across the cube and out of the door, but without the jerky skips that I remember. His voice is different too. Deeper. I suppose he's all grown up now. That's what makes the difference.

When he comes back, sure enough, he's holding more fotograms of my baby. He seems excited. Who would have thought he would take such an interest in what after all are female concerns. He studies each fotogram carefully and hands them to me.

'There are no mutations, as far as I can see. No doubt they will examine her thoroughly after she's born, do lots of tests to make sure, but, from the scans, it looks as if she's a perfect complete.'

'I was rather hoping she would have an extra arm like me and five extra tiny fingers.'

'Doesn't look like it.'

'Is it a good thing that she's got no mutations?'

'Some might think that.'

'What do you think?'

He wrinkles his forehead. 'Depends. In the long run it's good. It means that, in the future, in all probability, every baby will be a complete, now that the contamination from the plague has been eradicated.'

'And that would be a good thing?'

'For the future of the world, yes, but….' I can see he's trying to tell me something, but he asks me a question instead.

'Has Dionysus got many mutations?'

The question shocks me a bit but as it's Merc I answer him. 'When he's dressed, in uniform and that, you'd can't see anything different about him. A bit like you really. I don't mean you look alike but you both look more like humanoids used to look in the time before.'

'And out of uniform?'

I feel myself blushing. 'He's just perfect. Strong muscles

on his chest, arms and legs. He works out a lot you know and all that marching is good exercise.'

'But….' Mercury prompts me.

'I don't know if you'd really call it a mutation but he has three nipples on his chest.'

'Nothing else?'

'Nothing I've noticed.'

'And your only mutation is your little extra arm.'

'I don't think of it as a mutation. With a bit of practice I'll be able to knit more quickly than patients with only two hands.'

'Knit?'

'Baby clothes. I'll show you. Look.' I get out the wool and needles from the cabinet by my bed and attempt to demonstrate. 'I'm not very good at it yet, but with a bit more practice I'm sure I will be. Both Bridie and Gemma think I'm lucky to have been "blessed" as they call it with three hands. They're totally envious.'

Mercury isn't really listening. He's deep in thought. At last he starts to tell me what's on his mind.

'If your baby is indeed a complete you need to be prepared for a few things. For one thing, the Symposium – the Oasis government – are unlikely to let a complete go back with you to live in a compound full of mutants.'

'What's it to do with the government? She's my baby and I'm going to take her to C98 whatever they say.'

'I'm just trying to warn you that there may be some resistance to you doing that.'

I stare at the tiny blurred figure on the fotograms. 'I think I'll call her Penelope. That was my mother's name. At first I hated her for dying and leaving me all alone. I tried not to think about her. But lately, since I've been pregnant, I've begun to remember all the good things about her, how much she loved me and all that.'

I clasp my hands together. 'I wish she could be here now. She'd be a good grandmother. Still, I have to count myself lucky that little Penelope will have a grandfather.'

Mercury looks puzzled.

'Odysseus. He's my father. Didn't you know? Odysseus and Penelope. Get it? That's why I was sent to C55 when my mother died.'

'I didn't know. Didn't realise.'

'He didn't twig either. Not for years. For all you're both so blinking clever with your heads in books and on compus, there are some things you just don't get. Either of you.'

Mercury gives me his cheeky grin. 'Quite right, as usual, Isis.'

'I'll tell you something else. Thanks for the warning, but I can assure you that there's no way any doctor or Sympo-what-sit will ever separate me from my baby.'

Just before he leaves, Mercury gives me another bit of advice. 'Get Dionysus – sorry Osiris – to come as soon as possible. He should be here for the birth.'

'And if he can't come?'

Mercury hesitates. 'I'll stay with you. Just in case there's any trouble. I won't leave you alone.' And then he's off.

I'm not sure what he means by alone but it occurs to me that he means alone, except for completes. But they're all so nice and friendly. Is he really afraid they'll take my baby away from me?

I sit on the side of the bed struggling with the knitting. The wool is in knots and the bit I have done is a tangled mess. I throw the whole caboodle across the cube. Damn the bloody thing!

It was good to see Mercury. He's like a brother to me, but it's Osiris I need, my golden warrior, my lover, husband and father of little Penelope. Where is he? Why hasn't he come to see me? I put my head in my arms. I think I'll have a little cry. That will make me feel better.

No, I must pull myself together. I think about Mercury's visit and remember that I didn't ask him anything about his life. All we talked about was me. How selfish I am. Me, me, me, that's all I think about. And the baby of course. I didn't even find out what compound Mercury is in now or if anything interesting has happened to him. I don't suppose it has. He's not the type to have an adventure. I expect he's just jogging along like before, spending hours on his compu, studying hard for no reason at all.

He and Odysseus have a lot in common. They both love knowledge for its own sake. Odd that.

I should have asked him where he lives. Taken an interest, like.

A gush between my legs. It feels as if the bottom part of my body has broken off. Oh, don't tell me I'm going to lose this baby. I press the buzzer as they've taught me to do in an emergency and the old nurse, Gertie, comes in straightaway.

'Something terrible has happened,' I tell her. 'I feel as if everything has collapsed down there.'

She slips her hands under my robe. 'Everything's fine. Your waters have broken. That's all.'

She slips some sort of instrument inside me. 'You're almost fully dilated. That is one little baby in a hurry to come into the world. We must get you to the theatre immediately.'

Chapter Ten
You've got mail
(according to Bathsheba)

'I'm relying on you, Bathsheba to keep me informed on everything that happens in my absence,' Kat told me before he left for C99, 'It must be private – a communication that no one else can read.'

An auto-mail can be read by anyone, but a personal coded memo – a pcm – is a private device that no one but the recipient can read. That is how he wants me to communicate with him while he's away.

I'm honoured that Kata-Mbula has chosen me as his informant. I'm not officially his deputy. He prides himself on treating all members of our sectoid as equals, but I know that deep down he regards me as such. The pcm is easy to use. He sets up the code and, with one click I can write normally and, with another click it transforms itself into the pers-code he has set up.

I'm ready to begin, but am not sure how to address him.

My Beloved Kat,

I delete that greeting and start again. I try alternatives: *My beloved Kata-Mbula, Beloved Kat, Dear Kata-Mbula* and even a simple *Dear Kat* but none of them feel right. So, at the risk of upsetting him – not that he is ever upset, he's the most composed person I know – I go back to the first version. Why? Because, although it is not a quite accurate description of our relationship, it is how I think of him. To me he is and always will be *My Beloved Kat*.

I'm aware that this intimate greeting might bother him with its possessive undertones. He doesn't like shows of possessiveness. I have come to terms with that – or like to believe I have. He doesn't always share his innermost thoughts with me, just as he doesn't always share my bed. I try not to picture the intimacies we share being enacted with other partners.

But this propensity to share is part of his philosophy (and ours) in Compound Creative. We are all dedicated to community living and for this to extend to our sex lives seems quite natural.

I've noticed that Kat's affairs often begin during early rehearsals of a piece of theatre or dance and come to a climax (forgive the terminology) towards the end of the production and fade out soon afterwards.

From what I've read on line, I understand that these short-term relationships are quite usual in the world of the theatre. Intense all consuming passions at the time but after the last performance, the participants of these arrangements – let's call them arrangements – cease to operate and each half of the couple moves on without rancour.

This type of theatrical infatuation is a mixture of fantasy and reality, a confusion of the role and the actor who plays it. In the past, actors were likely to move on physically to act in different productions in different companies, possibly in different towns. Separation was inevitable and so the affair ended. In rehearsals with another group of actors another short-lived affair might start.

It's different for us. We remain here in the same compound and have to suffer the emotional hurt of witnessing our previous lover move on to someone else as a new play goes into rehearsal. We all, both males and females, have to cope with that rejection with varying degrees of success.

If the lover in question happens to be Kat it is somewhat different. In spite of our egalitarian beliefs, Kata-Mbula is our undisputed leader. There is honour in being sought out by him and after his affairs – some with females, some with men, some short-lived, some longer lasting – he moves on.

His partners do not. Or only rarely. And not easily. There is no taboo against this. We are, as I said before, believers in egalitarianism.

But the fact remains that most of Kat's partners do not make new alliances: or if they do, not until considerable time has passed. It's as if we keep ourselves untouched by anyone else ready to receive his attentions again should he decide to return. No compulsion. It just happens. Out of respect for him. And desire. We remain open to his needs.

To engage in an intimate relationship with another humanoid after knowing Kat would be less than satisfactory. Perhaps I'm exaggerating this tendency, imposing on others my own feelings, but I believe I'm sensitive to the emotions of Kat's ex-lovers, because they have known what I have known.

"Save your love for me," goes the old song. That's what I'm doing and that's what I suspect these others – especially the females – are doing too. I am saving my love for him and that's what I mean when I address him as "My Beloved Kat."

He knows I'm waiting. He knows I'm faithful to him and that I have never moved on, never taken another lover.

I also know that he relies on me. He trusts me to let him know what is happening in Compound Creative. This sectoid is more important to him than all his lovers – including me. I accept the limitations of his feelings, am pleased with the task he's given me and intend to carry it out to the best of my ability.

So – here goes. In spite of the opening greeting, I know I mustn't write a love letter.

These personal coded memos are to give him news about what's going on in Compound Creative and there's plenty to tell him without burdening him with personal matters.

Pcm One

My Beloved Kat,

I miss you. We all miss you. I'm sure you know that. We do our best to keep our spirits up, but without you here beside us, it is not easy.

I need to tell you about some of the problems we are encountering here, but I want you to know that we are coping with them. This is not a plea for you to return, much as we would all like that. We are aware that the work you are doing in C99 is important and will benefit us all in the long run.

Firstly, I must tell you that the arrival of Heracles and his sidekick, Sati, went off well, without mishap. You would have been pleased with the welcome we gave them, both the feast and the show afterwards. They were overwhelmed by the hospitality awarded them, so superior to anything they experienced before.

They arrived wearing what looked to us like sports-gear, the sort of sweat pants and tops that athletes in olden times would wear after physical exercise of some sort. I organised some of the women to make them more suitable garments before the evening's festivities. Sati and Heracles more than complied. They seemed delighted with the attention afforded them and their transformation. I've arranged for other costumes from our store to be at their disposal. Sati in particular has made full use of this facility. Her beauty and sexuality is much admired by both males and females and she has a good eye for choosing the costumes that suit her.

A word about Sati. There is something about her I don't

entirely trust. At first I thought she and Heracles were an exclusive couple and gave her a dormo-cube next to his. She uses this cube as a base, mainly to rest during the day. No doubt to get over her nightly exertions in the communal dormo-cube.

Heracles seems to accept her promiscuity. Mind you, he is not without other lovers himself, but – call me old-fashioned – I've always thought it more acceptable for a male to vary his bedfellows.

If you remember, we initiated the commun-dormo-cube in keeping with the spirit of the community we were building. Members of a theatre or dance group could develop relationships begun in rehearsals openly. This practice might cause suffering for the rejected partner, but a bit of anguish was considered a suitable price to pay for the sake of the play. The freedom awarded these new alliances, has worked well for the most part in spite of a few outbursts of jealousy. We consider this methodology, not an excuse for licence or promiscuity, but another method of "getting into the skin of the character." Exploring the sexuality of each other means the new couple could immerse themselves more deeply in their roles.

With the coming of Sati the original purpose of the commun-dormo-cube seems to have been forgotten. Sati, as her name suggests, is insatiable. As a lover she is voracious. As a female, she feeds on being the centre of attention.

I'm not sure of the ultimate purpose of the roles she is playing, but I have come to realise that it is not good for the health and growth of our creativity. There have been several falling-outs and several examples of non-attendance at rehearsals. A certain lethargy has set in as far as work is concerned. In my opinion, although I have no positive proof of this, Sati is determined to ruin the collective loyalty that we have worked so hard to achieve. I have no positive proof of this, because, as you know, I do not participate in the activities of the commun-dormo-cube. That is not my style. Nor is it my desire.

I'm afraid to have to tell you that there have been other problems in Compound Creative due to the change in leadership.

Initially, Heracles appeared amenable to my suggestions and agreed to consult the council before making any changes, but lately, he ignores its advice and mine. He laughs when I gently intimate that a change of policy might cause problems. For example, he no longer allows the competition for creative works for your office (now his) to be chosen democratically. He selects the winners himself and takes pleasure in announcing them in public. This causes great distress in some quarters. His choices tend to be – again in my humble opinion – not based on the best-executed work but on whether he fancies the artist who created it. There is talk of a "casting couch." Between the two of them, Sati and Heracles, seem to be turning our beloved sectoid into a den of debauchery. I am sorry to be the bearer of such bad news, but feel you should know what is going on.

You have probably heard about the coup at our neighbouring compound, C98. Jagadgauri has been replaced by the previous leader, Durga. As expected Durga has reinstated the golden warriors and they are practising their war games again as avidly as before, with the added advantage of being able to extend their marching and war games to the outside of the compound. Because of the previous rivalry between Durga and Heracles – she was after all his prisoner – not to mention between Durga and her so-called sister-wife, Sati, I just hoped that there would be no trouble coming from that sectoid.

With that in mind, I decided to attend Brahmin's funeral to restore good relations between us, but Heracles forestalled me, asked me to stay and hold the fort here so to speak while he and Sati attended the event in my place. I spent the entire day worrying about the dreadful things that might occur – but am pleased to say that nothing untoward appears to have happened. I did not receive any ill reports about the visit. I conclude Heracles was just checking up on the changed status quo.

Heracles continues his high-handed treatment of our colleagues, re-arranging the rehearsal schedules for no known reason and insisting on giving what he calls motivational speeches at the beginning, in the middle or at the end of rehearsals. Needless to say we are not used to such a cavalier approach and some resentment is apparent. No overt protests at the moment but there's an undercurrent of bitterness that is far from conducive to a good working atmosphere. All I can say is that his so-called motivational speeches do not have the intended effect. He seems to offend more than encourage. I have had words with him about it, but he laughs and tells me to "lighten up" whatever that means.

Another change. He wanders into rehearsals and sits at the back, usually with his arm round one of his favourite females and whispers to her, throughout. The other day a poor girl missed her cue and was scolded by Jeronimo, the Stage Manager. Heracles then undermined the SM's authority by telling him in front of the cast and stage crew that he should keep things in proportion. What he actually said was, 'don't get your knickers in a twist. After all, it's only a play.' Only a play!

How can someone with such insensitivity be in charge of Compound Creative? Even though it is only a temporary appointment, he acts as if it is a permanent one. Do reassure me by telling me that his power is limited. It will be disastrous for us all if he stays here much longer.

I'm sure you will think I'm exaggerating the gravity of the situation, but I swear I'm not. I'm sorry I haven't better news for you.

Meanwhile, I promise you that I will do everything in my power to make sure he and Sati don't ruin all your good work.

I hope everything is going smoothly with the design and construction of the new stadium and that Athene appreciates your extraordinary talent as much as we all do.

You know without me telling you that you have all my love and support.

Your ever loyal
Bathsheba

Pcm 2

My beloved Kat,

I hope all is well in C99 and that your plans are progressing smoothly.

Over a week now and no answer from you. I expect you're busy. Just because you haven't replied doesn't mean that I won't continue with my reports. You must be informed of what is happening here. It's just unfortunate that there is very little good news to tell you.

Things are a little chaotic here at the moment due to changes in routine and several problems in personal relationships concerning members of the cast.

The dancers, Dali and Lucretia, have announced that they are no longer a couple. Or rather Lucretia has. That's fine, in principle. Everyone is entitled to move on, but Lucretia is refusing to be in the same dance troupe as Dali. She says he's the guilty party and he must leave. She cannot bear to be in the same rehearsal room with him, can't bear to see his ugly face or see him prancing about like an arrogant pig as she puts it.

Dali tells her that if she feels that way she must be the one to leave, that he's not going anywhere. She stamps her feet and screams abuse at him.

As you know, Dali is the better dancer and we really can't afford to lose him. There's always a shortage of good male dancers and there's no one available to replace him; whereas it wouldn't be too difficult to find a substitute for Lucretia. I've tried to have a quiet word with her and have offered her another part in Troupe Two, but she turned her fury on me and told me she had no intention of dancing with "those losers." Where did she learn such language? I've never heard anyone use the word "loser" in Compound Creative before.

Before you ask, yes, Heracles is aware of the situation. He just shrugged, grinned and said, 'They'll get over it' and walked off. Maybe he's right. A good night's sleep and they may be back together again. I'll see what tomorrow brings.

Oh, I forgot to tell you. Dali's "crime" was sleeping with Sati. Apparently he's besotted with her and Lucretia is wild with jealousy.

I'm sorry to say that another problem has cropped up concerning Sati. She has decided she wants to be an actress. I told her she'd have to have some training first and she just laughed in my face. She's got her eye on a particular part – Juliet.

'I'm much prettier than that female,' she said. 'Actually I'm twice as pretty. I have two heads.'

You can imagine what our Juliet, Phaedra, had to say about that.

Heracles said, 'Oh let her have a go. It can't hurt. If she makes a mess of it at least she will have tried and then Phaedra can take over again.'

What a fiasco. Phaedra stalked out. Sati tripped up to

Romeo, ran her hands all over his body, bent him backwards and covered his face with kisses, with her two sets of lips, before thrusting her two tongues….

Well, I'm sure you don't want to hear the gruesome details.

The other actors huddled in little groups, whispering, deciding what to do.

Finally they attacked Sati, pulling her away from Romeo by her two heads of hair, all the while taunting her with mocking comments and laughter until she'd had enough and ran out.

Phaedra was brought back in and, after a bit, the rehearsal continued. Panic over.

A new notice appeared yesterday in various places all over the compound. It informed us that there would be an extraordinary general meeting at 8.0 pm. this evening. Attendance compulsory.

Naturally I asked Heracles what it was all about. He touched his nose and said, 'you'll have to wait and see. Just like everyone else.'

What a cheek! I thought of staying away to show him what I thought of his appalling manners, but of course I couldn't do that. I had to know what was going on.

First a group of male humanoids ambled on to the stage. About twenty or thirty of them, dressed in work fatigues similar to the way Heracles was dressed when he arrived. Then Heracles strolled on.

I can't remember if I told you but he has become a bit of a peacock lately. Everyday he dresses himself in a different costume. One day he's a Roman, another an Elizabethan, the next a sleek twentieth century businessman. He details some of the wardrobe mistresses to adjust the costumes to fit his broad physique and three muscular legs. The costumes are always brightly coloured. You certainly can't miss him.

For this extraordinary general meeting his costume was even more garish than usual: trousers and top in red and yellow stripes. He could have been one of Shakespeare's fools. Or anybody's fool for that matter.

He then proceeded to drop his bombshell. I still can't believe what he told us. The main point being that, from tomorrow, rehearsals will not start until 2.0 p.m. The mornings will be spent building.

Yes, Kat, building.

The fool has the crazy idea that we're going to build a city and that when the city is completed we will move out of the compound and live there.

He doesn't understand that communal living helps us to work as a team and produce creative work of a high standard.

You can imagine the stunned silence that met this announcement.

Heracles did concede that such a change would take some getting used to, but that now Earth is no longer contaminated we will have to leave the compounds and learn to live like true humans again. Unbelievable. Is he suggesting that we are not true humans now? Is he blind to all the work we've produced while living in a compound?

He told us that the males behind him – yes, they were all males, not a female in sight – were from C99, the top architects, designers, engineers and overseers on Earth. If this is really the case, why did Athene send for you to design and build the stadium? I can only suppose that Athene does not have the same high opinion of their talents.

I'm sure they can't be as skilled as you, my dear Kata-Mbula. I have doubts that these thuggish looking men have the ability to design a cave, let alone a city.

Heracles took pleasure in telling us that every member of this sectoid will take part in the necessary physical labour, males and females alike.

'That will ensure that the city will be your city, the buildings your buildings and this project, your project.'

That was his effort at inspiring the workforce. Pathetic.

'The humanoid in charge of the entire project is to be my good friend, Thor,' was his next announcement.

From the wings appeared the most ugly humanoid I have ever seen, grinning at us out of two mouths one above the other in the middle of a brutish face.

Maybe I'm being unkind, but the very appearance of this Thor made me shudder.

Kat, this is a bullyboy, a whip-master. I'm sure of it.

The idea of him being in charge of our sensitive actors and dancers, forcing them to do manual work appals me.

Heracles is not unaware of the fear he is creating. He seems to relish it.

Yours, very, very worried,
Bathsheba.

Pcm 3

Kata-Mbula, beloved leader,

Another week has passed since the construction began and I have no better news for you. I do wish you would contact me and give me some indication what I should be doing about this.

The new schedule is not going well. The members of our sectoid are working so hard in the mornings under bullyboy, Thor, that they are often too exhausted to do more than go through the motions of rehearsing in the afternoons and evenings.

Heracles says they will get used to the new routine in time. Two days running he congratulated them on working hard on the building project and cancelled the afternoon rehearsals.

'You deserve a rest,' he said and they were only too pleased to comply.

He's got his priorities wrong. If rehearsals are cancelled we shall never reach the standard necessary for the performances in The Big Event. But he's determined that Compound Creative should be the first sectoid to build and live in houses outside the compound.

In spite of Heracles saying that everyone has to help with the building project, one or two more mature humanoids, including myself, are exempt from physical labour; but this doesn't stop us going outside to watch progress, which, I grudgingly admit, is quite impressive.

Some of the workers seem quite keen on the project too. Several of the couples are looking forward to moving in to their own house. They've never shown any interest in doing such a thing before, but I guess times change and as they see the city taking shape, they visualise a different sort of life. I suspect living outside does have its attractions, but not for an oldie like me. I'm used to communal living and have no desire for change.

Today I noted a strange phenomenon. One of the buildings is very high. A tower. I asked Heracles what it was for.

'For?' he said. 'It's for me, Bathsheba. My house. The Heracles Tower. A big phallic symbol. Appropriate don't you think?'

He seems to enjoy winding me up. Is he flirting with me? I do hope he doesn't fancy me.

An update on Lucretia and Dali. She seems to have forgiven him and they are at least talking now. I hear that they are thinking of moving into one of the houses when it's completed. Maybe she thinks he'll be faithful to her if she keeps him away from temptation.

By the way, Sati is exempt from physical labour. She seems to spend most of her time in her own dormo-cube, lying on her bed, reading magazines or daydreaming. A lull in the storm. I suspect she's keeping well out of the way in case Heracles changes his mind and asks her to lift a brick or two. Ha!

No more for now. I'll keep in touch. I do wish you'd find a moment to contact me.

Ever faithful,
Bathsheba

Pcm 4

My dearest Kata-Mbula,

Great news. Lucretia is pregnant. And so are Hera and Phaedra. I say it's great news because it speaks well for the future of our planet. It makes the building project seem more sensible too. If there are to be children, the idea of living in family units appears to be a viable option.

The distaff side is that there will come a time when our pregnant dancers and actors won't be able to perform. At the moment Heracles is willing to let them off any heavy construction work. He too sees the advantage of making sure that the women are looked after and that their babies are born safely.

There was even some talk of asking Athene to intervene and ask if the births could take place in Hos-sat, as arranged for Isis from C98. When Isis returns perhaps we could pay her a visit and see the baby. Oh dear, I'm getting quite broody. Fat lot of good that is. My childbearing days are over.

Another good thing. Now Heracles has his city project to interest him he is interfering less with rehearsals. Consequently they are going fairly smoothly. I actually think that the city project has given the troupes a new interest and they're not so intense about their theatrical work. You may not like the sound of that, but to hear them chat and laugh and generally behave in a more relaxed way is, I believe, a bonus.

I have hopes that everything is improving at last. It's not the same without you, but it's not all bad. I suppose we've accepted the difference in leadership styles and are going with the flow.

Yours in a slightly more positive frame of mind,
Bathsheba

Chapter Eleven
Downs and ups
(according to Kali)

Stride, hop, leap. Stride, hop, leap. My signature movement. I've been practising it, trying to cross the compu-centre in three groups of three to land neatly on my shaper at my workstation. If I can achieve a smooth transition from leap to seat I will feel better about myself. That's what I'm reduced to: devising little tests to cheer myself up. Not bad this morning. Not dead on, but getting better. I slip on to the shaper and look around. No one else here. That's not unusual. I like to be here first.

I warm up my multi-screen compu and check the update news-stream from other compounds. Heracles, now head of C97, is building a city. I always thought that young man would go far. I miss him. He was supportive when I was in need of a friend, after losing my chief administrator role here. Another snippet of news. Durga, the sister-wife who helped me regain control of C55, is out of captivity and has taken over from Jaga at C98. Quite right. She's back where she belongs in charge of the golden warriors. She was also supportive of me and helped me regain my sectoid. No mention of what has happened to Jaga. The next piece of news concerns Odysseus. He's to be chief adviser to Athene as well as being the curator of the museum and chief chronicler. I'll send him an auto-mail to congratulate him. All good news this morning.

I only wish I had something good to report too. Unfortunately not. The message I look for everyday has not arrived. No news of Mercury, my little messenger. I don't understand it. Why doesn't he keep in touch?

Hugo tightens his hold on my neck as if to comfort me. Some humanoids cringe at the very thought of being touched by snakes. I have no such hang-ups.

I find their touch soothing.

Hugh and Hannah, Henry and Henrietta tighten their grip round my wrists and let out a gentle hiss of affection. Hugo, a scarf at my neck, gives me a reassuring squeeze.

The other workstations are still empty. Where are the members of my sectoid? They should be here by now. They arrive later every morning.

I hear some shouts from outside and leap across the compu-centre and out of the door to investigate.

A group of workers have collected twigs and branches as mock weapons and are marching up and down as if they are warriors. Others are engaged in mock fights. They are reliving the time when they marched to C99. Their co-ordination hasn't improved a jot. They have no idea how to march in time with each other or with the drum that one of them is banging. The rest of their colleagues stand around cheering, or perhaps jeering.

'Smarten up!' 'Fight the good fight!' 'Kill the enemy!' they shout.

Pitiful. There is no enemy and no fight. What do they think they are doing, this excuse for an army, with their erratic movements, makeshift weapons and ragged clothes? Why are they outside instead of sitting at their workstations?

The answer is – because they can. Ever since the front door of the compound has been open and they've known it's safe outside, that's where they want to be. Outside, in the fresh air. Problem is, they don't know what to do there. They only remember marching to war and they use that memory to play at being soldiers.

I'll have to think of something profitable for them to do outside. I think of Heracles and his colleagues building a city; but these pathetic creatures with their multiple mutations and lack of brain cells wouldn't be capable of such a project.

I sigh and am just about to call out to them to come in and start work, when a crash of thunder and a streak of lightening do the job for me.

They squeal and run inside, helter-skelter, arms and legs awry, as the sky opens and down comes the rain.

Like a mother shepherding her children, I hustle them indoors, tell them to take off their wet clothes and change into dry ones. 'Back to work,' I chide them. 'How are you going to meet your targets if you spend all your time playing soldiers?'

They scuttle off to change their clothes. Some of them return to the compu-centre, but not all. Others wander off to the games room to play bar billiards or table tennis, to the bowling alley or the gym. Others lounge in the RR and play pop music. All the leisure facilities that Sati helped design are now in place. They are only supposed to be used in the evenings, but lately slackness has crept in. I seem to have lost control.

Things have never been the same since I was reinstated as Chief Administrator. I read somewhere that it is almost impossible to return to the status quo of the past, whether in personal relationships or at work. It seems to be true. The depression I felt in Headculturedome is in danger of returning big time. I sit, head in hands, at my workstation and try to assess what has gone wrong.

The problem started when Sati seduced my workforce, when the rigour of my well-run sectoid was exchanged for the pleasure-based agenda favoured by Sati and Jaga. Long hours reaching targets for Worldwideculture were replaced by equally long hours devoted to sex, games and dancing. When I – with Durga's help – returned, I had no idea it would be so hard to regain control.

The first problem I had to overcome was the resentment caused by Jason's death. He was a casualty of war. One of Durga's warriors killed him when we attacked C55. Not so unusual for someone to be killed in a battle you might think, but mutant humanoids have no experience of war and even less of sudden death.

It was an accident, a shot fired in the heat of the moment; but the members of C55 would not accept that fact.

Jason was Sati's favourite and that's why she took Jason's body away with her to make sure he had a decent burial. Jason's colleagues in sectoid C55 had no funeral to help them come to terms with the loss. There was no closure for them. It was left to me to deal with the build-up of bitterness that Jason's death aroused. There was a craving for blood.

The morning meetings that I set up to listen to their ideas were never completely satisfactory. They became little more than opportunities for grumbling, a chance to air complaints without coming up with any solutions. Day after day the meetings deteriorated into sessions designed to bait me. I was blamed for Jason's death. In vain I told them his death was unintentional, an accident of war. They wanted revenge. But the captain responsible for killing Jason was in prison in C99 and so was Durga. In any case, in my opinion, this strategy of an eye for an eye never solves problems, only prolongs conflict.

I decided to hold a memorial service for Jason. His colleagues were to make little speeches reminding us of his good qualities. The main problem turned out to be that in life Jason had not been popular. He was arrogant and self-seeking.

He had never been a loyal friend or lover. To top it all he had always been Sati's favourite. When former friends, colleagues and lovers tried to record his good qualities, they remembered instead the numerous times he had let them down.

One by one the members of the workforce came to me, saying they couldn't deliver these little eulogies. They didn't want to be insincere and make up lies, but couldn't think of anything good to say about him. The truth was Jason was not a very popular humanoid. The result was that Jason didn't get his memorial service after all.

Somehow, because this matter had not been settled, it caused more bad feeling between them and me.

Another matter that caused trouble in the aftermath of Jason's demise and Sati's departure was the conduct of Hermione. She and Jason had been sexual partners on and off for several years before Sati came on the scene, seduced him and made him her favourite. Now they were no longer here, Hermione made her move to take over Sati's role.

One of Sati's innovations had been to construct an ornate dormo-cube to entertain her numerous lovers. Some referred to it as the brothel. When I first saw it on my return, I could hardly believe my eyes. It was decorated in the most vulgar – you could say tawdry – manner with swathes of gaudy wall hangings, rose-coloured satin sheets, cushion-covers and crude murals of nude male and female humanoids in sexual poses that left no room for the imagination. I am no prude, but I was quite frankly sickened by this display.

I had so many other things to attend to in order to restore law and order that I delayed having these cubes refurbished. Hermione appropriated them for her own use. She tried to emulate Sati's promiscuity and invited a series of males to visit her.

Hermione was quite an attractive female, but not as stunning as Sati. For a start, she only had one head to Sati's two. Her four eyes and two mouths were crammed on to the same face. The result was a rather crowded jockeying for position of her features, but apparently, the mouths were used to good effect when making "love-sex".

Hermione's attempt to take over where Sati left off was a far from popular move with the other females. It was one thing to be obliged to tolerate your partner's attraction to a charismatic stranger but quite another to accept his infidelity with someone you'd previously considered a friend. Who did Hermione think she was?

Serena suspected that her current squeeze, Apollo, was one of Hermione's conquests and organised an attack. In the middle of the night a gang of female mutant humanoids burst into the dormo-brothel, saw the naked male on top of Hermione and screeched at him to get out. Seeing the gaggle of ferocious looking females led by Serena, Apollo jumped off the bunku and beat a hasty retreat on his three stumpy legs, not stopping to retrieve his clothes. The females stayed behind to deal with Hermione. They stripped the bunku, tore down the wall hangings, hurled any objects they could find at Hermione and dragged her by the hair off the bunku, out of the cube and out of the compound.

The first I heard of the incident was a commotion by the compound door: strident, high-pitched voices screaming and shouting. I leapt out of my bunku and strode off to see what was happening. I arrived as the door slammed shut and the key turned in the lock.

'What's going on?' I asked.

All speaking at once they attempted to enlighten me. 'Hermione is a slut,' 'A slag,' 'She thinks she can do what she damn well likes,' 'We don't want her here,' 'She's banished,.' 'She can find somewhere else to go….'

I tried to calm them and asked exactly what had happened. They led me to "the brothel" and told me that

that Hermione, had set herself up in here as a second-rate whore and been "having it off" with anyone stupid enough to have her.

'We'd only just got our partners back when she decided to try her hand at being a Sati clone.'

'Imagine that. Plain little Hermione thinking she could take over from Sati.'

'And imagine our males being so susceptible.'

Rather shame-facedly, Serena's followers showed me the damage they'd done to the dormo-cube. The sheets and wall hangings lay in tatters. China and glass ornaments, powder bowls and perfume bottles lay in pieces on the floor.

'She'd no right to behave like that,' Serena said.

'No right at all,' said Aphrodite.

'You are right,' I agreed. 'She shouldn't have behaved in this way, but when you have a problem such as this you should come to me and let me deal with it.'

Serena, Aphrodite and the others looked at me doubtfully. They would need a lot of convincing before they would trust me to solve any problem for them.

'Where is Hermione now?' I asked.

'We've locked her out. We don't want her here,' said Serena.

'That is not your decision,' I told them. 'I say who leaves and who stays, not you.'

They looked at me as if I were crazy. 'Yes, but…'

'You should all go to your bunkus now. I don't want to hear another word from any of you tonight. Get some sleep. Tomorrow I'll give you brooms and cleaning materials and you can clear up the mess you've made. You can also give the walls a lick of paint while you're at it. Nothing fancy. Plain white.'

They exchanged looks. 'What about Hermione?' Serena asked.

'I am going outside to get her back. I'll have a talk with her and I don't think you'll find she'll give you any more trouble.'

They came to the front door with me. I unlocked it. In the distance a female figure lay slumped on the ground. 'Go to your bunkus, now,' I told them. 'Get some sleep. You've got a busy day tomorrow.'

They watched me as I strode, hopped and leapt towards the lone figure. I stopped, turned round and glared at them. Serena began to move off slowly, and the others followed.

As I approached Hermione she looked up at me. Her face was badly bruised and covered in blood. She was holding her arm as if in pain.

'I can't come back,' she said. 'They'll murder me.'

'They won't touch you again,' I promised her. 'Besides, where else do you think you're going?'

She started to sob as if she would never stop. I picked her up in my four strong arms and carried her back to C55, making sure I didn't hurt her arm. I strode out confidently, even adding a few leaps. My precious pets hissed and spat. Their tongues stuck out like spikes. Hermione looked terrified, but they didn't mean anything by it. They were only posturing, giving her a bit of a fright. That's all.

I took her to Sicku-bay and asked Emilia, one of the older females, to look after her. The setting up of Sicku-bay had apparently been Jaga's idea. She'd partitioned off a section near the gym as a kind of health centre or mini hospital. Jaga thought that with the installation of a gym and games room there might be accidents or at least a need for treatment. After all, she reasoned, the humanoids were exercising muscles that had not been used for years. Sicku-bay was one of Jaga's good ideas that had counteracted Sati's zany plans.

Sicku-bay came in useful to isolate Hermione. Luckily her arm was not broken but she had a sprained wrist and her arm was put in a sling for a while. I visited her every day and, when I felt she was up to it, gave her little pep talks about how she should behave in the future, as a responsible member of the sectoid.

The advice really wasn't necessary. She was ashamed of her escapade and terrified of seeing the other females again. My main job was to persuade her that she had no need to be afraid, that I would make sure they would not assault her.

After a few days, or possibly weeks, she came to work in the compu-centre. I kept my extra eye on her.

No one of either gender spoke to her; but no one harassed her.

The way I dealt with the situation must have restored some confidence in me. No further dramatic episodes have occurred, but I know the balance of power is not right.

It's not just Hermione that the members of the sectoid ignore. It's me as well. They feel no compunction to work at their targets. They spend their time doing what they damn well like and there seems little I can do about it. No wonder I feel depressed.

An unexpected visitor arrives. Athene. She doesn't address us impersonally each week on the big screen as Ra, the previous CEO, did. She visits each sectoid personally. Today it seems it's our turn.

She arrives by the transporter next to Man1 and makes her way down the silver cylinder to the compu-centre, a tall, elegant woman in a long sky blue gown. Apart from her hands and face there is not a bit of skin to be seen. She moves with an easy grace. She looks around and notes the number of empty workstations. Apart from myself, only Hermione is here and the compu-mad whiz kid, Damian.

'Kali,' Athene says, coasting up to me, 'can you spare me a minute?'

For Zeus's sake. She's the CEO. How can I not? I complete the line I'm typing, save it and reduce it. Nothing important, but I must give the impression that it is.

I look up at her, nod and smile. 'Athene. Good to see you.' I stand up. 'Shall we go to Man1? We can talk in private there.'

She raises her eyebrow, implying that it is reasonably private here. 'I'd like you to show me round the compound first, if you don't mind.' She's nothing if not polite. 'I haven't seen it since the renovations.'

I do mind, but I have no choice. I stride, hop and leap to the sliding doors and look over my shoulder to make sure she is keeping up. She's right behind me. The doors slide open and we step into the RR, side by side. Several couples are lounging on the double shapers.

'Oh dear, I've come during your mid-day break,' Athene says. Sarcastic bitch. She must know that the situation has become so lax here that whatever time of day she chooses to visit she would think it a break.

She drifts over to have a word or two with the humanoids on the shapers. They jump up as they see her approach as if caught with their fingers in someone else's food packoid. Pleasantries are exchanged.

We proceed to the gym and watch a game of badminton and some weightlifting. On to the games room where billiards, table tennis and scrabble are in progress. Athene waits for a suitable break in the action and has a few words with the players. She is all smiles, calm, friendly but business-like. When she considers she has seen and heard enough, she recommends we move on, not to Man1 as I suggested, but outside.

'Outside? But there's nothing there and it may be a bit cold. We've just had a storm,' I explain.

'That's all right,' she says sweetly. 'We can try it anyway.

Good to get some fresh air. You say there's nothing to see? Then we'll have to use our imaginations.'

It's not cold. It's muggy and there's a smell of damp. Not an unpleasant smell.

She glances at the sticks scattered over the ground where the "soldiers" dropped them when the rain started. 'I see you haven't started planting anything yet.'

'Planting?' I ask. 'What would we plant?'

'That's up to you. You'd have to find the type of plants that suit the soil and climate.'

She bends down and grabs a handful of muddy earth. 'It's quite loamy. Might be worth consulting Jaga.'

'Jaga?'

What's the matter with me? I seem to be speaking in monosyllables repeating her words as if I'm a moron. No wonder I've lost control of the workforce.

Athene half closes her large eye, shields it with a hand like a sloping roof on her forehead and squints at the horizon. 'Plenty of scope here for quite a big project.'

I think of how the members of the sectoid love being out of doors. I try to share the view she's imagining. I see rows of vegetables, fruit trees and bushes. I turn to her, feeling quite excited. 'We could cultivate this land. Grow our own produce.'

'It's a possibility. Now we are no longer confined to the compounds we should take advantage of our exterior resources. But we mustn't be too ambitious too soon. My advice is – start small and gradually develop. Oasis will continue to support us until we are ready to be independent.'

'Some sort of market garden or farm might be the answer,' I suggest.

She takes me by the shoulders and faces me, her one big eye looking deep into my extra eye in the centre of my forehead. 'Kali, everything you say is possible but I think you could do with some help.'

'Help?' I'm back on repeating monosyllables again and hate myself for it.

'I have taken the liberty of asking Jaga to come and see you. I think the two of you could devise a plan to make full use of this area. Come. Let's go in now. She'll be here soon.'

I'm gob-smacked. Why would I want help from Jaga, that traitor? She came to help me fight Sati but changed sides and betrayed me. She stole my sectoid. She and Sati ruled C55 together until Durga helped me win it back.

On the other hand it occurs to me that Jagadgauri is named after Shiva's harvest bride and she takes her role seriously. She's skilled in all things agricultural. Perhaps she could prove useful to me.

Athene continues to talk to me as we make our way back to the compound. She tells me that Jaga needs my help as much as I need hers.

She was Chief Administrator in C98 while Durga was in prison, but once Durga was released and initiated a coup, Jaga's power collapsed. Jaga had tried to turn the golden warriors into farm labourers and it just didn't work. They rebelled and supported Durga.

'Here in C55, it's quite a different scenario. I suspect your workforce will be only too pleased to work outside and learn to dig and plant things. With your cool head and good administrative skills and Jaga's agricultural knowledge, there is no reason why you shouldn't succeed. You both have so much to offer each other. Ah here she is.'

Jaga steps out of the transporter. My sister-wife and I greet each other somewhat coolly but Athene takes my hand in her right hand and Jaga's in her left and leads us into Man 1.

We sit on a treble shaper, Athene between us, Jaga and I turned towards each other.

Jaga looks as beautiful as ever with her straw-coloured hair encircling her bronzed face like a halo. I have no idea what mutations she has. I've never seen her without clothes but she can't be a complete or she wouldn't be living on Earth. I wonder what she thinks of my blue-black face, three eyes and dreadlocks and the mottled snakes at neck and wrists.

Jaga smiles her sunny smile and begins to draw for us a mental picture of her plan. Bit by bit she encourages us to share her vision of the future. She talks, not of a market garden nor a farm, but field after field of golden wheat.

She talks of a glorious harvest with the workers scything the corn, side by side in unison, of binding the sheaves into little tent-like structures and leaving them in the field to dry, of lifting them on long pitchforks to store them in stacks. She talks of sifting and grinding the seeds, of making bread, of cottages, a church, a shop, a village, of enjoying a rural life and, eventually, of being entirely self-sufficient and independent.

'It will be our place,' she says simply. 'Our own place.'

Such is the power of her words that I swear I can see those waving fields of wheat gleaming in the sun and the villagers, our colleagues from C55, living an idyllic life in the countryside.

It's an ambitious scheme and will take a lot of work to bring it to fruition. I can see that Jaga will need my common sense to take one step at a time. We will need experts and equipment to help us. Athene promises us all the support we need.

'At the moment,' Athene says, 'the completes on Oasis continue to provide us with nutri-food packoids and clothes, but they won't want to support us forever. Anything they can do to help us become independent they will do. They know and we know that change cannot take place over night, but it can happen. It will happen. And you can take the first steps towards making that dream come true here, starting tomorrow.'

We sit and talk a little longer, all three of us contributing ideas to what has become our combined plan. When Athene sees that our meeting is going well, she slips away and we two sister-wives talk on.

When we are ready, we leave Man1 and go to the compu-centre to share our news with our colleagues. Most of them are at their workstations now, heads down concentrating hard, shamed by Athene's presence into doing some work.

When they see Jaga, their faces light up. They spring up from their shapers and rush towards her. They pull up before they reach her and look at me warily, but I nod and make myself smile, encouraging them to greet her.

They crowd round her and ask her how she is. 'Are you just visiting?' 'Are you back for good?' 'How great you look' and to tell the truth I feel jealous of her popularity. I have never experienced such warmth from them.

News of her return travels fast and in come the others from other cubes to welcome her. I turn away, unable to watch any longer.

'Just a minute,' Jaga tells them and she walks across to me with strides almost as big as mine, puts her arm round my shoulders and says, 'Kali is still here too. My dear sister-wife, Kali. She and I are going to work together from now on. We have some plans, but they will only work with your support. We'll tell you about them now and you can tell us what you think.'

With her arm round my shoulders, she talks again of waving wheat and harvests and working on the land and building little cottages and living in villages, and a mighty cheer goes up.

She raises her hand and says, 'But I can't carry out this plan and neither can you, without Kali. She is a wonderful administrator and she will make sure everything is workable.

I tend to get carried away with big ideas but to make my dreams come true I need Kali. And we need your support too or this will not happen. Do we have it?'

Someone calls out, 'Yes, you have!' and others take up the cry, 'Yes, yes, yes.'

Jaga asks me if I'd like to say something and I find myself saying, 'This promises to be an exciting project, although, as Jaga says, it will involve hard work.'

A groan and someone says, 'Here we go again. She'll mention targets in a minute.' That comment provokes a laugh. What a killjoy they think I am.

I need to say something that will have popular appeal. 'From now on, those of you who wish to work outside can do so.'

A loud cheer.

'Those who prefer to work inside on your compus are welcome to do that too.'

A mocking cheer. But I note that Hermione, Damian and one or two of the others who are less physically able or have an aptitude for research nod and exchange smiles, pleased to have the option.

I can't resist adding. 'From now on you can reach your targets either inside or outside.'

'Those bloody targets,' shouts Apollo. 'What use are they anyway?'

'No more targets!' yells Serena and a chant starts up 'No more targets' and everyone claps in unison. I decide to let it pass. At least for the moment. After all they could be right. How has working towards targets ever benefited C55?

There's a buzz of excitement in the compu-centre. Things are looking up. Maybe power-sharing is not so bad after all. I hug Jaga and find I have tears in my eyes. I notice that her eyes are moist too. Tomorrow will be the first day of our new life.

That turns out to be true in more ways than one. An unexpected auto-mail from Durga arrives. She suggests that we four sister-wives, Durga, Sati, Jaga and myself should let bygones be bygones and demonstrate our solidarity at Athene's proposed Big Event.

'Bloody cheek!' says Jaga. 'She takes over my sectoid and expects me to co-operate with her? I don't think so. Solidarity? What a joke. She can count me out.'

'It might be worth listening to what she has to say,' I suggest.

Naturally Jaga is bitter about Durga's behaviour. It's different for me. Durga helped me get my sectoid back from Sati. I wouldn't be here now if it wasn't for her.

'Do what you like but don't expect me to join in one of her madcap schemes.'

Jaga throws back her head and straw-coloured hair flies all over the place. 'She talks about the power of us sister-wives, but what she really wants is power for herself. Sati won't agree to any plan by Durga either. Their personal history leaves a lot to be desired.'

'We've all got adverse history with each other, but if we can get over our differences and work together, as you and I have started to do, in spite of our past relationship, why not the rest of us?'

Jaga pulls a face. I can see she'll need some heavy duty persuasion to make her co-operate with whatever it is Durga wants us to do.

When Durga tells me her plans for The Big Event, I can see immediately that it will wow the spectators, fill them with awe and wonder. In fact I am so excited by her imaginative proposal, I know I must be part of it. I will have to find a way to persuade Jaga and Sati to put aside their grievances for one day and join in too. The four wives of Shiva are going to upstage every other presentation at The Big Event.

I suspect that Sati might be tempted by the prospect of showing off her beauty and sexual potency in public. Jaga will be more difficult to convince. But I will succeed in persuading both of them.

Things are looking up for my sectoid and the prospect of performing at The Big Event gives me something else to look forward to.

There is only one thing missing for my life to be complete. To be reunited with Mercury. I still have no idea where he is.

Chapter Twelve
Confidences and Conspiracies
(according to Michael)

Journal Entry

I ask Mr Spencer, the surgeon, for a postponement of the vasectomy.

Our conversation is polite but he can't understand why I should want to change my mind.

'Are you sure you want to do that, Michael?' he asks. 'I moved several appointments around to make you a priority.'

'I am sorry to upset your schedule, but, I've had second thoughts about having the operation. As I'm sure you will agree it is a big decision.'

His grey eyes study me across his desk. 'Your father led me to believe....'

'It's not my father who's having the operation. I am twenty-years-old and an adult.' I hear my voice rising. I must keep calm. 'The choice is mine, not my father's.'

He hesitates, taps his fingers on his desk and rests those steady grey eyes on my face again. 'You are right. You must be sure before embarking on this course. A vasectomy is not so easy to reverse as you might think. I would like to help you with your decision by making an appointment for you to see our psychiatrist. You can talk through everything with her.'

'Does she know my medical history?'

'She does. Dr. Atherton is a permanent member of our team. If you remember I suggested you should consult her before going ahead with your previous procedure. You said it wasn't necessary, that you'd already made up your mind. This time you appear to be less certain.'

'It's a big decision to deny myself the right to become a father.'

'It was a big decision to convert from mutant humanoid to complete,' he observes dryly. He pauses. 'Any regrets on that score?'

'Of course not,' I answer almost too quickly.

He's no fool. He narrows his eyes. 'But you do have some reservations.'

'I probably should have spoken to Dr. Atherton first. It might have helped me adjust to my new life more easily.'

'In that case I'll make you an appointment with her.'

'That would be great. Thanks.'

I stand up ready to leave. At the door I turn back and say, 'I don't want to rush my decision. I'm happy to stay on for a while and have several sessions with Dr. Atherton, if necessary.'

Mr Spencer frowns. It's clear that he finds my request for delay far from logical. Not in keeping with what he knows of my nature.

I'm sure he'll be on the phone to my father the minute I've left his office. These old boys always stick together.

I must get to Father first. I send him a text to tell him that I'm reconsidering having the procedure. I take a deep breath.

Now I have an excuse to stay in Hos-sat for a few more days.

I pop my head round the door of Isis's room.

Isis is not there. Only Gemma, the pretty nurse. She's changing the sheets. She looks up when she sees me, and smiles.

'She's been in there all night,' she says. 'A long labour.'

'Can I go and see her?'

'I don't advise it. She's kicking up quite a fuss, screaming and yelling at everyone.'

I pull a face. 'Maybe not then – unless you think I could be of help?'

'You? No, I don't think so. She's in good hands. Gertie is there and the obstetrician, Doctor Carter. Best leave it to the professionals, Mr Mercury.'

'Michael, please.'

She gives me an odd look. 'Michael? OK. Isis calls you Mercury.'

'It's a sort of childhood nickname.'

Another odd look. I've said the wrong thing. She's wondering how a mutant and complete can possibly have known each other since childhood.

I have no intention of enlightening her, but something keeps me there. I watch the efficient way she pulls the sheet tight across the mattress. She has neat, capable hands.

'I've seen the scans,' I tell her.

'But you're not the father?'

I find myself blushing. 'No. Just a friend. The scan….'

'Looks perfect – no sign of any mutations, but they'll examine the baby thoroughly after the birth to make sure.' She treats me to her lovely smile. 'No need to worry.'

'I understand the baby is female.'

'She is.' Gemma plumps up the pillows and spreads the top sheet across the bed, smoothing it with those compact little hands.

'If they don't find any mutations, do you think they will let Isis keep the baby?'

She puckers her little forehead. 'Why wouldn't they?'

'I just wondered if they would allow her to take a complete back to Earth?'

'Oh, I see what you're getting at.'

Gemma stops tucking in the sheet, stands up straight and thinks for a moment, pursing her mouth in a manner that is far from unattractive. She's pretty and intelligent too. A good combination.

'Could be a problem, I suppose,' she says. 'The idea of a complete human being brought up among mutants would be unconventional to say the least. There may be some against it.'

'What about you?' I ask.

She takes a moment to consider that then shakes her head. 'In my experience a child is always better with its mother.'

A good answer. 'I'd like to ask you a question. During the last few days, have you seen any unusual visitors here – official-looking people?

Gemma gives me a sideways look. 'Only you, Michael. Only you.'

I grin. 'I'm not an official. I'm a student.'

'At Oasis uni?'

'That's right.'

'You're so lucky. I'd love to go there. I studied to be a nurse here at Hos-sat, but what I'd really like to do is to study medicine and become a doctor.'

'You should go for it. If that's what you want to do.'

'I often think about applying. Thing is my mother can't really afford to support me through another lot of training. I'd need a grant or loan of some sort.'

'I could look into the possibilities for you, if you'd like me to.'

'You would do that for me?' She raises her dark eyes to mine. I note that she's a bit shorter than me.

'Sure. I'd like to help. I think having an ambition is important. Do you live here on Hos-sat?'

'In the nurse's home, yes, but I go back to my parents' house on Oasis on my days off.'

'Maybe we could grab a coffee some time?' I got that line from Jonathan. 'I could download the necessary forms, you could bring your CV and we could fill them in together.'

I hesitate. How far should I go to show my interest in her? Jonathan would tell me to just go for it.

'I'd really like to talk to you some more, get to know you better.'

She gives me a shy smile that makes my head reel. 'That would be good.'

We exchange mob-fone numbers and she says, 'I have to go now. See you later.' And she's off.

I call out to her retreating back, 'You will let me know when it happens?'

She looks over her shoulder. 'What? Oh, the baby. Yes, yes of course I'll let you know.'

There's a thing. A pretty nurse has agreed to have coffee with me. She wants to get to know me better. I say her name to myself: Gemma. I find myself giving a little skip along the corridor. I look over my shoulder just to make sure that Janey, the physiotherapist, is not around before I launch myself into a giant leap.

Journal Entry

A little old man is sitting outside the maternity unit. Not so old actually. Probably only about fifty or at the most sixty but he has the look of old age, a mixture of frailty and wisdom.

Close up I recognise that triangular face and shrewd central eye. I hesitate for a moment. Father has forbidden me to talk to mutant humanoids, but I've already broken that promise by making contact with Isis. And there isn't anyone I'd rather see. Apart from Kali.

'Odysseus!' I say. 'Great to see you.'

He looks up questioningly and an expression of wonder comes over his face.

'It's been a long time, Mercury,' he says.

'Nearly four years.'

Neither of us can stop grinning. With amazing agility he springs to his feet and puts his bony arms round me.

His body is thin and wiry. Not an inch of flesh on those bones. Isis used to call him a crinkly-crumbly but I have the feeling there is something in the constitution of this humanoid that is far from crumbling.

'No news yet?' he asks, acknowledging that we are both waiting for news of the birth.

'Not yet. No. You do know the baby is female?'

'I do indeed. Isis is going to call her Penelope after her mother.' His face lights up. 'I still can't believe it. I'm going to be a grandfather.'

Odysseus brought up Isis just as Kali did me and I consider her my mother. A sudden thought. If ever I do have a baby Kali will be a grandmother.

We sit down next to each other and Odysseus starts to ask me questions right away about where I've been and what I've been doing since we last met. I realise that the time for hedging is over. No more lies. At last I have found someone I trust enough to tell the truth about the changes in my life.

But not now. A text from Gemma tells me that Isis has given birth to a healthy baby girl. An odd twist in my stomach as I note that Gemma's message concludes with two little crosses – kisses. A personal message from Gemma to me.

Journal Entry

Isis is the picture of serenity, propped up on her pillows with the bundle that is baby Penelope in her arms. The pupils of her eyes roll upwards to show the whites in typical Isis fashion and she smiles the widest smile I have ever seen.

'Isn't she beautiful?'

Odysseus and I both nod and smile, but to tell the truth all we can see is a little screwed up face. Not much beautiful about it; but I suppose a mother sees her baby differently.

Isis looks totally happy. She doesn't even ask if Dionysus is here.

The old nurse, Gertrude, bustles in. 'You should get some sleep now,' she tells Isis and puts out her arms to take the baby.

Isis pouts. 'No, let her stay here with me.'

Gertrude yawns. Not surprising. She's been up all night and no doubt wants to catch up with some sleep herself. She's a bit tetchy. 'Don't be silly. You can't go to sleep with the baby in your arms. You might lie on her and crush her. We'll put her in the cot at your side. She won't run away.'

Isis gives the baby a last kiss on the forehead and, reluctantly, lets the nurse take her and settle her in the cot.

Gertrude is just as strict with us, dismissing us as if we are children. 'Off you go, you two,' she says. 'Let the girl sleep. Enough visitors for one day.'

Journal Entry

In the Hos-sat dining room, Odysseus and I sit and talk. For the first time I feel able to tell someone what has happened to me over the last four years. He is the right person to tell because I respect him and am fond of him. As well as bringing up Isis he always took an interest in me.

So I tell him how my father came to Headculturedome to find me and how he took me back with him to live a very different life on Planet Oasis. I explain that first I came here to Hos-sat to have my mutations taken away and to learn to speak and move like a complete. He listens carefully and congratulates me on the way I have mastered these skills.

'It was not just the physical changes that I've found difficult,' I tell him. 'I've had to learn to think like a complete and living on Oasis is very different to being in a compound on Earth. Sometimes better, sometimes worse, but always different. A lot to get used to.'

Odysseus listens to my story with such intensity and seems to totally grasp the nature of the ambivalent emotions I've experienced. But I'm not after sympathy. As Gemma said earlier, I'm one of the lucky ones. I'm studying at the University of Oasis, something I never in my wildest dreams believed could be possible.

Of course I tell him about my studies there and about Museum Oasis and its comprehensive collection of artefacts.

'All pillaged from Earth of course,' I add with a wry grin.

It's such a relief to be able to talk about my life openly. It makes me realise how frustrated I've felt, forced to keep this secret to myself.

He asks me about my father and I say that I believe Alexander Court to be a good man and that I've come to love and respect him. Odysseus presses his bird-like hand on mine and says how pleased he is to hear that.

My turn to ask Odysseus about his life.

He tells me about his new position as Chief Consultant to Athene. 'What an honour it is to be offered this position!'

His face glows with pleasure. 'Of course I'm still curator of Museum Earth although I've had to delegate much of the day-to-day work. And as Chief Chronicler I'm in the process of asking humanoids from different compounds to contribute to the archive. Sooner than we realise the compounds as we know them will fail to exist. I believe that some well-documented personal reports of what it was like living in those confined spaces should be recorded. What do you think, Mercury?'

'I think it's a must. Each contribution would be different and the collection of these reports would provide a great primary resource for future students of the history of Earth.'

I feel excited by this project. Accounts of life in each compound would make a fascinating read.

'I'm so glad you approve,' Odysseus says, adding with a keen look, 'would you be willing to contribute?'

'As a matter of fact, I've been keeping a journal for years. Just for myself, but the idea of it being part of resource in the museum's archive would make my ramblings really worthwhile.'

Odysseus's eyes light up. 'Excellent news. Your journals would chronicle, not just life on Earth, but on Oasis too.'

I hesitate. 'Some of the things I've been writing about are very personal. I'm not sure....'

'All the better. It's always the frank accounts that make the most compelling reading.'

I shake my head. 'No, I can't do it. Not yet anyway. What I haven't told you is that my transformation from mutant humanoid to complete is not known by anyone else apart from the team here in Hos-sat, my father and Stella.'

'Stella?'

'My father's partner.'

'Stella Jameson, the head of Worldwideculture?'

'That's the one.'

'I've met her. She interviewed a select group of us when considering who to appoint as CEO.'

I remember watching Stella's dramatic intervention on the Worldwideculture site during the meeting arranged by Athene. The individual interviews with potential candidates for the post were private. I hadn't been able to view those. 'What did you think of her?'

'Formidable. A powerful female, I imagine.'

I laugh at his description of the woman who considers herself my mother. 'I honestly don't know how much real power she has, but she does try to control my life.'

'Does she succeed?'

'Not always.' I think of the procedure I am supposed to have tomorrow that I've cancelled. She certainly won't be pleased to hear that.

'The thing is, Odysseus, my father and Stella would be furious if they knew I'd even talked to you or Isis. They don't want me to have anything to do with my previous life as a mutant humanoid. I don't really care that much what Stella thinks. It's Father's opinion I care about. He believes he has a lot to lose if it becomes common knowledge that he and his son were formerly mutant humanoids. I've already betrayed his trust by telling you my story. Don't think I regret telling you. I don't. It's a relief to be able to talk about this change in my life to someone who – well someone who has known me a long time, someone I respect – but I do have to ask you to keep my secret. One day I'm sure it will all come out, but until that time can I trust you not to say a word?'

'I promise I won't tell anyone what you've told me – but I would like to read your journals, to find out in detail what you've been through. I'm fascinated by what's happened to you, both as a historian and a friend. I can assure you if you afford me the privilege of reading them no one else will have access to them.'

He's very persuasive. Every writer wants his work to be read, but most writers are also afraid of revealing too much of themselves. Yet without that honesty what is the point of writing at all?

Odysseus promises my journals will not be put in the public domain until I am ready and I agree to let him read them.

A call from Father to discuss my postponement of the vasectomy. He knows and respects Dr Atherton, the psychiatrist, and finally accepts my decision to talk to her first.

A little later Stella calls and screeches down the phone at me. I'm obliged to hold the mob-fone well away from my ear to avoid being deafened.

Odysseus must be able to hear every word so I feel obliged to tell him that as far as Father and Stella are concerned my visit here is to have a vasectomy but for me it was just an excuse to see Isis.

'A vasectomy? Why? Have you got a girlfriend?' he asks.

'No. It's preventative surgery. They are scared I might father a mutant.'

He raises his eyebrow. 'And that would be a disaster?'

'Not for me. For them, yes.'

'Bit drastic to have that operation when you're so young.'

'That's what I think. That's why I'm not going to have it and that's why Stella was screeching down the phone at me.'

He shakes his head slowly from side to side.

Time to change the subject. I suggest we have some coffee and cake. They make particularly good chocolate cake here and I'm becoming addicted to it.

Once we're settled with our mid-afternoon treat, I ask him about Kali and he tells me that she has been quite depressed since returning to C55, but now Jaga has joined her she seems to have bucked up, determined to make a go of their new enterprise.

'That was the first piece of advice I gave Athene in my new role as Chief Consultant, to try to get those two together. I'd seen Jaga's enthusiasm for agriculture in C98 and although her attempts to use the warriors to plant crops and build cottages was misguided, I could see that her plan to cultivate a piece of land could be a worthwhile project. With Kali in charge of the logistics and Jaga overseeing the planting the project stands a good chance of success. Time will tell.'

Odysseus also tells me that Athene is trying to arrange for him to pay a visit to Oasis Museum. He's looking forward to it.

'Not only to see the exhibits but also to talk to the curator. I intend to invite him to come and visit our museum too so that I can show off a bit and demonstrate what we mutant humanoids are capable of doing.'

I begin to think Odysseus and I will never stop talking but there's a "ping" on my mob-fone. It's Father asking me to check my pcms. For some time Father and I have been sending each other private messages by personal coded messages and have devised our own pers-code for this purpose.

I ask Odysseus to excuse me, leave him to finish the chocolate cake and return to the privacy of my room to access my mail. There are several pcms from Father. The first reveals an image of man, with a caption from Father.

Do you recognise this person?

I stare at it. A brutish face.

I send a message back. *Yes, he's one of the men who arrested and humiliated me.*'

A message flies back. *Are you sure?*

Quite sure.

I sit quite still, remembering that big, ugly mug thrust into mine and the terror I felt as he manhandled me.

And this one?

And there is the other thug. No mistaking his coarse features.

Yes, that's the other one. Who are they?

Orlando Wolfe's henchmen. I have no proof as yet that Wolfe is behind the incident, but we have arrested them both and are playing one off against the other in the hope of extracting a confession. I have people working on them.

What methods are being used to "extract" a confession? What does "people working on them" mean? Torture? Can't be. Father wouldn't be party to anything like that.

The next pcm says he has found out that Orlando Wolfe is on his way to Hos-sat. He thinks he may be looking for evidence to see if I had an operation here to remove my mutations.

He's on to us, Michael. There's no doubt about that. I've

informed Mr Spencer and his team not to divulge anything. I'm sure they wouldn't, but Wolfe can be very persuasive.

Officially, his office says he's going to Hos-sat on quite another matter. As you may have heard Isis has given birth to a complete and Wolfe intends to stop the child being taken back to Earth. He says it's not right for a complete to be brought up by mutant humanoids. Michael, I've decided to come too and join in the proposed meeting with the surgeon, Mr Spencer and the paediatrician, Dr Carter.

I suggest you keep a low profile. Don't let Wolfe know that you're in Hos-sat. Better that you and I don't meet either. As you will appreciate, we must be very careful not to arouse suspicion at this time.

The third pcm informs me that Stella will be attending the meeting too. As the managing director of Worldwide-culture she says she wants to welcome the first baby born to a humanoid for twenty years.

Michael, it's difficult for me to admit this, but I don't believe that's why she's coming. There are lots of reasons for my mistrust but I can't go into them now. I'll discuss everything with you when you are back on Oasis.

I suggest you keep a low profile as far as she's concerned too. All this cloak and dagger stuff isn't my style, as you well know, but I feel that I must be at that meeting to keep an eye on what is going on and to intervene if necessary.

One more pcm.

One of my informants believes that Wolfe has a spy in Hos-sat, so do be very careful what you say to anyone who was not part of the original team.

A lot for me to think about: the lack of trust between Father and Stella, Wolfe's plotting and the possibility that he has a spy here.

A good thing I came to Hos-sat to look after the interests of Isis and her baby. No way will I allow them be separated.

I cannot take part in the meeting, but I must know what is said in it so that I can act accordingly.

I'm about to call Gemma to help me, but change my mind. Better not to involve her. Instead I go to see Janey and Moira, part of the original team.

I'm lucky. They're on a break. I tell them that my Father is on his way.

'He's already here,' Moira says cheerily. 'He's with a couple, a smooth-looking individual with sleeked-back hair and a woman made up to the nines.'

Why does she think that Wolfe and Stella are a couple?

'Where are they?' I ask.

'In Doctor Carter's consulting room and Mr Spencer is there too. Do you want to join them?'

'I don't think I'd be welcome, but I do want to hear what they're saying.'

I explain that I would like to have access to an adjoining room where I can set up my portable computer and hack in to the conversation.

Moira bites her lip, unhappy at the word "hack." 'I'm not sure I want to be party to something like this.'

'Father knows about it,' I tell her. This is not quite true. Well, not at all true actually, but surely the end justifies the means.

'Oh come on, Moira,' says Janey. 'This is our Michael. You know he wouldn't do anything wrong.'

I explain to them my concern about Isis's baby and that my real reason for being here is to make sure she's safe and goes home with her mother.

This wins Moira round and she takes me to a room adjacent to the doctor's consulting room, unlocks the door and leaves me to set up the necessary coordinates so that I can eavesdrop on the meeting.

Journal Entry

I adjust the sound and picture until I can see and hear what is going on in the next room. I haven't missed much. They're still introducing themselves.

Orlando Wolfe asks Dr Carter in his steely voice if he is sure the child is a complete.

'I've examined her thoroughly. There are no signs of any mutations.'

'In that case you must give her up to us,' Wolfe says in a voice that would freeze an equatorial forest. 'A complete must not be brought up by mutants.'

'Why not?' Father asks.

Fantastic question. Wow! Am I glad I decided not to have the vasectomy!

'Imagine how she'll feel as she gets older surrounded by those creatures on Earth,' says Wolfe, his mouth turning down at the corners.

'Hang on a minute,' says Father. 'You're on the integration committee. I thought you were in favour of mutant humanoids and completes sharing the same space.'

'I'm open-minded about it. I said we should give it a chance. Judging from the first experiment of mutants on Oasis it's a scheme headed for disaster. Anyway, back to this case. We have couples on Oasis who, for one reason or another, find it difficult to conceive. It would clearly be better for the child if one of these couples were to adopt it. We all know that it would have a better quality of life on Oasis than on Earth.'

'We know nothing of the sort,' says Father. 'A baby needs its parents.'

'Not necessarily its biological parents,' Wolfe declares. 'Research shows that adoptive parents who genuinely want a child are often better at parenting than natural parents who don't. This child was not planned. How could it have been? Mutant humanoids believed they were barren.'

'The child has not been rejected.'

'Yet.'

A close up of Father's face, taut, tight-lipped. 'This is a wanted baby. Isis is thrilled to be a mother.'

Yes, she is, I think. Totally thrilled.

'Is there a known father?' asks Wolfe with a note of sarcasm. 'I understand there's a lot of promiscuity amongst the mutants in the compounds.'

'His father is a warrior in C98,' Father says. 'I repeat, this is a wanted baby. We cannot in all conscience take her away from her legitimate parents. I'm sure Stella agrees with me. She knows more than I do about the situation.'

Stella hesitates and I see from her face that it is by no means certain that she does agree with Father. This a shock, but I am reminded of several instances when she has shown, if not fear of mutant humanoids, at least distaste: an incredible reaction from someone who professes to be dedicated to Worldwideculture and the well-being of humanoids. Not to mention her knowledge of our family history.

'Well,' says Stella speaking very slowly. 'The girl is OK. Not the sharpest knife in the drawer perhaps and very young to be a mother; but I'm sure she would love the baby and care for it to the best of her ability.'

She pauses and runs her tongue round her blood red lips. 'The Father is a different matter. He is, as Alexander says, one of the so-called golden warriors in C98. In fact he is one of the ten members of the advance guard who came to Oasis uninvited and landed up in the museum. You will remember that the warriors were returned as part of the treaty we made with Earth when the new CEO was appointed. Since his return, the warrior has been behaving oddly. They say it's post-traumatic stress disorder but that is a term borrowed from the past. In this context the label is meaningless but there is certainly something unstable about him.

'One interesting fact,' she goes on. 'He hasn't been to visit his partner here in Hos-sat, even though the leader of the compound gave him permission to do so. I've observed this young humanoid on my special website and believe there is something very wrong with him. Mentally. I would want to know more about his state of mind before allowing this humanoid near any child.'

Lies, all lies. She's the one who is mental, not Dionysus. Father looks shocked, as well he might. He expected Stella to support his argument in favour of the parents – mutants or not.

I note that Stella doesn't refer to any mutant humanoid by name. She prefers, as always to keep things impersonal. What kind of person is she to have so much control over the humanoids on Earth? I feel like bursting into the neighbouring room and confronting her. She's so cold, so unfeeling, my would-be mother.

Mr Spencer, the surgeon, speaks next. 'May I remind everyone in this room that I am in charge of Hos-sat. Any decision to take the baby away from the natural mother without her permission or mine is not going to happen.' Wolfe opens his mouth to interrupt but Mr Spencer continues, 'unless it can be proved beyond doubt that bringing up the child on Earth would be detrimental to the baby's well being. For the moment therefore the baby must remain with the mother until something is resolved.'

Father gives a sigh of relief, looks at Stella and smiles, but his smile soon disappears. She is not looking at him but at Wolfe and they exchange a look that implies complicity. What is going on? Father's face turns pale. He clearly didn't expect this reaction.

Wolfe turns to the surgeon, 'I don't believe you have the power to stop her removal,' he says coldly.

'I assure you I have.' The surgeon gathers up his papers and prepares to leave.

'I advise you not to engage in a battle with me,' says Wolfe, tight-lipped. 'You won't win. I will override your decision.'

I turn off the computer, slip out of the room and whiz along the corridor before the visitors emerge from the consulting room. I'll thank Moira and Janey for their help later. I don't want to run the risk of being seen lingering in this area. As I make my way back to Odysseus, I try to make sense of the events of the afternoon.

Thank Zeus for Mr Spencer and his insistence that he is in charge. This means there is no immediate danger of the baby being taken. At least not legally. But Odysseus should take Isis and Penelope back to C98 as soon as possible, just in case someone decides to abduct her.

I don't trust Orlando Wolfe. Or Stella Jameson for that matter.

Journal Entry

When I tell Odysseus what I've overheard he agrees that the sooner he takes Isis and Penelope back to Earth the better. 'If she is strong enough,' he says. 'But we must do everything properly, with the release papers signed.'

Odysseus and I go to see Mr Spencer.

I start to introduce Odysseus to the surgeon, to explain that he's a dear friend of mine, a brilliant historian, but the surgeon pre-empts me. 'I know who he is, Michael. Odysseus's fame stretches from Earth to the satellites. I'm delighted to meet you,' he says and they shake hands. 'Today of course you are here in a rather different role. As Isis's father.'

When we tell him that we've come to ask him when Isis will be fit enough to travel, he answers, 'As soon as you like. She's a big strong girl and with her father beside her I'm sure all will go smoothly.'

I decide to come clean and tell Mr Spencer that I eavesdropped on his meeting this afternoon.

'I know it wasn't ethical, but I'm not sorry,' I tell him. 'When I found that my father, Stella and Orlando Wolfe were here, I just had to listen in.'

He raises an eyebrow. 'You hacked in and accessed our conversation?'

'I have to admit I did. I was desperate, you see.'

Mr Spencer's mouth twitches as he tries not to smile. 'In the circumstances it's not such a terrible crime, I suppose. You know the situation then. I agree with you that Isis and the baby should go back to Earth as soon as possible. I'll get the necessary papers signed and she can leave.'

'You mentioned danger,' says Odysseus. 'You think Penelope really is in danger of being abducted?'

'Who knows when Mr Wolfe and his colleagues will be back with some sort of trumped up charge and fake papers to override my decision?'

'They would go that far?' Odysseus shakes his head in disbelief and I'm reminded how little corruption there is on Earth.

'I'm afraid so. There are some people on Planet Oasis, who will stop at nothing to get their own way and I'm afraid the motive is not always altruistic.'

Journal Entry

I see them off by the transporter. Isis is so excited to be going back to the place she thinks of as home. She can't stop chattering. 'Wait until her father sees his beautiful daughter. He'll fall madly in love with her.' She rolls her eyes up until the whites show and giggles.

Odysseus presses my hand and says we must meet again soon, moved by our reunion and the confidences we've shared.

'Maybe you could come to C98 for a visit,' Isis says to me.

'Maybe.' I remember that, as far as she is concerned, I

am still a mutant humanoid living in another compound. Better to leave it at that.

She has enough to think about, focusing on her new role as a mother, without worrying about me. I'm sorry to see them leave, but am sure it's for the best.

Gemma is not present to say 'goodbye' to Isis. It's her day off and she's gone to Oasis to see her parents.

She'll be back in Hos-sat this evening and we're going to watch a film in the nurse's home. Our first date, but I'm sure not our last.

But it's not Gemma I'm thinking of after Isis has gone. It's Father. He must be wrecked.

Such a cataclysmic division between him and Stella is bound to have devastating consequences. Her conduct was unforgivable. I remember the look she gave Wolfe and the way he almost touched her arm and then drew back and the way Father's face gradually drained of colour. I try to imagine how my father must be feeling and the massive fight he and Stella must surely have. The two of them have to sort this out. No good me going home. I'd only be in the way.

And I think of Isis and Penelope and Odysseus and am so pleased that they've returned to Earth and that the baby is out of danger.

Chapter Thirteen
The Heracles Tower
(according to Heracles)

I stroll round the top floor of the circular covered balcony of the tower, looking out of its curved windows. Lord of all I survey. No view to speak of. One or two half built houses, an indication of a central road sketched in the dust. Not a city yet, but give it time. Give it time.

Sati hovers behind me. My shadow. 'What's the verdict?' I ask her.

'High,' she says. 'Very high.'

I can see she's impressed. 'You want to move in – or stay in the compound?'

She's not my prisoner any more. It's up to her to do what she wants.

A frown on both her foreheads. 'What's the deal?'

'No deal. No conditions. It's your choice.'

'I can have my own aparto-cube?' she asks.

'You can.'

'With the circular bed you promised me?'

'Why not?'

'And a free hand to decorate the cube as I wish?'

'Of course.'

She wanders round the balcony, looks down at the arid ground and deserted landscape. The dull grey of the sky matches the dry soil. 'It would be good to have some greenery.'

I lay my hand lightly across her shoulders. 'I'm on it. Imagine a city with green parks and tree-lined avenues. And shops and cinemas, like in the filmograms.'

'But no buildings taller than this one.'

'You've got it.' I grin. 'We will look down on all the others.'

She giggles and raises her faces to mine.' I give her four kisses, one on each cheek.

To my surprise she kisses me back, with one pair of lips and then the other.

These are proper kisses, her tongues probing deep into my throat. It's some time since she did that. She's been spending most of her nights in the commun-dormo-cube and I've been otherwise engaged as well. Is this a sign that we're about to embark on a new stage of our ever-changing relationship?

'You know, Heracles, these actors are so shallow. All they think about is the play they're in and their particular part in it. They sit for hours talking about their characters and what they call "the dramatist's intention." How do they know what that is? Most of the writers are long dead. Thing is it's soooo boring. They go on and on trying to find "the "essence" of their character. It's a total waste of time. I'm fed up with the lot of them.' She looks up at me with two winning smiles. 'Yes, I'd like to get out of that compound and move into the tower.'

'The Heracles Tower,' I tell her.

'A symbol of your power.' She gives me a sly look from the blue eyes. 'I wonder what Athene will think of that?'

'I don't care what she thinks,' I tell her as I take her in my arms and give her the obligatory two kisses to keep both mouths happy. The deep penetration of these kisses seals some sort of pact between us.

My new office, part of my purpose built penthouse on the

top floor of the tower, is a rather special affair. I take Sati to see it, but she takes one look at the dark green paintwork on the curved walls, loses interest and insists on me showing her the cubes reserved for her use on the floor below. I present her with an e-tablet with a graphic design app and down we go to view the space that is to be her aparto-cube. She wanders round it, her four eyes busily studying its possibilities. She begins to sketch and select colour combinations.

I leave her to it and return to my office with its Harrods-green circular walls and ceiling.

Imagine an office in that historic store decorated like this and you've got the picture. I sit at my giant workstation with its multi-screen, lean back in my shaper and look around me. I adore this green cave and relish its windowless intimacy. It's a private place, a secret place. Mine. All mine.

I check the output of auto-mails from Compound Creative. Not many. Few humanoids in that sectoid are compu literate. That bitch, Bathsheba, has written another pcm to Kata-Mbula. Not difficult for an ace hacker like me to de-code.

She's moaning about the lack of time for rehearsals and says that some of the cast are losing interest. They're too exhausted after a morning of manual work to concentrate. Blah, blah, blah. Quite a few of them haven't learnt their lines. Boohoo. I trash it with the others. I can't have Kat reading these rants or, before I know it, he'll be transporting himself back here, snatching back his compound and reversing all my reforms.

I agree with Sati. The members of Compound Creative are obsessed with all this thespian stuff. They can't see that their preoccupation with all things theatrical reveals their own superficiality. Surely the most creative achievement so far has been the designing and construction of this tower. No one seems to grasp that fact but me.

Secure in my green cave, I check the long dialogue that makes up my communication with Orlando Wolfe.

In an early pcm I gently suggested that he take a close look at Alexander Court's eldest son. He acted on this information by arresting the young man and subjecting him to a strip search by a couple of his assistants, the same two louts who interrogated me, no doubt. He finds no evidence to confirm that the boy is, or was, a mutant humanoid and sends me a brusque message:

Please do not feed me false information. You are of no use to me unless you check the facts.

Mercury's transformation to Michael Court appears to have left no trace of this former status. I send this reply:

There is no doubt that Mercury and Michael are one and the same person. Mercury must have had his mutations removed in order to become Michael Court. There is only one place such an operation as this could have been done. Hos-sat. Evidence of the procedure must be stored there.

Wolfe decides to go to Hos-sat, determined to find some evidence of such a procedure.

While there he asks a lot of questions and learns that someone matching Mercury's description has visited Isis and was seen conversing with a one-eyed male humanoid. From a further description of his triangular face and gliding walk, I realise it must be Odysseus. I tell Wolfe that I will investigate further from this end. I don't want him to find out everything for himself or he won't need me as an informant.

It's not that I have anything against Mercury but I may have to sacrifice him to benefit my cause. The worst that could happen to him would be that he is returned to Earth. What's wrong with that? It's where he belongs.

Wolfe tells me he has recruited one of the nurses as an undercover agent. He asks her to research and report back to him on all surgical operations undertaken during the last four years. Apparently the staff at Hos-sat is so trusted that data of all kinds including scans, reports and doctor's notes can be accessed quite easily by anyone in the hospital. Wolfe is confident the nurse will come up with proof that such an operation was performed.

Apparently this nurse is extremely attractive and Michael is susceptible to young, attractive females. What young male isn't? Wolfe told this nurse that her first task would be to win the young man's trust and encourage his advances.

'If you tell him about your past maybe he will confide in you,' Wolfe told her.

At first she was reluctant. She clearly fancied the young man but once I had planted the idea in her mind that this Michael might once have been a mutant humanoid she agreed. A relationship with a mutant was, understandably, distasteful to her.

Wolfe took pleasure in telling me that. Mind you, Mercury was always a bit of weed. If this nurse met a handsome humanoid like me she might not be so prejudiced against us.

Wolfe's message continued,

It's also amazing what a bribe can achieve.

I know what he means. We don't have money on Earth, but there are other ways of bribing people. I bribe Thor with promises of promotion and Sati with pretty clothes and furnishings. And Wolfe bribes me with building materials.

It turns out from my own research that the purpose of Wolfe's strategy is to damage Alexander Court's reputation. If Mercury does turn out to be Court's natural son, it means that the Minister of Culture himself must have mutant genes. Or his first wife. Either way, if that knowledge is made public it will most likely bring Alexander Court down. Mission accomplished.

If Alexander Court falls, Stella Jameson's downfall must surely follow. Serve her right, the arrogant bitch. How could she not have had the insight to see that I would have made a stronger leader than Athene? Big mistake, Stella darling.

In exchange for further information from me, Wolfe dangles the carrot of finding me a satellite to populate with selected mutants. I am not naïve enough to believe that this is likely to materialise. Not in the foreseeable future anyway; but he hints at this to keep me sweet.

Meanwhile Wolfe supplies me with the resources to build this tower and a city here on Earth.

I look on this project as practice for the city in the sky. Or maybe plan B is becoming plan A and the city on Earth will suffice.

I'm so proud of my tower I send him an image of it to make it clear that I'm a humanoid to be reckoned with. Click. There it goes. It's on its way.

Ping. A pcm from Orlando Wolfe, written in his usual terse style, headed *Rescue Mission.*

A mutant humanoid named Isis has stolen a baby and taken it to C98. Not the baby she gave birth to which she rejected because of its mutations but a complete human being. She refuses to give it up. You must rescue the child and return it to Planet Oasis. Contact me when the baby is ready to be transported and it will be collected on arrival.

See what he's like? Not a gracious communication. This is not a request from one equal to another but a command from someone who considers himself superior to me. I pride myself that I have him sussed, that I understand this ruthless bugger. Why? Because we are alike, he and I. We both have our agendas and are determined to see them through. Do I trust him? No. Does he trust me? Of course not. He thinks he is using me and that I will do whatever he asks. But I am using him too. It is this clash of wills that makes our relationship invigorating.

I sit and think for a moment about his request. It doesn't seem likely that Isis would reject her baby and steal another.

Why would a mutant humanoid reject a baby because it had mutations? Doesn't make sense. Perhaps her baby died in childbirth. If that was the case, Isis, suffering from some sort of postnatal depression or grief, might have stolen another baby.

I must go to C98 to see the baby myself. If it is a complete, I may be able to persuade Isis to give it up, but I doubt it. She's always been an obstinate bitch. If she refuses I'll have to come up with a plan. I can hardly steal the baby myself. Too dangerous.

I need someone completely loyal to me to do it. Someone Isis doesn't know. Thor. It has to be Thor.

Thor has already proved invaluable to me, drawing up the timetable for the building programme, arranging the transport of materials and acting as overseer of the workforce. Thanks to him the work has progressed quickly and efficiently. The Heracles Tower is complete apart from a few refinements to the interior and the construction of the city has begun.

Thor is a meticulous planner and a hard taskmaster. Eichmann to my Hitler. The two Adolfs. It was Eichmann who, at Hitler's request, initiated the meeting that came up with "the final solution" to what Hitler called, "the Jewish problem." Not that I'm considering annihilating any group. The point is, Adolf Eichmann was in charge of the logistics of the scheme, synchronizing the times of train departures and arrivals at the camps. That's how I view Thor. A diligent manager, prepared to do the boring but necessary work to make my initiatives effective.

In this case, I'm sure Thor will come up with a foolproof plan for the abduction of the baby and carry it out successfully. If anything goes wrong, Thor will be the fall guy.

If Isis is the child's mother then of course I will refuse to have anything to do with this kidnapping. I'm not Wolfe's slave and he needs to know that.

Ping! Another message from Bathsheba. This time an auto-mail addressed to me. She tells me that I have a surprise visitor. Shit. Why can't she say who it is? She's such a devious female. She thrives on secrets. For all she pretends to be so bloody helpful I don't trust her one little bit.

I stand up, step up on to the circular balcony and stride round it, glancing out of the windows as I go.

Two humanoids stand looking up at me.

Two statuesque females in long gowns: Bathsheba in black and gold. Athene in white and silver.

I descend the circular staircase and greet my boss.

'Athene, long time no see. What a pleasant surprise.'

'Is it pleasant?' she asks, her one large eye looking directly in to my central one.

'Always a pleasure to see you, Athene, you know that.'

She raises her head towards the tower. 'I see you've been busy.'

'Amazing, eh?'

'You could say that.' She doesn't smile. 'Heracles, we need to talk.'

'I'll leave you to it.' Bathsheba turns and starts to walk back to the compound.

'I don't mean to drive you away,' says Athene.

Bathsheba faces us again. The little fingers at her neck are almost strangling her. 'No, no, I must get back. I have a rehearsal in progress.'

Athene and I watch her go. Bathsheba steps out purposefully, but her shoulders droop a little. She's not as confident as she looks. Waiting for replies from Kat that never come is having an effect on her morale.

I invite Athene to enter the tower, but she shakes her head. 'Let's walk out here for a bit. You can tell me what you are doing here.'

I don't need much encouraging. 'A city. That's my plan.

This will be the main street with department stores and offices and houses and a cinema – maybe even another theatre. Everything we need.'

'You've got it all worked out. And the tower?'

'It's the Heracles Tower. I will live here and look down on the city as its benevolent leader.'

'Is that so.' Her voice is cold. 'May I ask who is funding this venture?'

I shrug. 'I request materials and they arrive.'

'By magic?'

'It is rather like that.'

'Where do these – materials come from?'

'From Oasis, I assume.'

'Ah. Oasis. Has it occurred to you that all requests should come through me, that I am the only humanoid allowed to contact Oasis.'

I raise my three eyebrows in professed innocence. 'I didn't know that. I hear that, now it's safe outside, other sectoids have projects in process outside their compounds. Kali and Jaga are developing arable land and Durga has built a parade ground and barracks for the golden warriors. So I thought – why not a city?'

'You didn't consult me first.'

'I didn't think it necessary. I understood that I was in charge here.'

Athene doesn't answer. Her face is white, her lips tight.

'Did Durga consult you before embarking on her project?' I ask.

'Everything has to come through me. How have you managed to arrange this on your own?'

I smile. 'I have my methods.' I point out the proposed layout of the city. 'Over there I imagine a park full of trees and plants. Maybe even a water feature. A fountain perhaps.'

She shakes her head. 'Dream on,' she says.

'It's a good dream,' I tell her. 'A possible dream. It will take time but it will happen. Earth City will be built, with or without your approval.'

She takes a deep breath. 'Does Stella know about this?'

'Stella?'

'Don't insult me, Heracles. You know I mean Stella Jameson.'

'Oh her. I have no idea if she knows or not. I assume she does. She's head of Worldwideculture so she must know everything.'

'But she's not your contact?'

I smile. 'She is not.'

'Then who is?'

'No one you know. Someone I met when on Oasis.'

'One of your gaolers?'

I smile again. I will not let her rile me. We have walked some way. I look back and ask Athene to turn round. 'Just take a look at the tower from here. Isn't it the most creative design you've ever seen?'

The light is fading a little and the tower shows up, tall and dark, against a sky flushed with pink. The tower bulges at its tip, purple black, aggressive.

To my surprise, Athene bursts out laughing. 'Why, it's a penis,' she says. 'A phallic symbol. A statement of your power.'

'You might think that,' I reply. 'I couldn't possibly comment.'

She laughs out loud again at this apt quotation from a twentieth century TV series about a ruthless politician determined to reach the top at whatever cost.

She stops laughing and gives a little shiver. 'Let's go inside now, Heracles.'

'Into the tower or the compound?'

'The compound.' She tucks her hand into my arm and we

walk along together as if we are old friends. Which I suppose we are. Old friends, who have had a bit of a tiff and made up. Temporarily.

Just before we reach the door, a tiny animal runs out of the flowerbeds and over Athene's foot. She gives a little squeal and clutches my arm. We stop and look down at it. I bend over and try to pick it up, but it's too quick for me and escapes.

'I think that was a field-mouse,' I tell her.

'It made me jump whatever it was,' she says. 'It tells us that the animals are coming back, that the Earth is fertile again. Pity we couldn't catch it to see if it has any mutations.'

'It appeared to have the customary four legs but if there's one mouse there must be more. I'll catch one next time.' I look up at the sky. 'Once we have trees we'll probably have birds.'

She looks up at me with an amused gleam in her eye. 'Birds? That would be good. Oh, by the way, Heracles. I forgot to tell you. I brought another visitor with me.'

In we go. The hall is full. Every member of the sectoid must be present. And, in the centre of the crowd, towering over everyone else stands the ebony giant, Kata-Mbula.

Chapter Fourteen
Perfect Specimens
(according to Heracles)

Athene and I, mere observers, watch the crowd's response to Kata-Mbula. The excitement is palpable. I'll never be so admired, so respected or so loved. My mouth feels dry – stale. I swallow, but it makes no difference.

His hair has grown. Long corkscrew curls touch his shoulders. His embroidered robe, the coloured beads at neck and wrists, the wide calm smiles on both of his faces, all contribute to the joy he emanates. He is as delighted to be back as his fans are to see him. They try to get as close to the great humanoid as they can. They plant their kisses on any piece of exposed skin they can reach, his faces, his body and his limbs. Some crawl between the legs of their colleagues to lift his robe, kiss his feet and sink their greedy mouths into his ankles and calves. Others clamber over each other and cling on to his robe, his hands, his arms, as if they will never let them go. A sickening spectacle.

The incredible thing is that this Kat, far from objecting to their proximity, laps up their adulation. Even the long sour face is wreathed in a smile. No pop star ever had such a welcome. His reception is more like that afforded a prophet or Jesus Christ himself. Only more familiar somehow. A tad distasteful.

I think of Bathsheba's letters and her assertion that Kat has slept with many of his actors, all in the name of producing the best possible performances. I wonder if he and I have shared the same females and if so, which of us they consider the better lover.

Bathsheba stands apart. Her face transfixed on her hero. She's glad he's back but disappointed that he hasn't taken any notice of her.

Ah at last. Kat's eyes travel over the heads of the mob and rest on the lone figure by a pillar. He begins to make his way through the throng towards her. When his admirers realise what he wants to do they fall back to create a central aisle. It reminds me of how these same humanoids welcomed Sati and me on our arrival, dividing into two columns like the parting of the Red Sea, to provide a space for us to walk through.

Kat approaches Bathsheba, his arms outstretched. She doesn't hesitate but trots straight into those arms and presses her body against his, honoured that he is paying her such special attention. Undignified behaviour. Ridiculous in a female of her age. Tears stream down her cheeks. An embarrassing display.

He takes her to one side and they exchange a few intimate whispers. I know it won't be long before Bathsheba finds out that he didn't receive any of her personally coded messages.

Athene looks at me. I give her a questioning look. Is Kat back for good? Am I being replaced? She doesn't satisfy my curiosity. Not yet. She enjoys playing cat and mouse.

There is to be a celebratory feast for Kata-Mbula this evening, followed by the inevitable "show." Athene is not staying to participate, but gently suggests it would be politic for me to attend.

So I am not being recalled to C99.

Before she leaves, Athene asks to be shown round The Heracles Tower.

'It's not finished,' I warn her. 'Sati is designing her aparto-cube and most of the other cubes are empty.'

'You have a dormo-cube here?'

I look at her out of the corner of my central eye. I'm not sure if she is flirting with me or not. Difficult to tell with Athene.

'I have. Would you like to see it?'

'I would indeed but is there somewhere a little more formal where we can talk?'

'My office on the top floor.'

I show her round the lower floors of the tower, mostly empty cubes. 'I intend to have a small gym or exercise room, a salon, a kitchen and dining room.'

She nods. 'You intend to make yourself comfortable.'

'I hope you will think of this as your second home, Athene. You will always be welcome here.'

I leap up the circular staircase and she follows me at a more leisurely pace. On the penultimate floor a door opens and Sati's two heads appear.

'Hi,' the blond head says.

I continue on my way. Athene stops for a chat. 'Are you settling in, Sati?'

'I'm still busy deciding on colours.'

'You want any help?'

'Oh no. I'm perfectly capable of making up my own minds, thank you Athene.'

'I'm sure you are. I'll leave you to it then.'

The other head shakes out her sleek dark hair and giggles. 'Enjoy the view upstairs.'

Athene follows me up to the top floor and I walk her round the balcony. We look out of the curved windows. 'You have to use your imagination to see the splendour of the future Earth City.'

She stands very close to me. 'If I allow you to go ahead with your plan.'

'Are you threatening me?'

'Just stating a fact. I want you to realise that the outcome of your dream is dependent on my permission.'

A red flash lights up her eye. 'I could stop the project now. I could order this tower to be destroyed. Just like that.'

She clicks her fingers. 'You have exceeded your authority.'

She's annoyed with me for going over her head and building the tower, for contacting Oasis myself, for deciding to build a city without consulting her, for this blatant exhibition of my power.

I need her on my side. 'I'm sorry. I thought I was in charge here.'

'In charge of the compound, but that doesn't mean you have *carte blanche* to make the kind of decisions that affect other sectoids as well. A big city would encourage emigration from other compounds. It's an executive decision that only I am entitled to make.'

I am very tempted to take her in my arms and attain her support by seducing her. With any other woman it would work, but perhaps not with Athene. The flash of fire is still there in her eye. 'Come into my office and let's discuss this.'

She looks round the green cave with interest. 'All these years in a compound without natural light and you choose to continue to work in a windowless cube.'

I shrug my shoulders. 'No distractions. Just me and the compu. It helps me focus.'

I motion for her to sit down on a shaper. She chooses a single one. I don't make the mistake of sitting behind my desk. Too confrontational. I pull up another shaper next to hers. I must play her game. Let her believe that I'm loyal to her, that my intention was not to go over her head but to use my initiative, to do something useful for the community, something she would be proud of.

'Athene, tell me what I can do to win back your trust. Just tell me and I'll do it.'

Shit. I've never eaten humble pie like this before. But whatever it takes I will do.

I see the corner of her mouth twitching. She finds it amusing that I should be forced to beg for her forgiveness.

'Oh Heracles.' She shakes her head. 'What am I going to do with you?'

At that moment I know it's going to be all right. She won't knock down the tower or stop me building the city.

'You want me to come back to C99 with you?'

'Great Zeus no! I can't cope with you that near to me. Better only to see each other from time to time, don't you think?'

I don't insult her by agreeing with her. Instead I say, 'It's up to you. I will do whatever you want me to.'

The words sound false, even to me. Can she really believe that this subservient Heracles is for real?

She takes my hand in hers. 'I want you to stay here,' she says simply. 'Live in your tower, build your city.'

I look her straight in her eye. 'Really?'

'Really.' She takes her hand away, stands up and moves around the cube. 'But Kata-Mbula stays too. He has finished his work in C99. He has designed a magnificent stadium surrounded by houses and hotels. Not exactly a city. No competition on that score. More like an Olympic village. Those from our sectoid who wish to live in the houses can move out of the compound. Some have moved out already, but not as many as I imagined. I suppose we're all used to communal living. It's not so easy to start afresh. In time I'm convinced attitudes will change. Especially now we have several pregnancies. Some humanoids are bound to decide to live in family units again as in the time before.'

She pauses for a moment, as if to remember the drift of

what she was saying. 'The hotels are for the visitors we hope to attract to events in the stadium. The Big Event will be followed by other activities: conferences, sports fixtures, pageants, dance events, opera – spectacles of all kinds. I intend to show the completes what we are capable of.'

Inspiring stuff. Quite moving, if I were in the market to be moved.

I stand up and walk away from her. 'You say Kata-Mbula is to stay here and that I should stay here too. Who is to be in charge of the compound?'

Athene hesitates. 'Kat came to C99 for the purpose of designing and overseeing the stadium. He has never been entirely at ease there.'

She comes up to me and lays a hand on my arm. 'This is Kat's home. His heart is here. Compound Creative is his baby. And, more important, I need him here now to make sure the show for The Big Event will be the sensation I intend it to be.'

'But what about me?'

'You will live in the tower and build your city.'

'But I need the workforce of Compound Creative to be under my control to do that. They work here in the mornings.'

'Kat will need to rehearse longer hours now in the lead up to The Big Event, but I'm sure with your negotiating skills you will manage to persuade him to give up some colleagues to help with the construction. Or you may come up with a different plan. Your workers for the project may come from another source.'

'Are you telling me that that I am no longer the Head of Compound Creative?'

'These titles and labels are not important, Heracles. Let's call it a division of responsibility. The focus must be on preparing for The Big Event. If that means that your building work has to progress a little more slowly, you will have to accept that. I promise not to reclaim Thor. He can stay here as construction manager. I know how much you value him. And he you.'

She puts her hands on my shoulders. 'Don't be unhappy about this, Heracles. We have something even more important to do now.'

'And what is that?'

'If you are willing, I thought we might try to make a baby.'

My mouth drops open. I must look as flabbergasted as I feel.

Athene takes my reaction to mean that I need a bit of persuading. 'Just think what kind of humanoid our combined genes could produce.' She grins and smoothes her hands over my face, neck and shoulders. 'How could we not produce a perfect child, two perfect specimens of humanity like us?'

I stare at her but say not a word.

'If you are in accordance with my plan, Heracles, maybe this would be the right moment to lead me your dormo-cube.'

She's cool. I'll give her that. But I'm sure I'll be able to generate a bit of heat to warm her up. If our actions do produce a child so be it. If not, at least I can take possession of her incredible body at last. And, if I use my wits, of her mind too.

An hour or so later, she says, a little less coolly, 'You do realise, Heracles, that one session might not be enough. We may have to repeat this experience from time to time. Do you think you could cope with that?'

I don't answer. I remember the old adage, "actions speak louder than words" and take the opportunity to consolidate my rights to her amazing body.

Chapter Fifteen
Sati the Saviour
(according to Heracles)

'She spent enough time up there with you,' Sati grumbles as we make our way over to Compound Creative, after Athene has left.

Both of her mouths turn down at the corners. One thing I've always appreciated about Sati is that she is not jealous. Some females become possessive once you've slept with them. Clingy. They sulk when you so much as look at another female. I do hope Sati is not becoming like them. If so, she'll have to go. I can't be doing with that.

She perks up a bit when I tell her that we have to go to our aparto-cubes in Compound Creative to select some costumes to wear to the party.

'Let's go as Anthony and Cleopatra,' she suggests. 'Show these second rate actors how to make a fantastic entrance.'

I'm not looking forward to this evening. More adulation of Kata-Mbula. More invisibility for me. But as Athene said, it's diplomatic to attend.

We do cause quite a stir when we walk in. Sati stunning as Cleopatra, in a long, red, embroidered gown with gold coronets on her heads, and my three muscular legs topped by a short toga. Sexy beast. Our entrance is welcomed with a round of applause. Kat roars his hearty laugh and opens his arms to greet us.

'Come and sit here next to me,' he roars.

Two shapers have been reserved for us. Sati's next to Kat and mine next to hers.

On the other side of Kat sits Bathsheba looking smug, a pink after-sex glow on her dark skin.

The feast is just as elaborate as the one prepared for our arrival, but now we are used to richer food and enjoy it more.

Kat makes a little speech, thanking "the kitchen staff" for their wonderful efforts.

This remark is greeted by a ripple of laughter, everyone aware that every single humanoid in the sectoid – apart from Sati and I – have helped in the preparation of the feast.

It's certainly a magnificent spread. I've never seen blue rice before or red bread rolls. I just hope the colorants they've used aren't toxic.

It's just as well Kat gives them praise at this stage in the evening because, judging from the expression on his faces as he watches the entertainment that follows he is not impressed by the show. The forehead of his long thin face creases and the lips form themselves into a stern, straight line. Even his chubby face can't summon up a smile.

Even I, who profess to know little about such things, realise that the some of the dancers are out of step and the singing off-key. The show is thankfully short and over quite quickly. The singers and dancers look nervously at Kat as they take their bows. The audience clap half-heartedly.

Kat does not join in the applause. He stands up and motions to me to join him in the office. Bathsheba and Sati hesitate, not sure if they should accompany us or not. I nod at them to follow. Bathsheba must take responsibility for this shambles of a show.

Kat faces me without a smile on either face. 'Well,' he says. 'What's the explanation for this fiasco?'

'Bathsheba has been in charge of rehearsals,' I say, 'but

maybe I should have kept a closer watch on what was happening.'

'Maybe you should,' the thin head snaps. He turns to Bathsheba.

She looks at the ground and doesn't reply.

'Our colleagues have been putting some of their energies into another creative project,' I continue. 'Have you seen the tower they've built?'

'Tower? What tower?' He looks ready to explode.

'I am building a city for everyone to live in. The tower is the first phase of this development.'

Sati sidles up to Kat and raises her four beautiful eyes to his. 'You should come outside and see it. The tower is a beautiful structure. All the members of the sectoid have contributed. They spend the mornings building and the afternoons and evenings rehearsing.'

Kat's reaction is immediate. 'The members of this sectoid are not construction workers. They are actors, dancers and singers.'

Sati shrugs. 'In my opinion they are pretty average as performers. Amateurs. But they excel in bringing Heracles's vision of a golden city to life. That's their real talent.'

Kat looks bewildered. I can see him thinking: tower, city, building? What has been going on?

Bathsheba creeps up to the other side of him and says tentatively, 'I told you all about this in my pcms.'

'What pcms?'

'The ones I sent you to keep you informed.'

He shakes his heads, at a loss.

'You didn't receive them? So that's why there were no replies. I assumed you were too busy.'

Kat starts to pace round the office cube, one hand on each forehead, as if trying to weigh up the importance of this.

Bathsheba says weakly, 'They must have got lost in the ether.'

Sati gives me a quick glance. Bathsheba may believe they were lost in the ether, but she doesn't. And neither does Kat.

Once more Sati comes to my rescue. 'Know what? I think we have a code-breaker in our midst. Someone determined that you should not receive that information. We will have to investigate this properly, make whoever it is confess, then turn him or her out into the wilderness.'

Sati must have forgotten for a moment that the wilderness no longer exists, but we get the general idea. Never underestimate Sati, I remind myself.

She managed the coup in C55 and held on to her power for some time. She's a quick thinker, worthy of being my deputy.

Kat stops pacing. 'There are very few compu literate humanoids here, so it shouldn't take us long to discover the culprit.'

'Give me a list of their names,' I say. ' I will be only too pleased to look into this matter for you.'

Kat screws up his eyes and gives me a searching look. The moment passes and I realise that there is no way Kat will accuse me of sabotage without proof, which I'm ninety-nine percent certain he cannot get. Sati has saved the situation.

'I'm sorry, Kat,' wheedles Bathsheba. 'About the welcome performance. I didn't know you were coming until this afternoon.' She raises her dark eyes up to his, a sad attempt to engage his sympathy. 'I had to cobble something together as quickly as possible. I feel I must warn you that you're not going to be very pleased with our progress for The Big Event either. We really haven't had time to get the play or the dances up to scratch, but now you're back I'm sure you'll be able to whip it into shape.'

She puts her hand on his arm. He shakes it off. 'I do not whip, as you well you know. I inspire.'

'Yes, yes,' says Sati. 'We don't doubt that for one minute.

You can work your magic at rehearsals tomorrow. For now you should come outside and take your first look at The Heracles Tower. It's full moon so it will be bathed in a yellow glow. A wonderful sight.'

As the four of us stand outside the compound door and gaze up at the moonlit tower, I can't help thinking that Sati has excelled herself tonight. My decision to bring her with me from C99 has been justified.

She squeezes my arm and the eye in the blond head looks up at me with what looks remarkably like adoration.

My next job is to seek out Thor. I know he will do anything I ask, however unethical.

When Athene asked me to find out who had spread the rumour that she was responsible for the death of three-headed Ra, Thor came up a with a name pretty damn quickly and, sure enough, admitted to being the source of the gossip. Whether or not she was actually guilty or not was irrelevant. She was willing to confess. That was all that mattered. I'm sure he will have similar success in the present case.

Thor is in the compu centre killing off a few aliens in Kill Them All, his favourite compu game. He looks up at me and grins. '500 down today. Enough to get me to third level.'

'Good job!' I sit down beside him and watch his considerable skills as he plans and attacks and shoots with amazing accuracy.

'If I could drag you away for a minute, I'd like you to use your remarkable expertise in another direction,' I tell him.

He nods affably, ever willing to oblige.

I look around. Too many humanoids here to talk privately, so we wander off and find a quiet corner in the RR.

'Ok, Boss. What's up?' he asks.

'I need you to persuade someone to own up to the hacking of pcms between Bathsheba and Kata-Mbula.'

He nods his huge head and licks his two sets of lips. 'Male or female?'

'Not important but I must have a confession by tonight.'

'Leave it to me, Boss.'

I fill him in with a few more details and off he goes to carry out the task.

I go back to The Heracles Tower. Better not to be on the premises whilst the dirty work is done.

Sati is flushed with success and we celebrate in the usual manner using the talent she excels at the most: love-sex. She is as inventive as ever, using her two heads, four lips and two tongues in such imaginative ways that I know I will never tire of her.

The two females I've enjoyed today are very different.

Until last night, the only intimate knowledge I'd had of Athene's body had been through her exotic (and erotic) dances performed exclusively for me in her dormo-cube. Twice I'd watched as her naked, painted body gyrated with the aid of seductive music and light. My eyes had knowledge of her magical body, but there had been no physical contact between us.

I don't know how to describe this first experience of real sex with Athene, except to say that it was out of this world. We conducted ourselves in the same way that any couple do when making love, but there was a touch of magic about it that eludes description. Suffice it to say that it was unlike any sex I'd had before.

Athene's magic touch didn't stop me enjoying love-sex with Sati. Of course it didn't. I'm a highly sexed male humanoid. Sex with Athene is special, but like most specialities, too rich to be sampled every day.

How lucky am I to have pleasured myself with these two beautiful females, on the same day. Good job I've got the stamina.

I admit I do find it a little disconcerting when Sati whispers in my ear, 'just think what a fabulous baby you and I could make, Heracles.'

What is it with these women, so desperate to give birth? There must be something in the air.

In the early hours of the morning, I leave Sati's bed and go to my Harrods-green office. A pcm from Thor tells me that he has successfully completed the assignment I gave him.

A female called Lavinia who's always hanging around Thor has confessed to the hacking of Bathsheba's mail. I don't know how Thor persuaded her to take the rap. Better not to know. I admire his ability to fulfil my wishes so quickly, whatever the strategies employed.

There's a compu-gram of this Lavinia trotting off to Kat, weeping and wailing. She goes down on her knees, clutches at his robe and begs his forgiveness. She tells him she didn't read the pcms, only trashed them because she was jealous of Bathsheba. She promises she will never do such a thing again. Kat goes soft on her. As a punishment he takes away her small role in the play and suspends her from attending rehearsals for two weeks. Pitiful. Call those leadership skills?

I delete Thor's pcm. I don't want any evidence about this admission of guilt to be traced to me. I go back to bed. Not Sati's bed. My own. All this talk of babies is proving a bit of a turn off.

Rehearsals are to begin at 9.0 a.m. No more building will take place until Kat and I have agreed on a schedule to accommodate us both. At the moment Kat insists that the priority is for everyone to rehearse. I am forced to accept his temporary victory.

I leave them to it and Thor and I set off on foot to visit C98. I intend to suss out the situation with Isis and the baby.

Thor chatters away about his success the night before. We're in the open air and there's no one to overhear us.

'Remember, I slept with this Lavinia once and she's always lurking around wanting me to go with her again.'

There's no accounting for tastes. As it happens I don't remember her. Not my type, I guess. I can't be expected to keep up with all Thor's conquests.

Thor burbles on. 'Last night there she was there waiting for me, outside my dormo-cube. I told her I'd spend the night with her if she would do me a favour in return. It was as easy as that.'

He's all puffed up, full of himself and I praise him for his efforts and tell him how much I rely on him. 'There's something else I may want you to do.'

His eyes light up in anticipation.

I explain that I'm going to see someone I knew years ago who has just had a baby on Hos-sat.

He nods. It seems he knows about that. It's pretty common knowledge.

'It seems that she may have taken the wrong baby back to Earth by mistake – a complete. If so, I will try to persuade her to return it to Oasis. If she refuses then I may need you to kidnap it and put in the transporter. I'll provide you with the code.'

Thor is on a high, only too willing to carry out this task too. He strides out, keen to arrive at the compound. As we approach, we see the golden warriors on the parade ground outside. Some of them are sparring with each other with foils; others are at a shooting range and yet others are exercising on heavy-duty gymnastic equipment. An impressive sight.

'You can stay here and watch,' I say, 'but do try to be unobtrusive.'

Almost an impossible task for someone his size, but the

warriors are so focused on their work out, they take no notice of us.

'Squat down here behind this wall,' I tell him, 'and don't talk to anyone.'

I look around and note that since my last visit, the funeral of Brahmin, quite a bit of building work has gone on.

Nothing to equal the grandeur of my tower and city, just purpose-built stores for equipment and weapons and basic living quarters for the warriors, all austere, serviceable square structures.

Durga has decided to house the warriors in barracks outside the compound, no doubt to make sure they concentrate on their training.

Inside the compound The Great Hall offers the same barren welcome. With no one there, it is just a huge empty space.

Durga appears looking regal, unsmiling. I auto-mailed her earlier to ask permission to visit Isis. The two of us stand isolated in the centre of the hall. She welcomes me formally with a touch of cynicism.

'I understand you've become redundant, Heracles.'

'I'm afraid you've been misinformed, Durga.'

'But Kata-Mbula has returned.'

'To perfect the programme for The Big Event.'

'Not your bag I take it, this thespian stuff?'

'I am engaged in a more important project.'

'What can be more important than The Big Event?'

'Nothing at this exact moment, which is why I have time to visit you.'

'My golden warriors are taking part too you know. They practise day and night to reach perfection. Their performance will outshine your amateur dramatics, I assure you.'

'A bit of competition never hurt anyone.'

She changes the subject. 'I understand you would like to see the new addition to our sectoid. The first baby born to a mutant humanoid for nearly twenty years. We are very proud of her.'

'I hear she is perfect. A complete.'

'Your information is correct. She has no mutations.'

'But how is that possible?'

'Her father, one of my warriors, is a particularly beautiful specimen of humanity and I guess his genes have proved the stronger and cancelled out the mother's rather unfortunate looks.

'Come, follow me. I'll take you to see them.'

Outside the door to Isis's dormo-cube, Durga turns to me.

'I want you to know that I haven't forgotten the time I spent as your prisoner in C99. I promise you that one day you will be the prisoner and I the gaoler.'

If this is a threat, it doesn't frighten me. She thinks she's so damned superior, but if she knew what I was planning now regarding the baby she wouldn't look so smug.

Chapter Sixteen
Hard man, soft man
(according to Heracles)

Isis is sitting with the baby in her arms surrounded by several young women, all dressed, like her, in long flowing gowns. It doesn't take me long to realise that they are all pregnant. There is something about the formation of the group and the gentle expressions on their faces as they gaze on the baby that reminds me of a Renaissance painting I saw when I worked in the histo-lab with Odysseus.

The way Isis looks down at the babe in her arms makes her moon face look almost beautiful and I'm reminded that there was a time when I fancied her. Those days are long gone, but there is something in the tender way she studies the babe and strokes its face with the fingers of her extra little arm that tells me this is not the silly female I once knew. She has grown up. Her serene repose suggests she has found fulfilment. Motherhood suits her. There is no way she will willingly give up this baby, hers or not.

Isis looks up. Do I detect a shade of disappointment? Who did she think her unexpected visitor would be? She soon corrects her expression and looks happy enough to see me, all previous altercations forgotten.

'Hi Heracles. Come over here and sit next me. Take a look at the best baby in the whole wide world.'

The eyes of the other females are on me as I roll across the cube. An athlete in his prime.

'Isn't she a darling? Her name's Penelope.'

'Hello Penelope,' I say somewhat inanely. The child has a round moon face. I fancy I can see the likeness to Isis, but maybe all babies look the same.

Giggles from the audience.

'Look at her tiny fingers and toes. You can let her hold your finger. Go on. Hold it out. That's it. See how she grips it? Who would have thought that such tiny fingers could have such strength? Have you ever seen anything like that before?'

I have to admit I haven't.

'Isn't it just cute how she winds them round your finger and clings on as if she will never let go?' Isis leans forward, releases my finger, lifts the baby up and covers its face with kisses. 'Who's a beautiful baby then? You are. Yes you are.' The kissing continues.

By the law of averages I should be embarrassed by this female mother and baby stuff, but I'm not. Isis clearly loves her baby and is behaving naturally, unconcerned about anyone else who happens to be in the cube. There is something quite touching about her uninhibited spontaneity.

'Oh Heracles, I never believed that I would ever have a baby. And yet here she is. Mine. All mine.'

There is no doubt that Isis loves this child. I'm convinced it is her baby. I'll tell Orlando Wolfe he's made a mistake, that the baby is hers.

How stupid I am. Wolfe already knows that. He invented that story about her taking someone else's baby to persuade me to abduct it.

No way will I be instrumental in taking this child away from her mother. I give an inward smile. It seems I have a heart after all.

I ask Isis about her time in Hos-sat, how she was treated there and what the doctors and nurses were like.

She answers positively about everything and the other females hang on her every word, no doubt hoping they'll be permitted to go to this special place too to give birth. 'I just adored the nurses and they loved me. They were totally fascinated by my little arm.'

'Did you have many visitors?'

For a moment a cloud passes over the moon-face and one of the females puts her hand over Isis's in sympathy. Isis soon perks up and says, 'Odysseus came. And Mercury too. You remember him?'

'Mercury? Of course I remember him. Did he tell you where he's living now?'

'Would you believe it, I forgot to ask him. You're good on the compu, Heracles. Can you try and find out which compound he's in? I'd like to keep in touch.'

I promise to do my best and let her know.

'It must be good to be back home,' I suggest.

'Of course,' she agrees but the cloud returns. 'It's not quite how I hoped it would be. I thought Osiris – Dionysus – would be here, that we would be living together as a family. But Durga keeps the warriors separate from everyone else. They live outside in the barracks and spend all their time keeping fit and practising their battle skills. Penelope and I hardly see him.'

Her eyes fill with tears and the female next to her applies pressure on her hand to comfort her. Isis manages a smile and looks round at the other females. 'I don't know what I would have done without these good friends. They've all been wonderful. Dionysus has only seen me and Penelope three times. I don't understand it. We were so close before he went off to war. A proper couple.'

'What about Odysseus? Can't he find out what Dionysus is thinking?'

'Oh – Odysseus – he's totally as bad. He's Penelope's grandfather but he's hardly ever here. Since Athene appointed him as her deputy he's always in C99.'

Odysseus, Athene's deputy? That's news to me. I thought I was her deputy. The devious bitch.

'If he's not in C99 he's transporting himself off to the museum on Oasis, negotiating which artefacts they are going to let him have for Museum Earth.'

I try not to look surprised. I've been too busy with my own projects lately to keep up to date with what going on other compounds. 'He's still the curator here?'

'Yes, but he's got new assistants now. He doesn't need me any more.'

'Now you know that's not true, Isis,' says the hand-holder. She looks up at me.

'He's told her again and again that she can go back to work anytime she wants to. Be fair, Isis. He says there will always be a job in the museum for you, if you want it.'

'I know Venus. I'm being a silly bitch.' Isis sniffs through her tears.

'Odysseus comes to see you and Penelope whenever he can. You know that,' says Venus.

'He adores both of you,' another friend adds.

'Is he in the compound at the moment?' I ask. 'I'd like to see the museum. And him of course.'

'I'm afraid he's not,' says Venus. 'But we could show it to you. Isis, you and Penelope should come too. It will do you good to have a break from this cube.'

That's how I find myself visiting Museum Earth accompanied by Isis, a baby and a gaggle of females in various stages of pregnancy.

On the way, the female called Venus grabs my arm and pulls me to one side. 'I just want to tell you that they say that Dionysus has never been the same since he came back from Oasis. They say he's suffering from post-traumatic stress disorder. It's something soldiers get after being in a war.'

There was no war. Dionysus was captured, imprisoned and put on show just as I was. It's ridiculous. All this post-this and post-that. He sounds a neurotic weakling to me. Isis is better off without him. He's certainly not taking his responsibilities as a father seriously.

I stop in my tracks. Venus looks up at me. 'What's wrong?' she asks.

'Nothing I tell her. Nothing at all.' I can hardly explain that I am wondering how I will cope if I become a father. Not very well I imagine. I'd better think about using some kind of contraception. Unless it's already too late.

Thor emerges from one of the store-cubes with two parcels, one long and thin, one bulky.

As we begin our trek back to Compound Creative, he explains that he's been hiding in the store-cubes waiting for me and has come up with a brilliant idea. In order to enter C98 inconspicuously he will disguise himself as a warrior. He has sorted through a pile of uniforms and found one large enough to fit him. I have to admit that he has used his initiative to good effect, even though I now doubt the abduction to be necessary.

He has also brought a couple of rifles from the arsenal.

'One to take with me in case of trouble. The other for you.'

'I thought you understood I wasn't coming with you.'

'I do know that,' he assures me. 'I was thinking of the guns as a general backup for future emergencies.'

I think about what he has done. It is almost unknown for mutant humanoids to steal from one other. As a no money society we are supplied with anything we need by our brothers in the sky and, living communally, we've not been too interested in personal possessions. In a society based on sharing, locked doors are not necessary. Now we are allowed outside our compounds, changes are bound to occur. There is talk of re-introducing a monetary system on Earth. If that happens personal possessions will become important. Criminal activities such as robbery and even murder are likely to become more widespread. Thor's thefts may well be only the beginning.

'Now all I need is the code for the transporter and I'll be ready to do the job.' He's so pleased with himself I haven't the heart to tell him that I've been having second thoughts about going ahead with the plan. I don't want him to think I've gone soft. I'll wait a day or two before telling him that it's no longer necessary to do it.

'I'll give you the code later,' I tell him. Without the code he can't do a thing.

I have managed to resolve the labour problem. I will no longer be using actors as construction workers. Kata-Mbula can continue with his rehearsals day and night as far as I am concerned.

My visit to C98 gave me the idea. Seeing the basic housing provided for the warriors in the barracks made me realise that we could employ migrants – manual workers from other sectoids – to build the city. Their first job will be to build basic living quarters for themselves so there will be no need to accommodate them in Compound Creative. The city will be completely autonomous.

I put my idea about the use of migrants as labourers to Athene and she agrees that it is an appropriate solution. There has been quite a bit of unrest in some of the sectoids with workers keen for a change. She is to select suitable candidates for me. I impress on her that they must be strong, hardworking and intelligent enough to follow instructions.

Thor will be in charge of the day-to-day work as before, a position he was born to fill.

All my communications with Athene have been by pcm and restricted to business, with no mention of anything personal. I don't question the appointment of Odysseus as her deputy, even though I am far from happy about her cavalier conduct. First she moves Kata-Mbula back to take charge of Compound Creative and now Odysseus appears to have replaced me as her closest adviser.

One thing she has not taken away from me is my plan to build a city. I am making all the decisions regarding its creation. The proposed flats or houses for the construction workers are to be built well away from the residential areas planned for the more discerning city dwellers. I envisage a kind of barrio, a working class area where the workers can establish their own community.

The buildings will resemble those in the barracks, simple, basic structures, nothing elaborate. It will be an area where the workers can rest at the end of the day, but without many extraneous creature comforts. After all, they will be here to work.

When I tell Kat my new plan for building Earth City he is delighted. 'There,' he says. 'Everything is working out fine. I have Compound Creative and you have your own workers, the tower and the city. Not only that but we remain good neighbours, no?'

Kat's right. Everything does seem to working out satisfactorily. Until Thor drops his bombshell.

He comes to see me in my office in the tower, both his mouths stretched in wide grins. 'Mission accomplished,' he says.

'What do you mean?' I ask but I already know. The heaviness in my stomach tells me.

'I thought I might as well do it while I had time before the construction starts again,' he says. 'It all went very smoothly. No one challenged me when I went into C98. They saw the uniform, not the man, just as I intended. It wasn't difficult to locate the baby or the transporter….'

He starts to recount in detail what happened but I stop him.

'How did you get the transporter code?'

He gives me a cunning sideways look. 'Not too difficult. I remembered the code you gave me when you travelled from C99 to Oasis. A few adjustments and I worked out the one from C98. You're not the only humanoid on Earth with a brain.'

I check my auto-mail. Sure enough there is a pcm from Orlando Wolfe, saying the "package" has arrived safely and, in return more building materials are on their way. He even gives me praise.

Good job, Heracles. Good job. Just let me know what else you need.

Thor stands there like a zombie expecting me to congratulate him.

'You fool!' I splutter. 'I told you to wait until I told you to do it. That was Isis's own baby you stole, and sent off to Oasis. Her baby. How do you think she is feeling now?'

Thor can't believe my response. 'I thought you'd be pleased. I wanted to show you what I could do. That I could use my own initiative, that I'm not just someone who obeys your orders, but a real friend, a colleague with a mind of my own. I thought….'

'I don't want you to think. I want you to do what I tell you. Nothing more. Do you understand?'

His mouths quiver, his head drops. For a moment I think he's going to blub. 'I'm sorry, Boss.'

'Sorry doesn't do it. Don't you understand? You've abducted a baby and left a poor mother totally shattered.'

'Sorry, I just thought….'

'Get out! Get out! I don't want to see your ugly mug again until tomorrow.'

He makes for the door, shoulders and back bent. I almost feel sorry for him and want to call him back. But I don't. I hear his heavy steps as he trudges down the stairs.

I switch on the compu and search for C98. There it is. I pan round inside the compound until I find Isis's dormo-cube. The door is ajar. Can I see inside? Ah yes, there she is, curled up in the foetal position on the bunku. I turn up the sound and make myself listen to her sobs. There's her moon-face, streaming with tears. She sobs and sobs as if she will never stop.

Zeus, what have I done?

I switch off the compu. I can't bear to watch any longer.

I shall have to get that baby back. I have no idea how I can do that, but know that I have to do it. It's my fault this has happened.

Great Zeus. I've developed a conscience! But I do need to do something to redress the situation. If only to get some sleep.

Who can I ask to help me? A humanoid? Athene or Odysseus? Tricky. My role in this plot may come to light.

A complete? Not Wolfe. He won't change his mind. He has the proverbial heart of steel. Stella perhaps? No. She has the power to intervene but will refer me to Athene. There's really only one person who can help.

Someone half humanoid and half complete. Little Mercury AKA Michael Court.

Chapter Seventeen
Mercury Rising
(according to Michael)

Journal Entry

The moment I arrive back at Home-Court-Jameson I sense something is wrong. I have only been away from Oasis for a few days but the house feels abandoned. No one is in. Yet, at this time of day the children should be home from school and Stella there to give them an afternoon snack to keep them going until the shared evening meal.

The kitchen, dining room, terrace and garden are not just devoid of people but also of clutter, unlived in. I check the rest of the house. Many of the ornaments and hangings have disappeared. A quick scan of Stella's study, the hub of worldwideculture.inc, reveals that it has been stripped of its contents. Neither the multi-screen computer, nor the conglomeration of artistic items so valued by Stella remains. Further examination of other rooms reveals that the clothes and toys in the children's rooms have gone.

I enter the main bedroom. Stella's wardrobe door is open. Empty. With some trepidation I open Father's wardrobe. I give a sigh of relief. His suits hang there as usual. Stella and the children have moved out, but Father hasn't.

I check my room. Everything is as I left it: computer, books and clothes.

I suspect that Stella's defection must have to do with the

shocking altercation I overheard at Hos-sat, when Stella failed to support Father's viewpoint and aligned herself with Orlando Wolfe. Whatever transpired afterwards it must have led to Stella walking out, taking Stuart and Bella with her.

With hindsight I realise Father's relationship with Stella has been disintegrating for some time.

Was it my intrusion into this family that caused the breakdown? Should I have tried harder to cooperate with Stella?

I glance at my watch. Father won't be home for another hour. But I can't sit here brooding. I decide to go to the Rehabilitation Centre and see if I can find out about Lizzy and her family.

The building is a rather forbidding one, as unlike the glass and marble structures in the Plaza as our residential area is to the Project. It resembles an old-fashioned prison from the 19th century, its grey walls dotted with narrow, barred windows. I summon up courage and knock on the door. A grid slides open.

'Name and number,' demands a disembodied voice.

'I've come to enquire if a family called….' I hesitate, trying to remember Lizzy's surname. Surely she must have told me it.

'Name and number,' repeats the voice.

'Edwards,' I say. 'Elizabeth Edwards.'

'Number?'

'I don't know. I'm trying to find out if she's here or not.'

'Number,' repeats the voice. 'Can't tell you anything without the number.'

'Where can I find her number?' I ask.

'Ministry of Justice, Floor Seven. Are you offering employment?'

'Not exactly,' I admit.

I can't believe this. I'm standing in the street talking to a door.

'Doubt they'll give you the number then.' The grid slides shut. Interview finished.

I hang around for a bit, hoping that if Lizzy is on work experience, she will return soon. A few depressed looking individuals arrive, knock, give their numbers to the door and are admitted, but no Lizzy.

I make my way to the Ministry of Justice, but the admin section is closed for the day. Impasse.

I trot round to the university.

'Thank Zeus you're back, man,' says Jonathan. 'You've been away for ages. Let's go for a beer. Tell me what you've been up to.'

'I really should do some work,' I tell him, keen to start up my computer.

'Tomorrow is another day.' He slings an arm round my shoulder and marches me off to our usual haunt, a little bar in the park. He chats for a bit telling me snippets of university gossip and grumbling about his father's attitude to his long hair and untidy bedroom. It's all so petty compared with my problems.

He turns to me at last and asks me what I've been doing. What can I tell him? Not about my meeting with Odysseus and Isis, nor about overhearing Orlando Wolfe and my father arguing, nor that Stella has left.

'I've met a pretty nurse who wants to be a doctor. She has a day off on Saturday and we've got a date.'

Jonathan's eyes light up. 'Good for you,' he says. 'Can I meet her?'

'No way. I hardly know her myself yet. I don't want you messing things up for me.'

'As if I would,' he says, all innocence. There is something in the gleam of his blue eyes that makes me understand why girls are attracted to him. He's totally got sex appeal. I'm definitely going to keep him well away from Gemma.

Back home Father is sitting at the kitchen table shoulders slumped, reading or pretending to read his e-tablet. He stands up when I walk in, his face alive with a welcoming smile. 'Michael. Thank Zeus you're back.' His words echo Jonathan's and I count myself lucky to have at least two people on Oasis pleased to see me.

Father puts his arms round me and we attempt an embrace, but we're not used to such a show of emotion.

We begin to prepare a simple meal. He is to grill the meat while I chop vegetables and put them in a pan of water to boil.

He doesn't talk about the break-up. Not yet. But I can see he's upset, knocked for six as they say, and not at all sure how he is going to cope.

I try to chat away as naturally as possible and find that I am able to speak frankly about my stay at Hos-sat. I admit that I'd had no intention of having a vasectomy and that the only reason for my visit was to see Isis and make sure that nothing happened to the baby. I tell him that I suspected that the last thing the authorities wanted was to have more mutants in the world. In other words I feared for the survival of the first mutant humanoid born for years.

Father pauses in his task of sprinkling herbs on the chops. 'By the authorities you mean the Symposium?'

I feel the colour rush up my cheeks.

'I don't know. Yes. No. Certain members of it, a powerful group of subversives, I guess.'

'No need to guess,' he says grimly, placing the chops neatly on the metal tray. 'It amazes me how much you have learnt since being on Oasis. About the different factions, I mean.'

'Sometimes an outsider's eye can see more clearly,' I say, but I feel awkward, as if I'm talking in platitudes.

I hesitate and then decide it is better to be completely honest about what I did at Hos-sat. I tell Father how I eavesdropped on his conversation with Wolfe, Stella and the medical team and how I was instrumental in making sure that Isis and the baby returned to Earth as soon as possible. Father nods seemingly accepting my conduct. He doesn't even blanch when I tell him that I talked to Odysseus and told him how I became a complete and about my new life on Oasis.

'I'm sorry. I broke my promise to you but somehow – meeting him there – it seemed right to tell him.'

He nods again, seeming to take my confession in his stride. 'Odysseus is a good humanoid. You couldn't have found a better confidant. Stella – Stella always admired him.' He stops, turns away from me, as if saying her name sticks in his throat.

Father sits down, the meal we've been preparing forgotten. 'I had no idea what was going on, Michael. No idea at all. I mean, yes, there were indications that all was not well between us, but I didn't know it had anything to do with that awful man. That conversation at Hos-sat – the one you overheard – was the first indication I had that she….' He looks at me his eyes full of tears. He blinks them away. 'I loved her, Michael, adored her. And the children. We thought the same way about most things. Or so I believed. I just don't understand how she could do such a thing. Michael, she's been having an affair for months with Wolfe of all people. What a fool I've been.'

Zeus! Has she actually gone and left this good man for that cold, calculating lizard? I can't believe it.

'You're not a fool, Father. Or if you are so am I. We were both taken in by her.'

Whatever differences there were between Stella and me, I never dreamt she was deceiving my father with another man. Let alone Orlando Wolfe. And now she's left Father to live with him.

I think back to that meeting in Hos-sat. There was something about Stella's body language as she stood close to Wolfe that spoke of intimacy and there was that exchanged look of complicity. I saw Father's face drain of colour and his face muscles tighten. He must have known from that moment that there was something going on between them. I feel sick thinking of them together, so how much worse must Father feel?

I think of Wolfe's mansion, the biggest most luxurious home on Oasis. Will it be called Home-Wolfe-Jameson now? Or is Stella just a glorified mistress who will prove useful to him for a while and then discarded? I still can't believe that she's been having an affair with Father's number one adversary and has now moved in with him. But it's true. The thought that they are not only lovers but have been conspiring to bring Father down politically, is totally horrendous.

I am careful not to say anything too derogatory about Stella. Couples that split up sometimes get together again. I know that from books I've read. Would Father take her back if she decided to return?

Apart from the personal damage Stella has already done, the entire situation is fraught with the possibility of further disasters. Stella knows Alexander's secret. And mine. The danger caused by her duplicity is far from over.

Before they have the chance to hurt us, I think we should "come out" ourselves and admit our mutant origins. It's just a case of convincing Father.

My father sits, back rounded, head bent forward as if he hasn't the will to sit up straight. He needs a new reason to live. Having the courage to admit the past could be the way forward. I must persuade him that telling the truth about our origins is the best thing to do. Stella may already have been indiscreet enough to tell Orlando Wolfe that Father and I were born with mutations. If so, it won't be long before he tells the Symposium. We must tell them first.

I'm the only person in the world that Father can trust now. There must be no more secrets between us. Father and I talk into the early hours of the morning. He looks exhausted but he dreads going to bed. He knows he has little chance of sleeping.

When I finally go to my room and check my auto-mails, I find one from Odysseus.

More dreadful news. Someone has stolen baby Penelope. Zeus! Isis must be totally gutted. We thought we'd done the right thing sending them back to Earth, certain that the child would be safe there. How wrong we were.

Odysseus suspects that Penelope has been taken to Oasis and he wants me to help him find her and return her to Isis. He doesn't need to ask me twice. I'll make finding that baby a priority. Being Odysseus he adds, 'Everything must be done officially.'

Another auto-mail, this time from Heracles, also asks me if I can help find the stolen baby. What connection Heracles has with Isis I'm not sure. We all knew each other in C55 but I didn't realise they were still in touch. He gives me a name to help trace the whereabouts of the baby. The name is no surprise to me: Orlando Wolfe.

One thing I can be sure of. One way or another, baby Penelope will be returned to her mother. Before I fall asleep, I have a comforting thought. I don't have to tackle this problem on my own. I have Father to help me now.

Journal Entry

Two hungry men at breakfast time do the male thing. We send out for a take away: bacon, eggs, sausages, pancakes, mushrooms and tomatoes. We eat the lot. No conversation by mutual agreement until we've finished.

Father wipes his mouth and manages a smile. 'Well, we never did get to eat dinner last night.'

I smile back and throw the remains of the neglected dinner in the bin. Stella would never have allowed us to do that. Father frowns, having the same thought, then shrugs.

Father tells me the men who arrested and strip-searched me have resisted all attempts to persuade them to reveal Wolfe's role. 'Paid not to talk, I'm sure. But I haven't given up, Michael. I can promise you that.'

'There's something else for us to deal with first,' I tell him and show him the auto-mails from Odysseus and Heracles about the missing baby.

'Leave it with me. A few phone calls and we'll find the location of young Penelope. Getting her back might prove more difficult but we will succeed, believe you me.'

I like the way he says, we will succeed. We're a team working toward the same objective.

Off to uni for me while Father makes his calls. He'll contact me later.

A sharp shower of liquid glass and I dash into the shopping mall for shelter. I'm passing a supermarket when I catch sight of Lizzy. She's not wearing the blue dress I liked so much but rather dowdy overalls and there's a collar round her neck and bands round her wrists and ankles that are certainly not jewellery. Electronic security tags. She's stacking shelves with packets of cereals from a trolley.

She blushes when she sees me approach. 'Michael! I was hoping you'd come by.'

'I went to the Rehabilitation Centre. They asked me for your number.'

'Isn't it awful? No name any more. Just a number. And these dreadful things round my neck. They're so heavy.' She waves an arm. 'They call this work experience but if you ask me it's slave labour. I have to work here all day and in the evening I clean houses. No free time at all. Might as well be one of them mutants the way they treat me.'

There's no way I can answer that. I just stand there looking at her, wondering what the hell I can do to help.

'How are your family?' I ask.

'Banged up. Undergoing treatment,' she says.

'Treatment?'

She shrugs. 'You know, drilling into their brains to make them better citizens.'

I shake my head. Lizzie must have got that wrong. She must be exaggerating. Or is she? 'Your father and brothers?'

'Father yes. He's on the treatment. And my mother. Brothers? I haven't got no brothers.' She claps her hand to her mouth. 'You mean those boys in the Project. They're not my brothers. Thought you knew that. They kind of looked after me. After my interests. You know how it is. When we were taken, they bolted, haven't seen them since. I'm all alone, Michael. Can you do something to help me?' Her eyes widen but look a little less blue than usual.

'I don't know. I'll try. Give me your number for a start and I'll see what I can do.'

'You'll come back and see me, won't you Michael? I might not be here tomorrow mind. They move us on quite quick to different places. Look the supervisor's coming. Better not be seen talking to me or you'll be the next one to be tagged.'

She leans over and starts stacking the cereal boxes on the shelves again, a skinny pathetic figure so different from the pretty dancer I was once half in love with. I turn away. She calls out her number. '5978342106.' Good job I've got a good memory for figures.

I have yet to tell Father about my relationship with Lizzy. I'm ashamed now that I didn't obey him and keep out of the

Project. On the other hand, if I'm not aware of the problems in our society how can I be a reformer?

Because that's what I intend to be. A reformer, someone who sees the mistakes in the system and finds a way to correct them.

On my watch, there'll be no more Projects, no more Rehabilitation Centres, no more treating people like automatons.

No more arrests on the street by thugs. No more discrimination between completes and mutants. Michael Court on his soapbox, Do-gooder extraordinary! I can't help smiling at my temerity.

If anyone can help Lizzy it will be Father. She needs a job and somewhere to live. Not with us. That wouldn't do at all. My philanthropy doesn't stretch that far. I'll talk to him about it tonight.

At uni, Jonathan pokes his head round my cubicle. 'Tonight's the night!' he teases me.

'What?' So much has happened that I've quite forgotten about my date with Gemma.

He offers to give me a packet of condoms.

'It's not like that,' I tell him. 'I told you. I hardly know her.'

'That's the best time to go for it,' he says, 'before you know each other too well.' He raises his eyebrows up and down in comic mode.

But I'm not in the mood for his ribbing. I'm thinking of Lizzy. Jonathan is only person who knows of my friendship with her so I decide to share my concerns about her with him. We go to the junior common room for a coffee.

'I've just seen Lizzie,' I tell him.

'Two chicks in one day,' he grins. 'You are coming out of your shell.'

I tell him where I saw her and about the electronic tags and how she's known by a number. 'And guess what? Those boys weren't her brothers after all. They just looked out for her, she said.'

'They were her pimps.'

'She wasn't like that.'

'Wasn't she? Did she ever ask you for money?'

I don't answer.

'Did you ever give her money, Michael? You did. You fool. She was playing you. Forget her, man.'

'You should have seen her today. She looked so – downtrodden. Close to despair. I want to help her.'

'Not much you can do, man. Sad, but that's the truth. It's the system.'

'Then the system must change.'

'And you're the one to change it?'

'Yes, I rather think I am. I've been thinking about my life, the future, about what I want to do. Reassessing my plans. I want to seek out what is wrong with our society on Earth and Oasis and find a way to change it.'

'Wow. That's quite a challenge.'

'I might not succeed but I want to try.'

'So – you want to be a politician?'

I stare at him. 'I suppose I do. If that's the way to make a difference.'

'You're a good person, Michael, but you know as well I do that politicians are scum. Power crazy, ruthless and corrupt.'

'I'm going to be a different sort of politician.'

'They all start out like that, full of ideals, keen to change the world. It doesn't last. In the end they find they have to play dirty to win.'

'I'm going to win without playing dirty.'

Jonathan laughs. 'I'll believe it when I see it. You'll get sucked in like all the rest and lose your integrity.'

'My father's kept his integrity.'

Even as I say that I wonder if it's true. There have been

occasions when I've been critical of him. I think of the mutant humanoids on display in the museum and find it hard to believe that my father was a member of a parliament that allowed such a travesty. The Oasis Project for the unemployed must have started out as a good idea too but degenerated into a less than perfect scheme, a trap that restricts the freedom of its beneficiaries and, if my sources are correct, one that leads to the brainwashing of those who do not conform.

Maybe my father's too soft to stand up for his principles, too soft to fight for his beliefs.

Or maybe it's not that easy to make changes when others use unethical methods to oppose you.

Jonathan could be right. There may come a time when even I, full of ideals and good intentions, might be tempted to consider that the end justifies the somewhat dodgy means.

Journal Entry

Gemma and I meet in a little bar on the far side of town. We sit opposite each other, drink wine and look into each other's eyes.

She starts to tell me about her life.

'My parents split up when I was ten years old. I live with my mother. It hasn't been easy for her. Sometimes she's had to hold down two jobs to support us. She was determined to give me a good education and supported me through my training as a nurse. It will be difficult for her if I go to university and study to become a doctor. That's why I must be self-sufficient.'

I like her positive attitude. 'I've downloaded some papers about grants for you. Did you bring your CV?'

She blushes. 'Oh no, I forgot.' I can see that something is worrying her. 'Michael, I want to ask you something. I got the impression that you and Isis knew each other from way back. How can that be possible when you are a complete and she is a mutant humanoid?'

I look at her. Her little forehead is wrinkled. Her confusion seems genuine enough. She's curious that's all. But it's too soon in our relationship to tell her that I was once a mutant humanoid brought up in the same compound as Isis. Until Father and I agree about not hiding our past, I must continue to be circumspect.

My hesitation prompts her to continue. 'You seemed to know that other humanoid too, the old one, Odysseus isn't it? Have you taken a trip to Earth?'

'No, but I'd like to,' I say. That is true. I haven't visited Earth. I lived there.

She looks at me expectantly. I haven't answered her question.

'I'll tell you something that not everyone knows,' I begin.

Gemma leans forward, attentive.

'My stepmother, Stella Jameson, is head of a company called Worldwideculture. Her role is to be a benevolent overseer of life on Earth. She rarely intervenes. As you know, the humanoids have their own leader, the current one being Athene who visited Oasis not long ago.'

Gemma nods. She continues to stare at me, willing me to tell her more, but the intensity of her stare makes me nervous. She's a little too anxious to discover how I could know Isis and Odysseus. Does she suspect that I am not the person I purport to be?

Feeling like the devious politician Jonathan suspects I could become, I tell her about the Worldwideculture website and my access to it. 'Normally, I'm just an observer, you understand, but occasionally, Stella asks me to communicate with some of the humanoids. I can do that in a chat-room. But because we all happened to be there in Hos-sat at the same time, a live meeting seemed appropriate.'

'So you'd never actually met Isis or Odysseus before?'

'Not in the flesh no. Only online.' A lie, but a necessary one. Is this how politicians start to be dishonest, a little lie leading to bigger ones?

'But you seemed very close to Isis. She had a nickname for you. Mercury.'

I feel my heart beating fast. 'Heh – what is this – an interrogation?'

She blushes and smiles. 'Sorry. I suppose the truth is I'm a bit jealous of Isis, of your closeness to her.'

She's been fiddling with her glass, but hasn't drunk any wine. I lean across and take both her hands in mine. 'You have no need to be jealous,' I assure her. 'Isis and I don't have that kind of relationship.'

She withdraws her hands and clutches her bag as if ready to leave.

'Are you hungry? Shall we order some food now?' I ask her.

She shakes her head. 'Sorry. I have to go.'

'But I thought.... Tomorrow perhaps? Lunch or dinner?'

'I'm on duty tomorrow. The early shift.'

'When can I see you again?'

She stands. I stand too and move towards her. Her whole body is trembling. I'm about to kiss her lightly on the cheek, but she pulls away.

'I'm sorry, Michael,' she says.

'You don't want to see me again?'

She looks round, anxious to make her escape. 'I just can't. I don't know how to explain. The truth is being a spy is just not my thing!'

And off she runs with frantic little steps out of the bar.

I sit down again, dumbfounded. She cringed when she thought I was about to kiss her. Actually cringed. She's never done that before. She's found out I'm a mutant humanoid and the thought disgusts her. And what was that she said about being a spy?

Suddenly it clicks. Orlando Wolfe has bribed her to find out about me. That's why she's been asking all those questions. He is paying her to find out if I had an operation in Hos-sat, to get rid of my mutations. My case was so secret that she couldn't find the evidence. Instead she thought she'd try to find out directly from me, but found she couldn't do it.

Has our entire relationship been a sham? Or was she really attracted me at first? I'd like to believe that. The fact that she couldn't go through with her plan to spy on me surely proves that she's not a bad person. But she cringed when I attempted to kiss her. Bad news.

There's no doubt about it. Our relationship has ended before it has properly begun. I pay the bill and leave.

A pcm on my mob-fone tells me that Father has located the baby. Thank Zeus for that. At least one piece of good news today.

Chapter Eighteen
Mail box: Bathsheba

Auto-mail from Bathsheba

Dear Odysseus,

You will be surprised to hear from me, as we have never met. We would have done so had I been able to attend the funeral of Brahmin, as planned. In the event, Heracles and Sati took my place and I was obliged stay behind and hold the fort, so to speak, at Compound Creative.

The reason for this missive is that you have requested a report about the said Compound Creative for your proposed publication, the Chronicles of Planet Earth, Life in the Compounds. The obvious humanoid to write such an account would be our beloved leader, Kata-Mbula, but, as I'm sure you appreciate, he is too busy with preparations for The Big Event to undertake such a project at present. He has therefore asked me to deputise for him. I'm proud to be entrusted with this task and just hope I can do it justice.

I know who you are of course. Who doesn't? Although we are quite insular here, immersed as we are in our creativity, everyone has heard of the wise Odysseus. I have long followed your work as historian and museum curator, but I doubt you know who I am. Forgive me, therefore, if I spend a few lines telling you a little bit about myself.

You may be interested to know I too am interested in antiques, art and handicrafts of all kinds. I have even been known to dabble in a bit of painting and embroidery myself. One of my works was chosen to hang in our beloved leader's office, in prime position on the wall facing his workstation. He usually changes his pictures every week, but mine seems to have become a permanent fixture. In addition, a tapestry of mine adorns the wall adjacent to the entrance of Compound Creative, an honour that I truly appreciate.

I like to think of myself as Kata-Mbula's deputy, although this title has never officially been bestowed on me. The reason for this is because in Compound Creative we work as a team and consider ourselves equal. Nevertheless when our leader's talents were called upon to design and oversee the building of the stadium for The Big Event at C99, the main responsibility of looking after the sectoid fell on me.

Yes, I know Heracles was appointed temporary leader but he was new here and needed considerable guidance. I was content to assist him settle in and, when necessary, to advise him of our procedures. With Kat away I also took upon myself the job of running rehearsals – once I became aware that performance art was not really Heracles's forte. Frankly he showed little interest in this aspect of our work and I felt justified in taking it on. I believe he was duly grateful for my support.

I should perhaps draw your attention to the fact that when Kata-Mbula is here, I prove invaluable to him too. I do not take part in the plays, operas or dances. I am not an actor, singer or dancer and do not aspire to be, but I can turn my hand to all kind of backstage tasks and am always ready to take over when someone has to drop out through ill health or incompetence.

Kat will not tolerate the continued presence of anyone who doesn't pull his or her weight or is proved not to have the talent to execute something perfectly. This criteria applies not only to dancers and actors, but also to ASMs, whether stagehands or sound or lighting operators. If they are not good enough they are dismissed and I am only too happy to replace them until someone more suitable is found.

Actors are subject to the same rigid standards but they have understudies standing by, ready to take over if they do not come up to the mark.

As you have probably gathered, Kat and I have a close relationship, which works well for both us.

I don't expect him to spend all his spare time with me. That would be unreasonable. Currently, for example, he spends much of his ex-curricular time with the girl playing Desdemona. It's a complicated role and she needs lots of coaching and confidence building that only he can give. I don't protest. I know, deep down, that he has a homing instinct and, as soon as this production is over, he will spend more time with me.

Before you start feeling sorry for me or think me a victim of Kat's arrogance I must end such speculations. There is nowhere I would rather be than in Compound Creative and nothing I would rather be than an integral member of Kat's team. To suffer from his indifference towards me for a short period is a small price to pay for the pleasure of his company both professionally and personally when he returns to my side.

Odysseus, you ask me to tell you how rehearsals are going and I'm delighted to say that now Kat is back in charge they are going very well indeed. The only hiccoughs are those caused by the number of pregnancies that have suddenly come to pass. We're pleased about them of course. For humanoids to reproduce again is a dream come true. Too late for me I'm afraid, but the joy felt by the expectant mothers is something I can share. I look forward to assisting at the births and helping look after these offspring, if called upon to do so.

The problem is, that because of early morning sickness or other pregnancy-related health problems, there has had to be considerable re-casting. As the weeks pass, some dancers in particular have had to relinquish their roles, no longer able to leap or twist or move with the required agility.

Kat has shown considerable patience in dealing with these setbacks and spent hours training less talented dancers who, quite frankly, would not normally have been deemed good enough to be selected.

Nevertheless, all is well and I don't think Athene or the audience will be disappointed in the end result.

You ask me about Heracles and Sati. To tell the truth we don't see much of them now. They have moved out of the compound and live in the Tower, a quite spectacular building in the shape of what appears to be a giant phallus. Not exactly subtle as a symbol of virility. Or tasteful.

Heracles is busy supervising the building of his city and a few members of Compound Creative have started to live there. Those who have chosen to leave us are mainly pregnant females and prospective fathers, planning to live in family units. A lot of promiscuity has gone on in the past so the paternity of these babies is never quite certain. I have noted of late that females hoping to become pregnant have been confining their sexual activities to one male. The commun-dormo-cube is rarely used now. It may be worth us reassigning it as an extra rehearsal space.

Most of us have no intention of moving out of the compound to live in the city. Because of the nature of our creative work, we prefer communal living, with or without communal copulation.

A piece of news about Sati. She too is expecting a baby. Sati went a bit crazy when she lived in our compound. There are quite a few candidates who could claim fatherhood of her baby, but as far as she's concerned, Heracles is the father and that's that.

Some of the humanoid migrants detailed to build the city seem a bit rough. Poor stuff. Luckily they live on the other side of the town in a barrio especially created for them, so we don't see much of them. One day when the sun was shining, Kat decided to rehearse the opera outside. The singers' voices soared and the workers stopped to listen, Soon they began to join in, with raucous voices and lewd comments. Kat soon led the group back inside. Open-air rehearsals have not been resumed.

In case you are interested in the programme we intend to present at The Big Event, I will tell you that we are offering various extracts from Shakespeare's plays.

The balcony and death scenes from Romeo and Juliet; the shenanigans of Puck and the lovers from A Midsummer's Night Dream and Desdemona's death from *Othello.* A bit of a secret – but I'm sure it's fine to tell you – is that Kata-Mbula is to play Othello himself. A performance to relish, I assure you.

There's also a short opera, Lovely Ladies, in which the characters masquerade as bottles of wine. Just imagine the costumes. I supervised and helped make them. I'm a very hands-on type of humanoid and like working alongside the other members of the company.

As for the dances, the titles are unpronounceable, mainly in the French language, but they will be spectacular, I can promise you that. Between you and me, the female in charge of the costumes is not quite as proficient or as innovative as she believes herself to be, but we can't expect perfection all the time.

In case you have the impression that Kat is a rigid director, intent on imposing his own ideas on a production to the exclusion of others, you would be wrong. Kat is focused, yes. He has a clear overall concept of what a performance should be like, but he does leave space for the actors, dancers, musicians, designers, stage-manager and even the stagehands to be imaginative too.

He inspires us, draws us out and encourages us to offer our views to contribute to the whole: a rare talent. Under his guidance we are egalitarian in our work practices and have a strong sense of community.

Odysseus, I realise I've been rambling on and that this isn't an organised account of what life is like here. I do hope you can extract whatever you need and include whatever you consider appropriate in the proposed chronicles.

It's just my way to put my thoughts down as they come to me, including my doubts and fears. This tendency to write from my viewpoint may prove too personal for your purposes. I do try to be objective but realise it doesn't always work.

Maybe at The Big Event you and I will have a chance to meet at last. I look forward to it.

If you need any more information from me do not hesitate to let me know.

Best Regards
Bathsheba

Reply from Odysseus

Dear Bathsheba,

Thank you for your heartfelt contribution to the Chronicles. I assure you that your account is not too personal.

The best histories are written from an individual viewpoint. That is what makes them interesting and why the truth about the past is so difficult to pin down. The information is all there in the texts of the primary materials, but the differing perspectives of the chroniclers necessarily affect our interpretation of past events.

For me this is one of the joys of histo-research, trying to work out what happened from the varied versions available to us.

Here I am rambling on, boring you with my theories. What I'm trying to say is – don't worry about your account being "too personal." The narrative voice you use gives it validity. You have a gift for drawing the reader into the story, Bathsheba. A rare gift. Treasure it.

I look forward to your next letter and to meeting you at The Big Event.

Best Regards
Odysseus

Chapter Nineteen
Mail Box: Isis

Auto-mail from Isis

Dear Heracles,
I'm writing to you to see if you can help me find my baby. Someone has kidnapped her and taken her away to another compound. I don't know who else to ask to help and you were kind enough to come and visit us and seemed quite taken with her. She took to you too. Remember how she gripped your finger and wouldn't let it go?

Where is she? Is she safe? Who's looking after her? I can't stop worrying about her. I cry buckets very single day and am not able to sleep at night. When I look in her cot and see it empty I'm totally wrecked.

Odysseus is looking for Penny too but he's very busy doing important things for Athene and goes off to some planet or other at the drop of a hat.

As for Osiris, no one would think he was Penelope's father. He's turned totally weird. Quiet and sulky. Not that I see much of him. He's always in the gym or on the parade ground, practising for The Big Event and he sleeps in the barracks with the other warriors. Can you believe that?

Trouble is I can't sleep and I have a job to eat a thing and just go on crying and crying.

Heracles, I've always admired you. You know that. I believe that if anyone can find Penelope and bring her back to me it will be you.

Please, please do what you can to help me.

Your friend,
Isis

Reply from Heracles

Dear Isis,

I'd heard that your baby had been abducted and am already taking steps to try to find out where she is and return her to you.

You may be surprised to hear that I don't think she's been taken to another compound. I think some completes on Planet Oasis have taken her. Why? Because they believe a complete should be brought up by completes. If this is the case you can at least be sure that your baby is well cared for so you need have no worries about her welfare.

But the abductors have committed a criminal act. They have stolen the baby from her rightful mother and I'm determined that they will pay for their offence.

I want you to know that I am making the finding of your baby and returning her to you a priority. So put your faith in me and soon that lovely child will be in its mother's arms once more.

Your friend
Heracles

Reply from Isis

Dear Heracles,

Thank you for your auto-mail. I have to tell you that I am totally knocked out by your reply and feel better already. I have faith in your power to help me.

Something else happened yesterday to make me feel better as well. Osiris resigned. I mean from the army. He's no longer a golden warrior. Apparently he has been suffering from something called post-something-or-other syndrome, since that time he went missing. I don't know exactly what happened. He has never wanted to talk about it and I haven't pressed him.

Anyway, the thing is he can't bear to even practise fighting, not even for The Big Event. He finally plucked up courage and told Durga. She was spitting mad, went bright red, and spluttered over her words.

Imagine it. She can't understand why anyone wouldn't want to be a warrior, especially a captain.

No warrior has ever resigned before. But she has to accept it. No choice. She can't make him fight.

Osiris no longer lives in the barracks. He lives with me. Amazing. I have to admit it will take us some time to get used to each other again. For one thing this syndrome thing is like an illness and he needs a lot of support. He's the one who cries a lot now and finds it difficult to sleep. When he does sleep he's totally restless and has horrendous nightmares. He groans and shouts out in his sleep and wakes up in a cold sweat, his whole body shaking. I have to be the strong one now.

It's given me a purpose anyway. I have to help him get better for when Penelope comes back. When she's back I'm sure everything will be perfect.

Do let me know when you have news of her and when I will see her again.

Hoping for good news soon,

Your friend
Isis

Auto-mail from Isis

Dear Heracles,

I hope everything is going well. I've been a bit worried because I haven't heard a word from you. I realise you must be busy, not just with finding my baby but also with building your city.

Osiris and I had quite a shock today. Because he is no longer a warrior we have been told that we have to move to another compound. We're not sure where we'll be sent yet but I think it's for the best to make a new start somewhere else with no golden warriors strutting about to remind Osiris of the past.

He looks quite different out of his uniform in ordinary clothes. Smaller somehow. Still handsome, but not quite so stunning. One good thing, there's no chance of him going to war again.

More news. Odysseus came to see us. He looked very tired to me. Doing too much and I told him so. He talked about Museum Oasis for ages. Went on and on about it. Osiris walked out of the cube after a while. Bored I suppose. Well, you know what Ody's like when he gets excited about old things. But you'd think Osiris could have made an effort.

I've decided I've misjudged Ody. He does care about Penelope. Guess what? He's going to Oasis to try to find her. I thought you'd like to know that he's looking for her too, so that you can liase with him – is "liase" the right word? I think it is. I looked it up. The more humanoids looking for her the better, as far as I'm concerned. I can't wait to get her back.

Ody thinks we should go to live in C55 but I'm not keen. I'm not sure Kali would welcome us and anyway that compound is far inferior to this one. I just want to go somewhere that will be good for Penelope.

Well, Heracles, that's my news up to date. Do let me know when you've got some news for me.

Yours hopefully,
Isis

Auto-mail from Isis to Odysseus

Dear Ody,

Just to let you know we arrived safely. Kali actually seemed pleased to see me, treated me like a long lost friend. I couldn't believe it. We never liked each other much before. I thought her a bossy old cow and I know she didn't think much of me.

She showed Osiris and me round the compound. Lots of changes. I won't describe them to you because I can show you round when you come to see us, which I hope will be soon.

Kali took us outside and there was Jaga. Then I understood why Kali was being so nice to me. She was trying to get me on her side. The two of them were trying to prove who was in charge. It reminded me of you and Brahmin bickering all the time, when you both wanted to be curator of the museum. Remember?

Jaga stood straight and tall, the all-glowing harvest queen with her long straw-coloured hair, fearfully good-looking compared with squat blue-black Kali with her dreadlocks and built-in snakes.

Jaga pointed at the fields and asked me what I thought of them.

I imagined my little Penny running in those fields and eating those rosy apples.

'Amazing,' I said. 'Totally amazing.'

'All designed by yours truly,' said Jaga with a sideways look at Kali.

Kali put her spoke in. 'Couldn't have done it without me.'

'I'm not so sure about that,' said Jaga.

Kali turned to me. 'My dear sister-wife tried to do the same project once before at C98. Disaster. But with me controlling her wilder ideas we've managed to pull it off.'

Jaga shrugged. 'Better soil here. That's the difference.'

'And better management of resources.'

They went on squabbling like that for some time. Totally boring. I mean who cares?

'Are you going to show us one of the houses in the village?' I asked.

'Cottages,' corrected Kali.

Jaga strode off. 'Follow me.'

There were about twenty of them, most of them empty. Jaga and Kali almost fell over each other to show me inside one of these little white washed buildings. I knew there was no way I intended to live inside the compound. It was a cottage or nothing.

Oh, Ody, I loved it. With a bit of my flair, it could be made into the perfect home for my family. I didn't let my pleasure show on my face but to tell you the truth I was really made up by the thought of living there. The cottage has three cubes – two kitted out as dormos, one as a kind of private RR and place to cook, plus a lavat cube with a bath. Totally amazing.

I kept my face straight, not wanting to look too keen. I glanced at Osiris, but he wasn't taking much interest. I kept them waiting a bit for my decision. To discuss it with Osiris privately I said, but I knew we were going to live there. It even has an outside space of its own, called a garden. Just the thing for little Penny. I can imagine her running up and down there on the grass. And Osiris could grow things too. Vegetables. It would do him good to have a hobby.

Osiris seems to live in a bubble – a little world of his own – but that's fine by me. It means I make all the decisions. The cottage is really cute. Ideal for our family. Have I told you that already?

All I need to make it a special place is some of that red and gold material. Have you still got some? Oh and a few ornaments. No antiques. Just a few shiny, bright objects to brighten up the place. It's very plain at the moment – white walls and stone floors. It needs a female touch and I'm just the female to do it! I thought you, Ody, might be able to dig out some suitable bits and pieces for me.

As you see I'm feeling a bit more cheerful. I won't be completely happy until my Penny is with us again. I can't wait to see her and hold her and make her remember her real mother. Do you think she will remember me? It seems ages since I've been without her, although it's probably only a few weeks.

Heracles is supposed to be helping to find her too, but I haven't heard a word from him for ages. I think he's all talk, no action. So I'm relying on you.

Take care, Granddad Ody, and bring my baby back to me. I know you'll find a way to do that.

Your loving daughter,
Isis

Chapter Twenty
Think-Tank
(according to Michael)

Journal Entry

Odysseus glides down the marble steps of the museum. His one eye in the centre of his triangular face and his odd way of walking attracts quite a bit of attention. Whispers, sideways looks, that sort of thing. Odysseus appears unaware of these reactions, immersed as he is in his own thoughts. He doesn't notice me until I touch him gently on the arm and say his name. His face lights up.

'Michael, how lovely to see you. I've just been looking at the reconstruction of the Sistine Chapel. The original colours were restored in 2014, you know, and we are still reaping the benefit some two hundred years later. Have you seen it?'

'I've been meaning to but....'

'Don't put it off a minute longer. Come on. It needn't take long. I'll show it you.'

He grabs my arm and I find myself trotting along beside him as he sails back up the steps and into the museum. Curious looks from members of the public as they step to one side to allow us to pass. Odysseus knows his way through the museum better than I do. He winds his way past Greek and Roman statues and various Renaissance paintings until we arrive at the entrance to the chapel where he pulls up short like a skateboarder.

'Take a deep breath in. Prepare yourself. Now, in we go.'

In he slides, looking up at the ceiling. 'Just look at those colours! Note the burst of light, the contrasting shadows and the physicality of the figures with those bulging muscles. Michelangelo was the master – don't you agree?'

I can't help but be impressed. Every centimetre of the ceiling and walls sings with colour, a mystical mix of transcendental figures. Odysseus keeps up a running commentary, guiding my eye to each image and its story. His enthusiasm is infectious.

For a long time I've avoided coming into the museum, uneasy about the memories it conjures up; but there are no more live exhibits, humanoid or human, to disturb me.

By neglecting the museum I have been denying myself the pleasure of viewing our artistic heritage. I make a pact with myself. I will put aside a few minutes each week to explore the treasures of this amazing place.

It isn't until we are outside again that I have a chance to tell Odysseus the good news. 'I'm happy to be able to tell you that Father has located Penelope.'

Odysseus stops, puts his hand on my arm. 'Really? Where is she? Can we go and see her?'

'No, not yet. It's not that simple. But she's safe, Odysseus, and well looked after.'

'But when can I take her back to Isis?'

His hands keep clutching his robe. I sit him down on the bench in the Plaza to calm him down.

I tell him what Father has found out. Orlando Wolfe's sister, Jessica, and her husband, unable to have children of their own, have wanted to adopt for some time. When Wolfe found that Isis's baby was a complete he was determined to acquire her for his sister.

'As you know, we forestalled him by taking Isis and the baby back to Earth.'

'We had the right forms, did everything legally,' says Odysseus, 'so how could this happen?'

'They abducted her. I have no idea how. Once she was here no doubt Wolfe was able to wangle some sort of permission for Jessica and John Hutton to keep her. Whether real or fake I don't know.'

'We had the right papers,' Odysseus repeats.

I try to explain to Odysseus that some of the completes are not as honest as humanoids. 'Orlando Wolfe is one of the most corrupt politicians, but he has a lot of power in the Symposium. There's not much anyone can do to stop him.'

'I will stop him. He's not going to get away with this.'

'No he is not,' I agree. 'And Father and I are going to help you.'

I call Father and suggest that we invite Odysseus to Home-Court that evening to work out a strategy in the privacy of our home.

Note, we've changed the name, dropped the Jameson, and Father is now going along with my plan to be more open about our past. We haven't actually "come out" and announced our original status in public yet, but we've certainly stopped being over cautious about people knowing that we are sympathetic towards mutant humanoids.

Father sends me a reply suggesting I bring Odysseus to have to have supper with us.

Without Stella around, Father and I have taken to having our meals in the kitchen. We enjoy the informality of the new arrangement. This evening, Odysseus shares our snack of pasta and ice-cream and the three of us continue sitting round the kitchen table and brainstorm what we can to do to get Isis's baby back to her.

'Whatever is done must be done legally with the adoptive parents' consent,' Odysseus says. 'Without official sanction

Isis would never feel safe. She'd always be afraid the baby would be snatched back again.'

Father agrees. His plan is to make a moving speech in the Symposium, to expose Wolfe, bring all the facts of the case into the open and insist on an immediate vote. 'I'm sure I could persuade my colleagues to vote in favour of returning the child.'

Odysseus exchanges a look with me. We both know a speech, however articulate and impassioned, will not suffice.

'It's too risky,' I say. 'Suppose the Symposium votes against the motion. What then?

'We need to come up with a foolproof strategy, affirmed by lawyers,' Odysseus says. 'Now, tell me, Michael, how do you think Wolfe and his colleagues have justified their actions?'

'By saying that they don't think it fair to the child – a complete – to be brought up on Earth by mutants.'

'So – this Jessica and John Hutton – only want this child if she is a complete.' Odysseus looks thoughtful. 'If Penelope proved not to be a complete after all, you think they'd be willing to give her up?'

'I can't think of any completes who would willingly bring up a mutant humanoid,' says Father. 'Not at present.'

'But she is definitely a complete,' I burst out. 'The best doctors in Hos-sat examined her. Dr Carter, the obstetrician and Mr Spencer, the surgeon.'

'But suppose there was an oversight, that we could prove that a mistake was made….' Odysseus leans forward eagerly.

'Those doctors don't make mistakes,' I reply. 'But, hang on a minute….'

A sudden flash, a reminder of the conversation I had with Stella when she tried to persuade me to have a vasectomy. The one thing she was terrified of was that I would father a mutant. Isn't it likely that every complete would feel the same?

'But we could point out to the adoptive parents that, because the child's biological parents are mutants, there is the distinct possibility – let's say a probability – that, their adopted daughter could give birth to a mutant humanoid. If they understand that their grandchildren are likely to have mutations, that might be enough to make them have second thoughts about wanting to keep the child.'

'Brilliant, Michael,' says Odysseus. 'I think you've cracked it.'

Father gave me such a proud look that I felt the blood rush up my cheeks.

'We just need a signed document from a doctor to state that this is a probable outcome and – abracadabra – we're in business!' Odysseus mimes the waving of a magic wand.

An old proverb comes to mind. I am going "to hoist Stella with her own petard." She has been afraid I would father a mutant. Now she and Wolfe and his sister, the adoptive mother, will have a similar worry.

Father wastes no time contacting his lawyer, Mr Arnold, and our plan starts to become reality.

Journal Entry

A quick summary of what we did next.

The three of us, plus Mr Arnold, make another trip to Hos-sat and relate the situation and our proposed solution to Mr Spencer. He prepares a document explaining that future generations of Penelope will, in all probability have mutations. He signs it and Doctor Carter and the solicitor, countersign it.

I suggest that Father, Odysseus and I should accompany Mr Arnold when he presents the family with the document.

Mr Arnold disagrees. 'Not a good idea, Michael. Better to avoid a confrontation. I will arrange for the interested parties to come to my office and deal with the matter on my own. I assure you I will do my best to make certain of the right result.'

Mr Arnold makes an appointment for a day or two later. For us the wait seems never ending.

At last he summons us to his office and tells us what transpired.

He explained to the assembled family, including the parents and Orlando Wolfe, that when their adopted daughter grew up and had a baby herself, the likely outcome was that he or she would have mutations.

Wolfe said this was some sort of trick to get the baby back. Even when he perused the signed the documents he said he was far from satisfied and insisted on getting a second opinion from his own doctors and lawyers. This would entail another long waiting period while Wolfe procrastinated.

But the damage was already done. Doubt had been planted in the minds of the adoptive parents.

At first Jessica became hysterical and said she would not give up her baby. Her husband, John, horrified by the thought that some mutant genes lay dormant in the tiny body ready to emerge in a future generation, took a different view.

He asked his wife outright if she was really strong enough to face the consequences. 'Imagine how you would feel if our grandchild had three eyes or an extra arm.'

Once these images had been planted in her mind, Jessica became even more hysterical. Mr Arnold admitted it was quite distressing. Obviously the mother had bonded with the baby and couldn't bear to part with her, but John Hutton told Mr Arnold that his wife was very highly strung and had recently been suffering from growing paranoia about whether the baby was really a complete or not. She'd had horrendous nightmares in which the child developed "terrible abnormalities" as she grew older. Medically they were assured there was no basis for this supposition. But the nature of Jessica's fear meant that the latest news about the possibility of mutations appearing in the next generation was too much for her to handle.

No matter how often Orlando Wolfe said they should get a second opinion on the veracity of this medical prediction before making such a decision, the parents were adamant that they couldn't live with this uncertainty hanging over their heads. And as DNA technology was no longer available absolute proof of the existence of mutant genes was impossible to ascertain, just as it was when I was arrested.

Finally they said they couldn't keep the child and wished to sign the agreement to return the baby immediately.

Mr Arnold said Orlando Wolfe's face was a picture. Purple-faced with anger he stormed out of Mr Arnold's office.

Today the necessary papers and the baby are to be handed over to Odysseus to take back to Isis.

Before I get all weepy and sentimental, I'd just like to say, without being too bigheaded, that I am proud of what we achieved. My first piece of negotiation between Oasis and Earth has gone well.

All it took was a kind of think-tank of three, sitting round a kitchen table, to work out a viable plan. Odysseus knew we needed doctors and a lawyer to make it work and Father proved himself willing to put his career on the line to fight for what he believed was right. As for me, well, if Stella hadn't told me I mustn't father a child because it might be a mutant, I might never have come with the idea that proved the key to claiming Penelope back. Congratulations all round are in order, in my not so humble opinion.

An added bonus was that we defeated Orlando Wolfe.

Journal Entry

It is Father's suggestion that I go with Odysseus to return the baby to Isis. I can't believe my luck. I can't wait to see Isis's face when she sees Penelope again.

I'm so excited about my first trip to Earth since living on Oasis that I can hardly sleep. Excited and nervous. Why nervous?

Because I learn that Dionysus and Isis have moved out of C98 and are now in C55, the compound where I was brought up.

I am going to see Kali again, the only mother I've ever known. I can't wait to see her, but am afraid that she might not want to see me.

After all, I abandoned her, left Earth without telling her, without saying goodbye, and I haven't contacted her since. I have no idea if she will forgive me or not.

It's four years since I left Earth. I may not have grown much taller but I'm a different person now, physically a complete, but emotionally still part mutant humanoid.

I've experienced things Kali couldn't begin to imagine. It was out of loyalty to my father that I have never contacted Kali. Now, with my father's blessing, we are to meet once more. I've no idea what sort of greeting to expect.

Journal Entry

It is Jaga, not Kali, who greets us as we step out of the transporter. My heart beats fast against my chest. Could it be that Kali doesn't intend to see me?

Odysseus, with Penelope cradled in his arms, looks as if he will never stop smiling. We walk at Jaga's side through the compu-centre, but there are only one or two humanoids sitting at the workstations. No Kali. I wonder where she is. Jaga leads us outdoors to what was the wilderness.

A profusion of colour assails us. Fields of golden wheat,

orchards full of oranges, lemons and red and green apples, and a little village with whitewashed cottages surrounded by banks of brightly coloured flowers. The members of C55 are working in the fields.

Jaga guides us to one of the cottages and knocks on the door. Isis opens it.

As soon as she sees Penelope she gives a little cry. Her eyes fill with tears as Odysseus transfers the baby with great care from his arms to hers.

I too feel tears threatening to appear I'm so moved to see them together again.

Osiris hovers in the background. Isis walks up and down rocking Penelope, unable to take her eyes off the little bundle in her arms. Odysseus continues to beam with pleasure.

I turn away trying to control my tears. I'd no idea this reunion of mother and child would affect me so much. I suppose my emotions are all mixed up with the disappointment of Kali not being there to greet me.

Isis looks up from the baby at last and sees me the first time. 'Mercury! You're here too. Thank you, thank you so much for all you've done to get my baby back.'

'Not just me,' I mumble. 'We had a kind of think-tank of three, Odysseus, my father and I worked out a plan together.'

'A think-tank? What's that?' she giggles, but doesn't wait for an answer. She doesn't want to know how we found her baby. Not yet anyway. She's just glad to have her back. That's all that matters.

A little later she does say, 'Your father? I didn't know you had a father, Merc.'

And I realise that I have so much to tell her but that this isn't the moment. This is Penelope's moment, the time for mother and baby to bond again.

'I've missed you so much, little Penny,' she says, planting a kiss on her forehead.

'Do you think she looks a bit pale?' she asks, but we assure her she doesn't. 'We'll soon put roses in your cheeks. No more stuffy old compounds for you. Not like it was when we were kids eh Merc, sitting at boring old compus inside all day. Here, she can grow up in the fresh air.' She cups the baby's tiny foot in her hand. 'Just look at that. Have you ever seen anything so small, so perfect?'

She chatters on, concedes that Penny does look healthy and well-cared for, that she's grown a bit too, but otherwise is just the same as before, just as beautiful as ever.

Eventually she runs out of steam and asks me what I think of the cottage. I look round. I find myself thinking how small and basic it is, but of course Isis hasn't any knowledge of anything different.

'It was a bit bare,' Isis says, 'but I've prettified it. Ody sent me the bits and pieces I asked for. Red and gold, my colours.'

'You've always had an artistic touch,' I tell her. Compared with Stella's flair for home decoration, Isis's efforts lack sophistication. 'It looks great,' I add to cover my unkind thoughts. 'Totally awesome.'

She laughs, delighted with my response. 'Mercury doesn't really understand such things,' she tells Osiris. 'He's always on those old compus learning useless facts. He knows nothing about making a nice home. And Ody is just as bad. He lives in the past but it's the future that's important.'

Odysseus doesn't argue with her, doesn't attempt to explain as he normally would that the future is dependent on our knowledge of the past.

It is, after all, Isis's day. Today we allow her to get away with any provocative remarks she cares to make.

Jaga and I leave Odysseus with his little family and stroll back to the compound together.

She tells me about C55's contribution to The Big Event. 'Our workforce can't compete with the physical antics to be put on by the golden warriors or the theatrical performances from Compound Creative, but we are to be in charge of the floral and wheat displays around the balconies where Athene and the visitors are to sit.'

'I'm sure it will be spectacular,' I tell her.

'All home grown,' she says.

Kali is standing in the doorway of C55 as we approach.

When Jaga catches sight of her, she says, 'I'll leave you to it,' and steps out towards the fields to supervise the workforce.

Kali is staring at me, her black eyes shining out of her lovely, familiar blue-black face. Hugo peeps out from her neck and hisses. He uncoils his body like a concertina, withdraws, spins out again and peers at me, button-eyes gleaming, tongue flicking. At her wrists Henry and Henrietta, Hugh and Hannah, peep out too, unwind their slippery bodies and flip out their lethal tongues.

'It's all right, boys. Calm down,' said Kali. 'It's our little Mercury.'

And she opens her arms wide and I run into them, put my arms round her and press my bony body against her solid one. That warm, comforting Kali smell reminds me of the times I used to creep into her bed after a nightmare. Hugo licks my face, slithers round my neck, shoulders and back and the other snakes lick my arms with sticky, rough tongues, acknowledging that their old mate, Mercury, has returned.

Time for another weep. What's the matter with me today? All this emotion is so unlike me.

'I'm so sorry,' I sob. 'So sorry I rushed off without saying goodbye. And sorry I haven't been in touch since.'

I give no reasons, no excuses, for my neglect. I long for

her unconditional forgiveness. It seems that is what she is giving me. She rests her cheek against mine and strokes my hair.

She runs her hands over the top of my back but can't find the stumps of my wings. She frowns, pushes me away and holds me by the shoulders at arm's length and scrutinizes me. 'Let me look at you. No wings? No sticking-out ears? Are you really Mercury?'

'I really am,' I tell her, tears flowing freely now.

'I'm still Mercury but I'm also Michael Court. It's a long story.'

'It must be. Four years long. Come in and tell me exactly what has happened to you.'

That is exactly what I do.

We sit on a double shaper together in the empty RR. I try to make my description of Oasis light-hearted. I make her laugh when I describe the rain that falls down like transparent liquid metal and cuts into your skin if you don't make it to the shelter in time.

I can see how pleased she is when I tell her that I still sit at a "compu" but now it's at the University of Oasis.

But I make sure that she doesn't think everything is perfect in my life. I wouldn't want her to think I haven't missed her.

In her turn, she tells me how she came back here, to C55, as Chief Administrator and how difficult it has been to settle in again and get respect back from her old colleagues.

We smooth over how upset we were with each other just before I left Earth. We leave the serious stuff for later.

'Let me show you round C55 now,' she says and, with a hop, skip and jump, she leaps across the RR, through the sliding doors, intent on showing me the changes.

The innovations – the RR itself, the gym, the games rooms and the hos-unit that she's so proud of – are, in my opinion, poorly designed and equipped, but then I'm used to the high standards of Hos-sat and Planet Oasis. The entire dome is very cold and bleak, claustrophobic with no windows. How depressing to have to live in a building like this. I can scarcely breathe.

I can't help comparing everything with the light and airy buildings on Oasis, but I have to pretend to be impressed. For Kali's sake. She shows me the dormo-cube where I'm to sleep tonight. It's small and airless. I'm sure I won't be able to sleep there.

We pass very few humanoids as we do the tour of the compound. She seems quite proud that they are working hard outside. 'We are growing things for The Big Event at the moment.'

I gather that she and Jaga are getting on well together, working towards the same goal, until Kali says, 'Jaga envisaged a kind of harvest festival service with religious music and songs, but it just wasn't practical. Too ambitious. Keep it simple, I told her. "We don't want a fiasco on our hands.'

She tells me that the females are to carry bunches of flowers or baskets of fruit and the males, bundles of wheat and put them, under Jaga's supervision, in the designated places before the ceremony begins.

'Jaga wanted this to take place in public once the audience were seated with some sort of music so that the workforce could keep in step. To make a kind of show of it.' She raises her three sets of eyebrows. 'Did you ever hear of anything so stupid, Mercury? Can you imagine this lot keeping in step? I had to say no to that. I can't have the members of C55 making fools of themselves in public.'

I smile to myself. Kali hasn't changed.

'We are doing something else at The Big Event. A surprise item.'

'What is it?'

'It won't be a surprise if I tell you, will it?' she grins. 'Besides, it's early days yet. We haven't rehearsed it and others are involved, so it might not come off.'

Everything seems to building up to The Big Event. Athene is determined for it to be a showcase for the talents of mutant humanoids.

Father has received an invitation to attend and I'm to go with him. Another opportunity to see Kali.

Kali asks what I think of the cottage where Isis lives.

'Really cute,' I tell her. 'Are you thinking of living in a cottage yourself?'

'Not me,' she says. I prefer to stay in the compound where I've always been. I can keep control of the compu-centre better if I'm on the spot. Keep an eye on the targets.'

I'm right. She hasn't changed. She's still on about those damned targets!

'Well, Mercury, I suppose we'd better go and join the admirers of baby Penelope. I mean, as leader of the sectoid I must show my face.'

'Aren't you fond of babies?'

'I'm glad the child is back of course, but there was only ever one child I was interested in and even he was a bloody nuisance at times.' She grins at me.

'A nuisance? I thought I was perfect.'

'In your dreams.'

We laugh and I think how good it is to be with Kali again, to tease each other and enjoy each other's company.

Isis has put Penelope down in her little bunku-cot. She's fast asleep. 'Come and look at her, Kali,' she says. 'Isn't she just beautiful?'

I'm pleased to say that Kali plays the game and bends over the bunku-cot to look at her. 'Just beautiful,' she agrees.

'See what long eyelashes she has,' whispers Isis. 'Her

eyes are flickering a bit, but no, she's not waking up. Just dreaming. I hope they're pleasant dreams. I wouldn't want her having the sort of dreams her poor father has.'

'All children dream,' says Kali. 'Mercury did. He had terrible nightmares, but he got over it. And I'm sure little Penelope will too.'

Isis fetches drinks for everyone and she and Dionysus pass them round. I notice that his hand shakes. Poor humanoid. He's been traumatized by the time he spent on show in Museum Oasis.

I'd like to tell him that I saw him and the other warriors there and understand how demoralised he must feel. But I can't. It's not the sort of thing to say in public and I have no opportunity to talk to him alone.

To my surprise, Kali raises her glass and says, 'You've all seen old filmograms on your compus so will know that a toast is a drink to wish good health and success to someone. It's also a celebration of success. We certainly have something to celebrate today – the return of Penelope to her rightful mother. We drink to her future health and happiness.'

We raise our glasses and take a sip of whatever it is Isis has given us. Some sort of wine, I think, but I'm not sure. If we were on Oasis it would be champagne.

'To Penelope!' we all say in unison. 'To her health and happiness.'

'Shush!' says Isis. 'Not too loud. You'll wake her up.'

'Nonsense!' says Kali. 'You shouldn't go tiptoeing around babies and talking in hushed voices. They have to get used to noise.'

'Like I had to get used to you snoring when I was a child,' I tell Kali. Hugo sticks his tongue at me for being rude to his mistress.

Isis decides it's her turn to hold court. 'Thanks, Kali, for the toast to little Penny. One day when she can talk I hope she'll thank you herself. I still can't believe she's here. I have to say she's been looked after well. Thank her adoptive parents for me, Mercury. I understand you know them. They must be devastated to have had to give her up but quite honestly I can't feel too sorry for them. They shouldn't have taken her in the first place. She doesn't belong to them. Anyway, she's back with her real Mummy and Daddy now. And it's great to have Ody here, her totally amazing grandfather. And Mercury too of course.'

'That was a nice touch, Kali, to think of having a toast,' says Odysseus, sliding across to her side.

'Oh I haven't finished yet,' Kali informs him. 'I have more to say, more to celebrate.' She raises her voice to speak to us all.

'Everyone in this room has different talents. Isis, I'm sure, with a bit of practice you will be a good mother and homemaker, in spite of being a bit of an airhead.'

We all smile and Isis gives a nervous giggle.

Kali continues. 'I want you to know, Isis, that you and your family are welcome here in my sectoid. As for Odysseus, we all know how clever he is and how well he has done in his career: Curator of Museum Earth, Chief Chronicler and Chief Consultant to Athene. Not bad eh? But never forget he started here in the histo-lab in this compound, C55. We are all rightly proud of his success. We should drink to Odysseus and wish him all the best for the future.'

'To Odysseus.'

We all take another swig of the strange tasting liquid.

'As for little Mercury, remember he started here too. He sat at a compu at four years old, taught himself how to use it and learnt everything he could. And now he is at the University of Oasis, doing very well indeed and planning to be a big man in the Parliament there. I know he'll make it. We're all proud of you, my son. To Mercury!'

They raise their glasses to me. 'To Mercury!'

I'd like to say thank you to Kali but I can't utter a word. I have a lump in my throat as big as a golf ball.

I'm ashamed of myself for my critical thoughts about the compound and the cottage. I'll have to watch out that living on Oasis doesn't make me consider myself superior to my old friends. All I can think of at the moment is that Kali called me her son and that she's proud of me. That makes me feel worth a million dollars.

'Are you back here for good now Mercury?' Isis asks.

Before I can answer, Kali says. 'He certainly is not. He's got to finish his university studies. But he isn't leaving here until tomorrow. He's staying the night in the compound.'

I need not have worried about not being able to sleep in the small dormo-cube. Kali and I don't go to bed – or bunku. We stay up all night talking. There are things we both need to say, to apologise for, but we don't dwell on them.

We talk about the future. The one thing we are agreed on is that we will not lose touch again. Her precious pets confirm our promise. They cling to my neck, arms and wrists as if they will never let me go.

Chapter Twenty-one: The Big Event

Extract from the Chronicles of Planet Earth: according to Michael Court

Athene had planned The Big Event carefully. The stadium looked superb, its layers of raked seating arranged so that everyone had a good view of the circular arena. The colourful arrangement of flowers, greenery and wheat placed round the podium where Athene was to sit was a credit to Jaga, Kali and C55. The buzz of anticipation among the spectators marked the importance of the occasion.

Odysseus had told me that, after much discussion, he and Athene had come to the conclusion that completes and mutant humanoids were to be offered seats in separate stands. Segregation was a concept neither of them favoured but neither did they believe that members of Oasis and Earth should be forced to sit side by side. There were, therefore, designated seating areas. But if some members of the audience decided to mingle there was nothing and no one to stop them. No barriers. No police. A good compromise.

Father and I had only just taken our seats in the section assigned to completes when an incredible thing happened. A figure leapt over the barrier, hopped over the benches and strode out towards us. I couldn't mistake that signature movement. Kali had arrived in typical style. She threw her arms around me and her snakes flicked out their tongues and hissed, delighted to see me again.

How brave she was to jump those barriers, both real and symbolic, determined to watch the performance with me.

I sat with my father on one side and Kali, my mother, on the other. Amazing. I was so proud of her.

And proud of my father too for understanding how important she is to me.

This was the first time Kali and Father had met. Father was charming, Kali warm and chatty. We took no notice of any odd looks from completes around us, but sat there together as a family unit. What a break-through.

My eyes skimmed the stadium. The benches and seats that rose up around the arena were full. Among the completes I recognised several members of the Symposium, representatives of various businesses connected to the Arts and curators from Museum Oasis.

I was shocked to see Orlando Wolfe and Stella Jameson arrive together. As a member of the Symposium he was entitled to attend, as was Stella as owner and director of Worldwideculture; but it was far from tactful or kind of them to come as a couple.

I glanced at Father and noted the muscles in his face and neck tense as he caught sight of them. He soon recovered, at least outwardly, and continued to listen to Kali as she told us that Isis was at home with the baby. Dionysus, unable to face the ordeal of watching his ex-colleagues, the golden warriors, perform, was with them.

A trumpet. Athene, with Odysseus on one side of her and Heracles on the other, moved swiftly on to the podium. The spectators rose as one and applauded.

Athene, resplendent in a white robe that fell in elegant knife pleats to the ground, couldn't stop smiling. The gown was voluminous but failed to hide the fact that Athene was pregnant, a surprise to most of us. There were gasps, exchanged looks and a ripple of animated whispers.

Athene went on smiling, serene, confident. Heracles held his head high, a possessive hand on her elbow and grinned broadly. Who could doubt he was the father? Athene, Odysseus and Heracles settled themselves on the shapers on the dais.

Like the Roman Emperors and their entourage at the Coliseum, they were placed so that they could be seen.

The air of excitement spread through the spectators. Like the Romans, we were all waiting to be entertained. We were not going to see gladiators fight to the death or Christians thrown to the lions.

Our world might not be perfect but we no longer considered it amusing to watch others suffer. I found myself thinking with a certain satisfaction that we had learnt something after all these years.

The lights dimmed. Music rose to a climax.

The show was about to begin. And what a show it was. In spite of what happened at the end, we must remember that.

The blare of a bugle. Durga enters in her chariot, red hair flowing like a lion's mane out of her golden bull-helmet, a magical hybrid creature, holding the reins high urging the golden calves to go faster. We can almost believe they are real, as if they, not a motorised engine, are causing the chariot to whiz round the arena in that cloud of dust. Durga pulls up short and faces the entrance.

Drums increase in volume to herald the appearance of a phalanx of red and gold warriors, marching, dividing and coming together, always in straight lines, always in step, faces looking straight ahead, impassive, emotionless. Shining animal helmets – tigers, lions, panthers – glint in the sun. The warriors halt and stand as rigid as toy soldiers. Durga encircles them, inspecting her troops. The drumming increases. Trumpets sound.

Displays of fencing, marching, shooting and other training exercises follow, all impressive for their meticulous timing. Durga and the warriors leave the arena to thunderous applause.

A terrifying crescendo of strident brass and timpani as a giant screen unfurls, filled by a blood red sky. Out of the fog rises a tall cylIndracal building. A caption appears: THE HERACLES TOWER.

The sky turns from red to orange, to magenta, to green to violet. A camera encircles the tower, revealing its height, its solidity and the prosthesis that caps it. There's no mistaking its intention. It's a symbol of virility, of masculinity, of power.

The screen clouds over. A dark city looms out of the haze. Another caption emerges: EARTH CITY.

Tall black skyscrapers, silhouetted against the purple smoke-laden horizon. An electronic shriek, rotating amber searchlights, dazzling street signs, the revving up of engines, screeching brakes, gunshots, screams of terror. The camera pans out to show The Heracles Tower dominating the city. Blackout.

That's it. A short, sharp, powerful film, designed to shock and awe. It's greeted by a stunned silence, followed by a half-hearted attempt to applaud.

I wonder how Heracles has got away with this exhibition of power? Didn't Athene vet the film before it was shown?

I look over at her, but she's smiling up at Heracles, amused, as if this display of his power is a joke.

I'm not amused. I find myself wondering if the human

race is about to make the same mistakes again. Heracles is power-crazy and the tower and the city are demonstrations, not only of his present power, but also of his aspirations for the future. It warns me that if I am to liase between Oasis and Earth in the future, it is Heracles I may have to contend with.

The dark city fades and is replaced by whirling colours on the screen to match the swirling movements of dancers in the arena, images full of light and colour accompanied by mystical music. A piece of magic from the dancers of Compound Creative.

Two Shakespearean death scenes follow, both unnecessary deaths, triggered by misunderstandings.

Firstly, the suicides of the doomed lovers, Romeo and Juliet, in the marble vault, depicted in monochrome, black and white, as a kind of live film noir. Heart-breaking. Not a dry eye in the house, as they used to say.

Secondly, *Othello*. As directed by Kata-Mbula, becomes a truly frightening piece. My heart pounds against my chest throughout the scene. Othello's anguish in his belief that Desdemona has been unfaithful to him shatters him and us. Our pity for his innocent victim is absolute but also for this misguided, vulnerable man.

In contrast, we laugh at the lovers in *A Midsummer Night's Dream*, at Puck's mixing of the potions and the couples professing love to the wrong partner. All is resolved happily to our relief.

Warmed up by this gentle comedy we are ready to ache with laughter at another dance, a pastiche of the dying swans in *Swan Lake*. As they expire, they shed their feathers all over the arena. Like all the best comedy, it's hilarious and sad.

The mess of feathers take some clearing up. But even

that becomes an act in itself as the dancer/cleaners, sporting headscarves and aprons, trip each other up, swing their brooms and dustpans round horizontally, knock each other down and tip over each other's buckets of feathers to sabotage the others' efforts. Slapstick humour straight from Edwardian pantomime.

Kali whispers in my ear. 'Save my seat. Surprise, surprise, remember?' And hop, skip, jump and she is striding away and leaping over the barrier. She's off backstage to prepare for the promised surprise item.

That's why she misses the final act from Compound Creative, an astounding solo from Kata-Mbula himself.

Who would have thought that such a big man could step and leap so lightly and execute such acrobatic spins and somersaults? He's the master of illusion. A bird on giant wings soars through the air, a flickering silver fish weaves through glittering water, a tiger ever ready to pounce prowls through the jungle. Kat's body, flexible, athletic, supple, is transformed again and again, from fish to fowl, from lizard to leopard, from male to female, as he tells stories through his own physicality that are both disconcerting and moving. Finally, he collapses concertina fashion in a heap on the floor. The lights snap off.

When they come up again the amorphous mass of darkness remains on the ground. Silence. We hold our communal breath. The mound begins to shift and slowly, very slowly unrolls to reveal the silhouette of a two-headed giant with legs astride and arms held high, fists clenched. A beat. Another moment of stunned silence, followed by a roar of applause as Kata-Mbula takes a deep bow, turns and slowly walks out of the spotlight.

What timing. What theatricality! We have never seen anything like this before. For a while no one can speak.

Then a mighty shout of appreciation is taken up, calling for his return. Are we going to be disappointed?

No, there is to be a grand finale and on come all the performers to enact a short reprise and take their bows. The dancers twirl, Romeo, Juliet, Desdemona and a bedraggled swan die, the lovers in the forest are reunited and Kata-Mbula is transformed into a silver fish once more. He receives the biggest cheer, not just for his acting and his dancing but also for his direction.

But all is not over. Surprise, surprise!

A bugle sounds and on comes Durga in her chariot, red hair streaming from under her bull-helmet. Two triumphant circuits of the arena and she halts at the far side, directly opposite Athene and the platform party.

Another burst of sound on the bugle and a second chariot enters, driven by Jaga, straw-coloured hair flying from beneath a black helmet in the shape of a horse. She too circles the arena and pulls up next to Durga.

Where there are two, the other two sister-wives of Shiva must surely follow.

In comes Kali in her chariot, standing proudly, dreadlocks swinging round her blue-black face under a cobra helmet. She makes an impressive figure as she finishes her circuit of the arena and rests her chariot next to Jaga's.

Everyone focuses on the entrance again and in comes the last of the sister-wives, Sati. Two fierce tigers snarl from her helmets. She holds her heads high, the sun catching her blond curls and the long glossy sheaf of her dark hair. She leans back and we can see that Sati, like Athene, is pregnant. She halts next to Kali and all four sister-wives of Shiva smile.

I imagine rehearsing this has not been all smiles. For Durga to persuade the others to join her for this spectacle cannot have been easy. Although who would not be tempted by a ride in one of those chariots? I imagine the arguments and jockeying for power that must have gone on during rehearsals. No doubt I shall hear the details later from Kali.

It's the turn of the warriors to march on again, glorious in their uniforms of red and gold, their animal helmets, shields and swords gleaming. They line up next to the four chariots.

The arena is full now, full of dancers, actors, warriors and the four warrior queens in their chariots.

That was it. That was The Big Event. I hope I've done it justice. It's not easy to describe visual representations in words, but I've done my best.

Suffice it to say that we were all, completes and humanoids alike, on our feet, clapping and cheering as if we would never stop. The Big Event was indeed a triumph. Until....

Athene stood up and moved to the edge of the dais. The applause increased. Father and I were on our feet like everyone else, applauding. Odysseus and Heracles remained slightly upstage of Athene. This was Athene's moment. She had pulled off the impossible and was receiving a well-deserved accolade.

As if in ironic reply to the general euphoria, over the noise of the crowd, came a sharp, short shock. A bang. A gunshot.

Screams from the crowd. Panic. Pandemonium. Those in the stands and in the arena, sensing danger, started scrambling over seats and over each other, desperate to escape.

For a moment I was unsure what had happened. I saw Odysseus move forward. Before he could reach Athene, her body had slipped to the floor. Her white gown with its knife pleats lay around her, spread out, like a fan, with what looked like red paint splattered over it. Not paint. Blood. She lay on the podium, her head to one side. A hole in the middle of her forehead oozed dark liquid that streamed down her cheek and neck. Her one eye had become a useful target for the assassin to shoot accurately. There was no chance she was still alive.

Odysseus was kneeling by Athene's body. Heracles had disappeared from the dais. Maybe he thought there were more shots to come and he might be the next casualty.

Or maybe he had orchestrated the shooting. I thought of the images of the looming city and the tower, blatant images of power. Was it possible that this was a coup, a bid for power?

Or was it ambitious Durga who sought a takeover? As far as I knew the only humanoids with guns were Durga and the warriors. Had she secreted a gun in her chariot to produce at the opportune moment? The shot had certainly come from that side of the arena where the chariots stood.

Maybe Durga had planned this show of strength with her three sister-wives and the warriors at her side. Flushed with her recent coup at C98 where she'd ousted Jaga she might have thought another attack would be just as successful. If so, I was sure she was acting without the knowledge of her sister-wives. Kali would certainly not have colluded with such a plan.

My mind was in a spin.

I looked towards the far side of the arena, opposite the dais. Who else could have done it? My original suspicion returns. Someone acting on orders from Heracles.

His loyal right hand man. Thor.

Extract from the Chronicles of Planet Earth: according to Odysseus

I lowered myself to a kneeling position and looked at the inert body. I couldn't believe what had happened, couldn't believe that our popular leader, the beautiful, clever Athene, was no more.

A hand touched my elbow.

'Come, Odysseus, come inside.'

I didn't recognise the voice immediately. It was some time since I'd heard it. But there was something about its calm authority that made me obey. I started to get up but felt shaky. The hand on my elbow steadied me, helped me to my feet. I looked up, my eye blurred by tears. A miasma of blue and gold. Stella Jameson.

'Come, Odysseus. We have a lot to arrange, you and I.'

She supported me to a bench in the mini-museum that I'd set up for the spectators to view in the covered part of the stadium.

Looking down on us were the special pieces I'd selected to provide a visual overview of the centuries, set out in a manner that was aesthetically pleasing. I'd planned it as something for the audience to view after the performance. No chance of any visitors seeing it now.

Stella told me what had already been done. Durga and her warriors were in pursuit of the assassin.

'They will succeed in catching him. There is no doubt about that. Once he's caught, we must set up an official enquiry. There may be more than one person involved in this. I'd like to chair that enquiry – if you don't mind.'

I was confused. Why should my opinion matter to her? And why should Durga be trusted to go after the culprit? Wouldn't she be a suspect herself?

Stella was still speaking. 'Normally I don't interfere in Earthly matters as you know, but in the circumstances….' Stella opened her hands and shrugged her shoulders.

The shiny gold epaulettes and cuffs stood out against the deep blue of her jacket.

'We need to make a list of people, completes and humanoids, who we think would be the right team to look into this dreadful business.'

She mentioned several names and looked at me for approval.

I agreed to them all with a nod. I couldn't think straight, couldn't speak.

I kept hearing the shot over and over again. I saw that white robe splashed with Athene's blood and her face, rigid, lifeless, a hole where her eye should have been.

Stella paused, aware I was not really with her.

'You poor man,' she said. 'You're in shock. It's not surprising. You can leave the list to me if you like. No problem. I assume you're willing to be on the enquiry panel?'

I nodded yet again, a wooden puppet.

She closed the tablet where she'd been making notes and stood up. I thought she was about to leave, but she turned round and said, 'There is one more thing. I know it's awfully soon, but I have to do this.'

She took a deep breath, looked me straight in my one eye, and said, 'Odysseus, I would like to offer you the position of CEO of Worldwideculture, starting immediately.'

I stared at her, not able to believe what she was saying.

'Please say you will do it. There is no one else I can trust. I know it's too soon for you to think about this, but for the sake of a smooth transition, we must have a new leader at once.'

I went on staring at her.

'I know you're in grief. We all are. But remember how much Athene relied on you. She thought so highly of you, Odysseus. She made you her Chief Consultant. This is what she would have wanted. For you to continue her work.'

That's when I realised that there was no way I could refuse her request. I had to take on the burden of leadership. As Stella rightly said, it is what Athene would have wanted.

Chapter Twenty-two
Aftermath

Extract from the official enquiry investigating the death of Athene the CEO of Worldwideculture, chaired by Stella Jameson.

Statement from Heracles:
As soon as I heard the shot and saw Athene fall I suspected the identity of the assassin. That's why I left the podium so abruptly, intending to look for him, hoping my fears were unjustified. By the time I arrived at the other side of the stadium, where the shot had come from, he had fled and Durga's warriors were in pursuit. Congratulations to them for a speedy arrest.

Why did I suspect Thor? Because I knew how his mind worked. He was always thinking about what would be best for me. He thought too much, actually. I told him time and time again to follow orders, not to act on his own initiative. But he's always been impulsive.

You ask me to explain how Thor could have acquired the murder weapon. I've thought a lot about this. I remember that he accompanied me the day I visited C98. I went inside the compound to visit Isis and her baby. Durga can vouch for that. Thor stayed outside watching the warriors training. That's when he must have discovered the weapon store and decided to steal a rifle, but I swear I knew nothing about it. All this is mere supposition on my part.

You also asked me if I had any prior knowledge of Thor's plan to shoot Athene. I wish to state categorically that I did not.

I do remember Thor saying that if The Big Event were successful it would consolidate Athene's position as CEO and that something should be done about that. I thought no more about it at the time, never dreaming what he was planning to do.

It is difficult for me to come to terms with he's done, to admit that Thor was responsible for this dreadful deed. The frightening thing is that he would honestly have believed he was doing it for my sake.

He'd always thought I would make a better leader than Athene and had not hesitated to tell me so. He continually urged me to take control. I thought he was crazy to suggest such a thing. Sure, some of Athene's ideas and methods differed from mine. There were times when I was openly critical of her decisions but I'd never contemplated a takeover.

I had certainly never contemplated murdering anyone. Let alone Athene, who was not only our leader but was also expecting my child.

You ask me about the filmogram shown at The Big Event and the show of power it denoted. I can only say in my defence that it was a joke. One in bad taste, perhaps, but Athene had sanctioned its inclusion in the show. She appreciated its irony.

I would like to add one point. Up to that time Thor had proved a loyal friend and assistant to me. How he could have believed that I would condone such an act as this I do not know, but I have no doubt that he did this terrible thing because he believed he was helping me. I repeat that this was far from the truth, but his intentions were based on his loyalty to me.

For this reason I ask you to judge him with a degree of leniency that the seriousness of such a crime wouldn't normally warrant.

Once more I wish to assure every member of this enquiry that I had no prior knowledge of this plot to shoot Athene and am as shocked and dismayed by what happened as everyone else.

Result of the official enquiry into the death of Athene: summarised by Stella Jameson:

The enquiry finds Thor guilty of the assassination of Athene. After interviewing several other persons suspected of being involved in the murder plot, we find there is not enough evidence to prove complicity.

We confirm that the murder weapon has been recovered and returned to C98. In future the weapon stores are to be kept locked.

Thanks must go to Durga for detailing her warriors to capture Thor and for keeping him in custody for the duration of this enquiry.

The members of this enquiry wish it to be known that our objective is to reform rather than punish. In view of this it has been unanimously agreed that, as Heracles appears to understand the workings of Thor's mind, he should be responsible for this reformation.

We deem it right therefore that, until further notice, the prisoner should be confined to house arrest in The Heracles Tower under the close supervision of Heracles. This ruling will be reviewed regularly.

I would like to thank my colleagues on the panel for their contributions to this enquiry.

Extract from the inaugural speech of our new CEO: Odysseus.

As is her right, Stella Jameson has appointed a new CEO of Worldwideculture. She made her decision swiftly to make sure that life would go on smoothly on Planet Earth after Athene's sudden death. I promise I will do my best to fulfil both Stella's and Athene's faith in me.

My first task is to express my personal sorrow for the loss of our beloved CEO, Athene, who was as wise as she was beautiful. It will be difficult for us to get through the next few weeks as we mourn this exceptional humanoid. Athene will be given a state funeral followed by a month's official mourning. I suggest you use this time to reflect on her qualities and consider what we can learn from them. Let's try to take away something positive from this tragedy.

As is my wont I would like to refer you to history, to assure you that it is normal after a tragedy such as this for those left behind to be in a state of shock. After the assassination of President Kennedy in 1964, a report from Washington declared: 'There is horror, there is bewilderment, there is confusion, and there is that drawing together that comes after a catastrophe.'

It is natural for us too, to experience horror, disbelief and confusion and turn to each for support.

Now for a piece of good news: As most of you are aware, Athene was expecting a child. It was at the suggestion of Michael Court that her body was removed to Hos-sat in the hope that the baby could be saved. I am pleased to report that the wonderful medical team there have achieved this miracle. We now have a new life to celebrate. Athene's spirit will live on in this child. Please do not ask if the child is a complete or a mutant. It is not something that should concern us. When Michael and I went to Hos-sat to see her, we found that she has very healthy lungs and a voice that cries out to be heard. She promises to be just as determined as her mother.

It was Athene's wish that The Big Event should be imprinted on our communal memory as a celebration of our progress, resilience and talent. Of course our memory of that day will be forever overshadowed by the tragedy of her death. But we mustn't forget the effect of the performances we witnessed at The Big Event. They demonstrated our creativity, our power. We may have been locked up in windowless domes for two hundred years but who can now have reservations about our abilities as members of the human race? Let's remember The Big Event as a celebration as well as a tragedy, just as Athene intended.

One more thought I'd like to leave with you. The Big Event was shared by completes and humanoids alike. Let's have more shared events such as this in the future.

Kali, a mutant humanoid, showed us the way. She leapt into the stand reserved for completes in order to sit with her son, now a complete. Let's all take similar leaps whenever we can. Think positively, be strong and journey into the future with optimism.

To be your leader was not something I looked for and certainly not in these circumstances. To quote Lyndon Baines Johnson who became President of the United States by default after Kennedy's assassination, 'I will do my best. This is all I can do. I ask for your help and God's.' I endorse those sentiments and promise to do my best to be the leader you deserve.

Auto-mail: from Bathsheba

Dear Odysseus,

What a terrible shock for us all to have to witness the tragedy that ended The Big Event. Everyone in Compound

Creative admired Athene and respected her. She often visited us and took a personal interest in our creative work. A lovely, sensitive and wise humanoid. We shall miss her.

As this tragedy occurred at the end of The Big Event, you and I had no chance to meet as planned. I hope that can be rectified soon with a visit to Compound Creative where you can be sure of a warm welcome.

I'd like to congratulate you on your new role as CEO of Worldwideculture. However, in the unlikely event that I had been the one to select our new leader, I would certainly not have chosen you!

My choice would of course have been my beloved Kata-Mbula. He assures me that to be CEO of Worldwideculture is not a position he has ever coveted. But when I think of all those months he stayed in C99 designing the stadium and being Athene's number one adviser on all kinds of matters, I cannot understand why Stella Jameson did not at least consider him as leader.

Kata-Mbula would be perfect for the job. He's clever, creative, sensitive and loved by everyone who knows him. I could go on forever extolling his virtues. Look how he inspires all of us in Compound Creative. Just imagine what good work he could do if that creativity were extended to the other sectoids.

I concede that your inaugural speech was well thought out and sensible, a good mix of sadness and optimism. It was academic too – perhaps too much so – with its references to parallel events in history. But let me ask you one question. Was it inspiring? I'll answer that. Not in the least. You haven't got what I would call "the common touch." Your words won't touch the heart of the populace. It seems to me that Stella made the appointment too quickly, without giving a thought to Kata-Mbula's superior abilities.

I'm sorry to sound a bit disgruntled. Put it down to the

menopause if you like. All these fecund females around me are making me grumpy.

Odysseus, please ignore what I've said. I've been rude to you without cause. Come and visit us soon, meet, not just me, but Kata-Mbula himself. I'm sure you and he have much to learn from each other. You could make him your adviser, your partner even. Don't dismiss the idea out of hand. Explore the possibilities. Come and meet him, get to know him.

If nothing else I am sure you will make a new friend.

Please don't be offended by this letter. It's just my way to write what I feel.

Do come and see us soon.

Please be assured that I do wish you well.
Best Regards
Bathsheba

Comment from Odysseus on receiving the above auto-mail from Bathsheba

I have to admit that of all the missives I received after becoming CEO, most of them congratulating me, this one moved me the most. To gentle laughter. And to tears. Bathsheba, although not the most tactful humanoid on Earth, certainly has a gift for expressing what she thinks and feels.

I will write to Bathsheba, tell her I am far from offended by her communication, but, on the contrary, admire her loyalty to Kata-Mbula and look forward to meeting him and her. I will make my visit to Compound Creative a priority.

An amusing thought occurs to me just before I go to my bunku. Bathsheba is as loyal a friend to Kata-Mbula as Thor to Heracles. I do hope she doesn't let her ambition for him get the better of her and attempt to murder me. I'll have to watch out that she doesn't pop some poison in my food or drink during my proposed visit.

As I endeavour to drop off to sleep, tossing and turning from one side to the other, throwing the bunku covers on and off, that thought seems considerably less amusing than it did before.

Extract from The Chronicles of Planet Earth: Out of the Closet by Michael Court

Father and I considered that Kali's leap over the barrier to join us in the stand for completes at The Big Event was a sign that we should follow her courageous example and go public about the secret of our past.

We were both nervous about exposing our personal lives to the press but knew we must do it before someone less scrupulous fabricated a distorted version of our origins.

We published our story on the Oasis News Site, outlining the simple facts of our lives.

The article was accompanied by one photograph of the two of us together. Our account and photograph went viral.

As expected, we did receive a number of negative reactions, both written and spoken, and our home was vandalized on more than one occasion. We repaired the broken windows and defaced walls without comment. To tell our story once was sufficient, we decided. Any further remarks could exacerbate the situation.

There were positive responses too, from friends and strangers. A man stopped my father in the street, shook his hand and praised him for his honesty.

'What kind of society is it where we feel obliged to hide the secret of our birth?' he asked. 'No one should have to live a lie. Well done for sharing your personal history with us.'

There were other unexpected consequences. Our

"confession" encouraged others to "come out." A spate of disclosures followed ours. More articles appeared on the Oasis website making public the fact that many other completes were born mutant humanoids. Many of them had disguised their mutations in order to gain access to the satellites, the safe havens in the sky. These further revelations had the effect of taking the focus off us. Our tale became just one of a plethora of confessions.

Father did not lose his ministerial position in the Symposium, as he had feared. At first his colleagues were a little wary of him; but it soon became cool to show how open-minded they could be. The human rights groups supported him and others followed their lead. Editorials were written applauding our integrity.

'None of us are perfect,' read one piece. 'Our ancestors were responsible for what happened on Earth and we must all take responsibility for that. We are all contaminated, if not physically, then at least emotionally.'

On a personal level I found it a great relief to be able to confide in my friend, Jonathan. Just before the article was published online, I told him my past history. I was apprehensive about doing this, but felt it was better to tell him face to face. His reaction was very much in keeping with his character. He listened carefully and said: 'I always thought there was something weird about you, man.'

'What do you mean weird?' I asked.

He punched me on the shoulder. 'I'm saying – so what's new? Tell you what. You show me yours and I'll show you mine.'

For a moment I thought he meant he had mutations too; but then he grinned, gave me another friendly punch and said, 'Lighten up, man. It's not like you haven't always been different. I kind of like that about you.'

That's when I knew that nothing had changed. We were

still friends even though he now knew that I had been born a mutant humanoid.

The tragedy of Athene's death will never be forgotten on Earth or Oasis, but now there is a new CEO of Worldwide-culture, Odysseus, a humanoid I really respect.

In spite of Stella's appalling treatment of my father and her association with Orlando Wolfe, she did remain clear-headed enough to choose a leader who is knowledgeable, wise and trustworthy.

One thing does concern me. Odysseus has allowed Thor to remain with Heracles. Surely that is a recipe for disaster? Or was that Stella's decision? Is she even more devious than I think?

Stella and Orlando Wolfe are still together. My father is, naturally, deeply wounded by this fact and finds it impossible to come to terms with her intimacy with Wolfe.

I try to be supportive but his hurt is so deep that there are times when I cannot reach him.

We have not been able to prove that it was Wolfe who had me arrested and interrogated but there is enough circumstantial evidence for us to know that he was indeed the power behind the incident. There is no secret for him to expose any longer, but that doesn't mean he has given up finding methods to discredit my father. The two men continue to be enemies, politically and personally. That is unlikely to change. Wolfe continues to play dirty, but, for the moment, Father's career is safe.

Once I become a member of the Symposium I'll be on Wolfe's case and will not give up until I've exposed all his corrupt ways.

Yes, readers of these chronicles, I have made up my mind to become a politician. I'm determined to get myself elected to the Symposium and systematically get rid of all the corruption that seems to have crept in there like a sneaky virus. I intend to restore the ideals of the original charter and do my best to make Oasis as close to a Utopian state as possible.

When I tell Jonathan my plan he laughs.

'You will have to become President to do that,' he jokes.

'If that's what it takes,' I tell him. 'Then that's what I'll be.'

'The first hybrid mutant/complete President of Oasis?' He shrugs. 'Well, anything is possible.'

'Would you vote for me?' I ask him.

'Oh come on, man. That's asking too much. Who in his right mind would vote for an oddball like you as President?'

In spite of him baiting me, he has put an idea into my mind that refuses to go away. The best way to get rid of corruption and make sure of good relations between Earth and Oasis is to become President of the Symposium. It may take me years to achieve this position, until I'm quite old in fact, about forty or even fifty. However long it takes I'm determined to do it.

I have another dream. To see Athene's daughter, Jocasta, grow up to be as wise and beautiful as her mother and inherit her role as Leader of Planet Earth. Not as CEO of Worldwideculture. With a bit of luck the latter organisation will be defunct by then and Stella's influence no longer in operation.

Sounds far-fetched? Maybe. But I can dream.

The End

About the Author

Brought up in a village in Northamptonshire, Jeannie van Rompaey has lived in London, The United States and Spain.

Jeannie considers herself an eternal student. She trained as a teacher at St Gabriel's College and studied Speech and Drama at Rose Bruford, both London based colleges. She has a BA from the Open University, a Diploma in English as a Foreign Language from the Bell School, Cambridge, and an MA in Modern Literature from the University of Leicester.

Her varied career includes teaching, lecturing and running drama and creative writing workshops. She is also a theatre director, actor and voice-over. As Jeannie Russell she is a senior member of the Guild of Drama Adjudicators and adjudicates drama festivals in the UK and Europe.

Jeannie is married to historian and artist, TJ. They live on the subtropical island of Gran Canaria where she spends much of her time writing and painting. She makes frequent trips to London to see her daughter, Anieka, attend literary events, visit art galleries and go to the theatre.

Acknowledgements

I would like to thank the following people for their support during the writing process.

Hedley Alcock, my first reader, for his interest and enthusiasm, as ever.

Maureen Blundell, my editor, for her invaluable advice.

Hayley and Gareth from Authoright for their thoroughness in every aspect of the publishing and marketing process.

My husband, TJ, for his practical and personal support.

Author's Note: I'd like to invite you to take a look at my website. If you would like to be informed when my next book comes out please leave your name and email on the Contact Page. http://jeannievanrompaey.com/

www.ingramcontent.com/pod-product-compliance
Lightning Source LLC
LaVergne TN
LVHW091113080826
845145LV00008B/1894